MW01178866

— Aaron L.
Poe

SAINTS
AND
MARTYRS

To Katherine.
Welcome to English 201!
We'll have a super fun
semester.
— Aaron

SAINTS
AND
MARTYRS

AARON ROE

atmosphere press

To my family

TABLE OF CONTENTS

Oh, where oh where can my baby be? The Lord took (him)
away from me (S)he's gone to heaven,
so I got to be good.
So I can see my baby when I leave this world.

—*"Last Kiss" J. Frank Wilson, 1962*

PART ONE

CHAPTER ONE
ORIGINAL SIN

Christ appeared dejected, which made Damian feel guilty. He was studying mathematics in his basement bedroom and struggling to ignore the erection that pressed painfully against his tight uniform pants, when the mailbox outside clanked shut. He looked up from his textbook to the crucifix hanging above his desk

Maybe it's just my math module, Lord, he prayed. He caressed Christ's pierced feet and sincerely tried to hope that the schoolwork he'd mailed to the Alberta Homeschooling Centre last month had returned, graded. But surely Christ, and Damian's deceased father in Heaven, knew that deeply, secretly, he wanted The Bay's catalogue to have arrived. Gazing down from above, they'd seen him fight off lustful thoughts the past few weeks, and they knew as well as he did that The Bay delivered its spring edition in February. So, with today being the end of the month, trying to hide his desire was futile. He felt like Judas as he kissed the crucifix before rising from his desk.

But his bedroom, like everywhere in Grandma Schiller's house, was so crowded that when he shoved back his chair it hit the bed he shared with his five-year-old brother James and crashed to the cement floor.

"Damn it!" he said, then immediately he held his breath, worried that his family upstairs had heard him curse. Already six-foot, three-inches tall at seventeen, his head nearly touched the basement's low, drooping ceiling.

He raised himself onto his toes, pressed his ear against the moulding, paper-thin ceiling panel, and listened carefully.

"Darwin was known to cheat at backgammon . . ." his mother was telling James and his two sisters, Mary (seven) and Bernadette (twelve), educating them in the same Bible stories, creation science, and warnings about socialism that he'd received at their age, ". . . which reveals his moral character and casts doubt on his theory."

Her voice hadn't wavered, so he sighed, relieved, but didn't yet lower himself from the ceiling. In case one of his siblings had heard him curse and felt inclined to tattle, he said loudly, "I mean *darn*."

There was momentary silence upstairs. They'd heard him *that* time. His mother, unwilling to interrupt her teaching from 9:00 a.m. to 3:30 p.m. on weekdays, resumed: "Fossils, despite what some *experts* claim . . ."

He could've recited the lesson verbatim. He lowered himself from the festering ceiling and wiped the mould from his ear. The slimy black dots smeared across his hand. How could something so disgusting figure into an intelligently designed world? Perhaps the smear was an omen, marking his hand that would likely soon lead him to sin. He could cut it off and pluck out his eyes, guarding himself from temptation. He could pray to his father for spiritual strength and try to hold out against lust for another day.

Or he could run upstairs, tell his mother he was checking the mailbox for schoolwork, and then, whatever happened, confess to Father Dennis, his parish priest, tomorrow. His frustration in this cramped, moulding house made some relief necessary. He cleaned his hand with a tissue, hoping that sin could be as easily removed from a soul, then picked up his chair, which miraculously wasn't broken, and hurried from the room before guilt held him back.

As he crossed the crowded basement, dodging lawn furniture, greying stacks of the National Catholic Register, and towers of rain-wrinkled encyclopaedias, his mother's voice travelled clearly through the ceiling: pressing his ear against it had been needless—an anxious act. Now he knew the mould *had* been an omen, a harbinger of sin. His desire persisted, however, so he moved faster.

The ancient stairs creaked under his 250 pounds. At the top he threw open the door, forgetting his strength in his anxiety over his soul, his eagerness to reach the mailbox. The door crashed against the kitchen wall.

"Damian!" his mother yelled from the living room. He stood in the doorway, crossing his hands in fig-leaf position, trying to appear contrite but also hiding his erection from his siblings who sat in a neat row, making him feel guiltier yet with their wide, innocent eyes.

Bernadette and Mary, hands clasped on top of their desks, wore matching grey jumpers, long brown hair in pigtails, and starched white shirts with Peter Pan collars. James' hair, dark brown as his father's had been, was parted to the side and slicked down. He wore a white, short-sleeved, collared shirt, a navy tie, a red cardigan, and grey slacks that fit him well. Damian's version of the same clothes was tight and uncomfortable, particularly in his present state.

His thin, pale mother wore her chestnut hair in a bun, and her starched blouse and grey skirt were so flat she matched the blackboard she stood before, chalk in hand. She'd mounted the blackboard on the wall four years ago, just after his father died. Damian had helped her hang it, doing what his father would've done, except he'd hung it slant. Since then his always-pious mother had heightened her fervor, no longer checked by his father's calming presence, and their family life became a flurry of Mass, prayers, catechetical instruction, and readings from *Butler's Lives of the Saints*. They hadn't bothered to adjust it. The crooked blackboard, he often thought, seemed to belong in a house that'd suffered an upheaval and had never been restored to order.

He stepped forward, stopping at the edge of the kitchen where the curled squares of smoke-stained linoleum gave way to the worn beige carpet that demarcated Grandma Schiller's living room, or, as his mother had named it since moving her children into the house, The Academy of the Immaculate Conception. She said, "What have I told you about slamming doors?"

"Not to," he replied, slightly sarcastic. He anticipated her next question by readying the answer he'd prepared downstairs.

"Where are you going?"

"The mail. My math module."

"Why now?"

"To review it for mistakes," he said. "To improve for . . ." He pointed up, implying God. He didn't want to take the Lord's name in vain because perfection in God's eyes, his family's constant goal, wasn't driving him to the mailbox that afternoon. And since he'd already cursed downstairs, possibly giving a bad example to his siblings through the basement ceiling, he didn't want to add blasphemy and lying to the sins he'd confess tomorrow.

His mother, however, seemed to interpret his gesture

differently, in a way that furthered her designs on him, which had been growing increasingly insistent of late. She said, "To prepare yourself for seminary."

He suddenly grew angry. Why did she try to control him like this? While the priesthood attracted him with its commitments to prayer and celibacy, her pressure spoiled its appeal. But he wanted to avoid conflict right now, so he resigned himself to her manipulation (at least for the moment) and said, "Yeah, the seminary. Probably."

She furrowed her brow, showing she acknowledged the legitimacy of his quest. "Next time wait till we're done."

He nodded and hurried past his siblings. He opened the foyer door and then *quietly* shut it behind him so his mother had no further grounds to criticize his disruption.

Inside, stagnant clouds of Grandma Schiller's smoke filled the dark, cramped space, and the afternoon sun beat against the tightly tin-foiled windows so that, though it was frigid outside, the air within sweltered like Hell. As he waited for his eyes to adjust, coughing and waving his hand before his face, Grandma Schiller mumbled prayers from across the foyer.

"Hi, Grandma."

"Damian," she said, her gentle German voice soothing after his mother's loud reprimands.

Why was his mother so harsh, compared to her mother? One day he'd ask Grandma Schiller.

"Saint Antony, patron of lost zings, help us findt God's pass to zalvation."

Her pious words and cigarette smoke hung in the air like incense. Though he could only see shadows now, he knew, from crossing Grandma Schiller's space when the door was open or the light on, that the walls around her were covered with brightly-coloured holy cards: small rectangles of laminated paper with saints drawn on the front and intercessory prayers on the back. Grandma Schiller claimed to have memorized these prayers decades ago, and now the words faced the wall, leaving the drawings on display. He'd studied them so closely when he'd moved in, he could now picture them vividly. The images of long beards, flowing robes, knotty staffs, uplifted eyes, pale complexions, and thin, floating halos haunted him because they reminded him of his father, whom he considered a saint as well. According to family lore, his father had died without having committed a mortal sin, and so they believed he was in Heaven and could see them always, something Damian cherished except for times like now, when his intentions were shameful.

Part of him wanted to return downstairs and continue studying. Doing so would preserve his soul from stain. But what was in the mailbox? His fingers tingled at the thought. He couldn't turn back now; he'd ask his father for forgiveness *immediately* after his excitement had been extinguished.

So, before the smoke cleared, revealing his eager eyes to Grandma Schiller, he opened the front door, gasped at the cold, and stuck his hand inside the mailbox. He sighed in relief as he felt the four-hundred-page, plastic-wrapped apple that'd arrived in his dismal Eden. The catalogue's soft, bulky shape was familiar from previous editions that'd arrived the months before fall, Christmas, and spring: the only times his habitual chastity collapsed into what his mother's ancient manual on male adolescence referred to as "self-abuse." He pulled out the catalogue before his conscience caught up with him, then shut the front door and hurried from the foyer leaving Grandma Schiller's smoke and mumbled prayers behind.

Back in the living room his mother was discussing the Cambrian explosion, a topic that animated her greatly. She faced the blackboard, drawing a hand that emerged from the sky, a globe under the hand, and then a tumbling assortment of animals streaming from palm to planet. Furiously she sketched birds of various sizes, a giraffe, and then began a whale (he guessed) while he tucked the catalogue behind his leg and tried to pass her.

"The Bay!" James said gleefully from his desk. Their mother turned to face her class and leaned around Damian to see what he was hiding.

"That's not your math module," she said. He quickly held the catalogue in front of him to appear innocent.

"I'm looking for a new weightlifting belt," he said, hating himself for lying.

"The Bay doesn't sell those."

"They do," he said, and then he knew how to proceed. Standing before his siblings, blocking their view of the crooked blackboard, he slowly tore open the catalogue's plastic wrapping. "See, look. They're right—"

"All right, all right," she said. "I'm not disrupting the Cambrian explosion for this."

This was adequate permission. He hurried past the desks just as Bernadette raised her hand. His slick-heeled dress shoes, the worst part of his uniform, nearly made him tumble down the stairs, and they clacked across the basement's concrete floor as he dodged a birdbath and brushed a hat rack. He stopped to steady it and heard his mother through the ceiling: "Yes, Bernadette?"

"Mommy, what's in Damian's pants?"

"Kleenex," his mother replied sharply as he entered his bedroom and pulled another tissue from the box on the night table. Bernadette's question broke his heart (he was such a sinner!), but he shut his door anyway, wishing it would lock. He removed Christ from above his desk and laid Him face down on the bed. The crucifix left a cross-shaped mark on the wall; he couldn't escape God's presence. Self-deception about his current intention was indeed futile. He was about to sin, and he wanted to get it over with. He flipped open the catalogue near the front, to the women's wear. Experience told him he wasn't far from the lingerie, and he skipped the pages quickly.

Upstairs, James asked, "Mom, why is Damian so grouchy?"

His heart sank deeper. Poor James! He stopped on a beautiful brunette model leaning against a hallway wall in a black bra and matching black panties. Her lacy bra appeared transparent, though he couldn't see her nipples. Her panties were tiny, so tiny.

"Teenagers are just . . . emotional," his mother replied to James.

Her covering for him—he *was* grouchy, he knew it as well as she did—made unzipping his fly seem like a desperate grasp at release.

"He never smiles," James said.

"And when I ask him to play with me, he won't," Mary added.

A tear fell from Damian's eye. He'd gone soft in his hand, but his need for satisfaction, for escape, for anything other than sorrow grew so great he felt like he'd burst.

"Well, why don't we end our science there," his mother said. "Who wants to read a saint's life?"

"Me!" his siblings, the little victims of his sadness, replied together. Compared to their innocent enthusiasm, was his desire for sanctity serious? They eagerly pushed their desks against the living room wall and then sat—*thump! thump! thump!*—on the carpet for today's reading from *Butler's Lives.* Damian, still pulling on himself, was already halfway to Hell, so he tore the tissue he'd been holding in his left hand and shoved it in his ears: he did *not* want to hear a saint's life while sinning.

Breathing hard now, his habitual unhappiness faded away as he stared at the model's crotch. He fantasized that she was his wife and their bedroom was at the end of the hallway featured in the photograph. She beckoned him to follow her to bed in a soft and enticing voice. And now *her* hand, not his, was working his renewed erection. . .

After glorious release came furious guilt, and without zipping up or closing the catalogue or even cleaning his hand, he collapsed onto his desk.

I'm sorry, Lord, he prayed. *Sorry, Dad.*

How could he have let this happen? He wanted more than anything to get into Heaven. Like the prodigal son and his father after the son had repented. Never to be separated again . . . But now all that was lost. He'd never rejoin his father unless he repented for this sin.

"Damian!" his mother called from upstairs, her voice muffled. Did she want him to come listen to the story from *Butler's Lives*? He quickly unplugged his ears. "Look whose feast it is!"

"Oh no!" he whispered. His heart froze. He slowly lifted his eyes to his calendar. A star adorned each day of

February but the 28th, today. He'd drawn the stars, which extended back in unbroken succession to the first day of the year, to signify each 24-hour period of perfect chastity. But today would remain blank: *on the anniversary of his father's death!* An abomination. He'd been so consumed with remaining pure he'd forgotten to mark this most solemn date.

"Come read us Dad's story!" his mother called. She was referring to the biography of his father he kept in his journal, which, with sin so fresh on his hands, he didn't want to even touch.

"Okay!" His voice wavered. He wiped back tears and cleaned his hand with the torn tissue, then threw it away and zipped up. He pulled his journal from where he hid it under the bed and placed the catalogue there for now, planning to destroy it later. Before he left his bedroom, he hung the crucifix back above his desk. Christ's face was turned away. He suspected his father, up in Heaven, had also turned away, but Damian was too sad to issue another apology.

I'll confess, he prayed. *Tomorrow.*

And he ran upstairs.

His siblings were sitting cross legged on the floor now, their desks in a row behind them. His mother had pulled a chair from the dining table, and she sat before the blackboard, her back rigid, her knees together. On it she'd written, *We love you, Dad!*

He forced a smile.

Beside his mother, Grandma Schiller sat in the low, boxy chair she used in the foyer. It was made of thick wood—a light tan that, he could've sworn, had gained a greyish hue from being pickled in the foyer's smoke.

Considering its weight and Grandma Schiller's arthritis, James must've helped her move it. The chair, which, like so many items in the house, appeared to be the lone survivor of a long-lost set, accommodated her bulk without any spare space, and she'd added two foam pads to the seat, so her black, low-heeled, lace-up shoes hovered just above the stained carpet.

Grandma Schiller's plain white dress fit her squat form perfectly, and he wondered, as he pulled up a chair and joined the circle his family had formed, if that was because she'd molded herself into it by wearing it daily, or if she wore it exclusively because it fit so well. Sitting calmly, mumbling prayers even now as she waited for him to begin reading, she signified the stable, loving leadership that this house so desperately needed.

Encouraged, he opened his journal. There, taped to the front cover, was a black-and-white photograph of his father in his rugby uniform, taking a knee on a playing field. At nineteen, his wide, tanned face and curly brown hair resembled a Māori Michael Landon from the reruns of *Little House on the Prairie* that his family was allowed to watch on the wood-encased, crackly television in the living room. He caressed his father with his fingertips and then flipped to the pages he'd worked on ardently.

Damian had composed the first draft of his dad's biography shortly after he'd died, on the advice of the hospital's social worker who'd helped his family deal with their grief. She'd instructed him to ask his relatives for their favourite memories of his dad and then to record their responses in his journal. Doing so had proved soothing, and then Damian had added his own fondest memories. He'd poured over his pages, revising and updating them until he'd clearly narrated the kindness, hard work, and sacrifice that'd defined his dad's life.

When the story seemed complete, he read the final draft to his family, anticipating satisfaction at his accomplishment but while the pages restored a comforting sense of his father's presence, as the social worker had said she hoped they would, they'd failed to describe him as the brilliant saint Damian knew—and *desired to show him to be.*

After that first reading, the biography's purpose had changed. He now wanted it to match *Butler's Lives* to prove his father was also worthy of Heaven's highest honour. Despite his efforts, his dad's life seemed mundane when compared to famous saints because it lacked the daring feats, asceticism, and miracles that marked those officially canonized. Nevertheless, over the past four years, he'd persevered, studying *Butler's Lives* daily, trying to adapt its content and style to his father's experiences, and seeking to emulate such saintliness himself.

His present version would have to suffice for now. Damian dispelled his guilt about the catalogue so he could give proper attention to reading this noble tale, the most important story in his life.

"George Kurt," he read aloud, his voice almost steady now, "was born July 18, 1960 on a sheep station in New Zealand. His father, George Sr., had immigrated from England, and he and his wife, a Māori named Whina, had six sons—George the eldest. As a boy George was known to be virtuous, and by age six he was so strong he could perform the work of a full-grown man. As he grew . . ."

And suddenly his father's deep voice returned: that rumbling baritone and Kiwi accent had, after all, been his original source for much of the story he now shared. Since he didn't want to cry—grieved that this afternoon's sin had jeopardized the prospect of ever hearing that voice again— he read quickly and loudly to drown out the memories: "By the age of sixteen George was renowned for hurling hay bales that normally required two men to lift. And George had also grown wild—as *his* father had supposedly been in his youth."

His siblings, at the mention of their fathers' wayward adolescence, smiled confidently, for they knew his short span as a rascal led eventually to lifelong piety and restraint.

In early drafts, Damian had referred to him as "dad." But, in addition to studying *Butler's*, he had for the past year written summaries of saints' lives for the parish bulletin, and he wanted his father's story to strike the same formal tone as those other, less personal pieces. So, he'd recently replaced "dad" with "George," which had accomplished his goal but sounded strange now as he read aloud. He wanted the biography to seem objective, and he'd asked his mother for documents left by his father— letters, a journal, receipts. Perhaps these would indicate valiant, even heroic acts that his father had been too humble to ever mention. She had none.

Another chance for information on his father was Uncle Rick, his mother's brother who lived a secret, secluded life in his bedroom on the main floor of Grandma Schiller's house. Once a Trappist monk, Uncle Rick left his monastery soon after Damian's father died; he'd returned home and not ventured out again, and was the only family member to refuse to share a memory of Damian's father when he was writing the first draft of his story.

"George and his brothers worked the station by day," Damian continued, "but drank gin and smoked in town at the Māori bar at night. They were suspected, however, by the other Natives for being half white, and totally rejected by the local whites for being half Māori."

"But he never hated anyone." His mother chiming in was expected, but still grating.

Damian cleared his throat, straightened himself in his chair, and glanced at his fly to ensure he'd zipped up in his haste downstairs: he wanted nothing to interrupt what came next.

"One day George and his brothers attended a rugby match, the All Blacks versus Australia's team, The Kangaroos," said Damian. "The crowd roared for the All Blacks as they ran onto the field, and George noticed some of them were white, some Māori. Suddenly, in the sea of screaming fans at the stadium, he had a plan for his future."

That last sentence sent shivers down his back and arms: he, too, needed a plan for his future, one that elevated him to sanctity by helping him avoid temptation. And if only his father had been inspired by a scripture passage, as had Saint Augustine, or a voice from above like Saint Paul, his epiphany to reform would fit Damian's intended story perfectly. But still, drawing on his father's youthful courage, he continued: "So George slowed his drinking and, instead, practiced rugby on his family's station with his brothers. When they went to the bar, he ran laps around the fields, chinned himself on the barn's rafters, and did push ups with bags of feed on his back. At eighteen, he made the All Blacks and traveled around the world."

As if the family sat in the stadium bleachers at one of their father's long-ago games, they now clapped and cheered and smiled—die hard fans, unwavering in support for a foreign team only because that team included the star of their lives, the hero that justified the Kurt's family pride.

James beamed and Damian found himself mirroring the same family loyalty. Despite the sufferings, reclusive living, and poverty incurred by the Kurts since their dad's death, their father had been a source of joy to the family: a professional athlete—mighty, successful, famous—and while nothing could erase such lofty status, Damian's story reinforced their collective memory of what honours his dad had attained. This memory dwelt now as a truth they each cherished.

His siblings gazed at him. Damian knew they'd perk up even more with the next section of the tale, but he worried: athletic dominance didn't correspond directly to holiness. Certainly, nights of watchful prayer would better describe saintly striving. Nevertheless, he read with flourish. James sat statue-still.

"In the late 1970s he came to Alberta for a series of exhibition games against the local teams, *all* of which the All Blacks, *of course,* won."

He'd deliberately made the All Blacks' victories sound inevitable, and now he smiled knowingly at James, who grinned back: they shared a belief that their father's former team had been unbeatable and that he'd been invincible, or nearly so.

After hearing his siblings' complaints through the ceiling earlier, he was happy to see how their father's story had gladdened them now. Their gazes fixed, relatively quiet and still as they awaited, whispering about their father's might, virtue, and many achievements, likely instigated by his story. Even Grandma Schiller peered off at some distant memory, it seemed, her expression placid. And his sisters grinned expectantly: their favourite part was coming up.

He paused a moment to heighten their anticipation, and then read further: "After the final match in Edmonton, he and some teammates drove across the province to see the Rocky Mountains. The farm fields he passed reminded him of his childhood in New Zealand. And then, on that drive—"

"I'll tell this part," his mother said, and the girls clapped and squirmed. He didn't mind letting his mother take over. Looking down at her daughters and softening her voice, she described how she'd met their dad when his team's bus stopped at the small-town gas station her family owned. She'd been working the till, and in walked a tall, burly man with a dark complexion. He pretended to peruse the store but kept stealing glances at her.

"He grabbed a bouquet of roses," his mother said, "paid for them, and then handed them to me. Well, how could I not look up into those big, brown eyes?"

Those eyes were impossible to forget as they now shined on his siblings' faces. His mother continued to relate that first meeting, telling how their future father asked her out to dinner that night but she refused because she needed to help her family at the station.

"But my refusal," his mother continued, "didn't deter your dad. Not a bit. He turned around and went out to speak to his teammates. Minutes later two other players entered the store and told me they'd do my job that afternoon, that another two had agreed to handle the evening hours. The bus's horn honked, then again—this time longer. The players raised their eyebrows and took my place behind the till as I ran outside to find your dad at the wheel of the bus. He drove us to dinner in Calgary that night, and the rest, well . . ."

A tear rolled down her cheek, but she smiled, clearly transported to the past. Damian imagined that day as it would appear on a holy card: his muscular father in an All Blacks uniform, pulling away from the gas station with a thin, smiling passenger, a halo above his head.

"Daat evening," Grandma Schiller said, describing the part of that day she'd been present for, "our customers ver shocked to haff dare tanks filled by such huge men!"

His siblings giggled with Grandma Schiller. Damian flipped the page to skip the parts in his story that his family had just shared, and then he resumed reading: "Within the year George moved to Calgary—his rugby career ended by a knee injury that some teammates suspected he had faked. After being baptized a Catholic, he married the young woman from the gas station and opened a plumbing business. And then the first of four children was born. And then, um . . ."

He sniffled, and his voice broke as it had downstairs.

"Why don't we end there?" his mother said. He nodded, reluctant to read any further because the joyful scenes from his childhood would only make him sad, and quite quickly led to the awful day his father died. *That* horrible event, which still largely defined his life, was missing; he'd never been able to write about it.

"Who wants to visit Dad?" his mother asked. His siblings jumped up to put on boots, coats, and mittens—the winter gear required to visit the graveyard in

February. Damian replaced Grandma Schiller's chair in the foyer, where she resumed her prayers and lit another cigarette. Then he put on his coat and followed his family to their white station wagon.

He got in the third, rear-facing seat, grateful for the privacy. The snow-covered city appeared grim as his mother pulled away from the curb, and he opened his journal to a fresh page:

Friday, February 28th, 1998

It happened today. I knew it was coming—my thoughts, my dreams, have been of bodies and skin. . .

He completed his account of that afternoon's sin and immediately felt more control over his spiritual life. With his lust extinguished, he could concentrate. As his mother slid and spun down the snowy roads, stopping only once at a grocery store to buy a single flower for his father's grave, he prepared his confession list for tomorrow, when Father Dennis would absolve him. He scoured his memory of the last week for moral failings, and when he'd listed them all, he placed checkmarks beside the faults he'd committed more than once so he could tell the number of offences.

The long list of sins disheartened him. How could he improve? For now, all he could do was press his pen firmly onto the page and make a solemn pledge:

Today's sin was my last, Dad. By this day next year, I'll be a saint. I will. I'll do whatever it takes so I can join you in Heaven.

When he looked up from his journal, they were at the graveyard.

CHAPTER TWO
SHATTERED SANCTUARY

The next day at Roy's Gym, Damian reached into the chalk bin behind his platform, grabbed a chunk, and crushed it, wishing, as he whitened his hands, that his soul was also white. He sighed as he shook the excess flakes into the bin, watching them fall and settle like so many souls into Hell. He would be damned if he died before confessing yesterday's sin, and though he'd tried to earlier that morning before Mass, he hadn't confessed it yet.

The loaded bar waited at the centre of the six by ten-foot platform. As he stepped onto the wood surface and spaced his feet shoulders' width apart his pulse slowed, his fingers steadied, and his breathing replaced the gym's noise, but still his concentration was blurred, so he shook his head, clearing it, and then closed his eyes.

He visualized a clean and jerk: *Drag the bar up your shins and thighs, and then explode upward, thrusting your hips forward and shrugging with the bar. As it rises, dive under it and catch the bar on your clavicle, shooting your elbows forward. Having racked the weight, stand up.*

Now bend your knees slightly, and then push with your legs. As you push the weight overhead, drop under it into a split-legged stance: left foot forward, right leg straight back.

Straighten your arms to lock the bar overhead. Then shuffle your feet together. Pause a moment; drop the weight.

His mental lift completed, he bent over the bar and rubbed his palms on the knurling to coat it with chalk. Then he gripped tightly, tensed his thighs, and lifted the bar smoothly from the floor. He racked the weight, and though his legs shook as he stood, he jerked it and held it overhead. Three seconds passed before he dropped the rubber weights. They hit the platform with a muffled slap and bounce.

"Stand up faster," Scott, his coach, said from behind him. Damian found him leaning against the gym's mirrored back wall, eating a banana. Damian's attention drifted to his own reflection. Dark circles saddled his eyes, and his cheeks were pallid. He'd barely slept last night. Shortly after turning out the light and saying goodnight to James, he dreamt that the body beside him was the model from the catalogue, lying on her belly, showing him her backside that the photo had hidden. He ran his fingers up her smooth legs, traced the curve of her buttocks, growing more and more excited until James, lying on *his* belly, had shaken him awake and said, "Why are you squeezing me?" Damian, his erection tenting his shorts, had found his hand on his brother. He'd not allowed himself to fall back asleep, fighting off lustful thoughts, praying rosaries on his fingers. . .

"Damian!" Scott said, his blue eyes fierce as he swallowed. "Focus! And why were your legs shaking with 220?"

"Just horn—hungry," he said. "Just hungry."

Scott tilted his head. "Did you just—?"

"Should I redo?"

"No," Scott said, still looking puzzled. "Just sit and rest. Then we'll go to 242."

Damian nodded and tried to act natural. He stepped off the platform and smelled the lingering aroma of Scott's banana as he sat on the creaking wood bench against the back wall. His stomach gurgled. He'd rushed his family out of the house that morning, begging them to postpone breakfast until they returned from Mass so they wouldn't be late for confession. Traffic, however, had been slow because of the thick snowfall that'd descended on Calgary last night, and when the Kurts finally arrived at Canadian Martyrs Roman Catholic Church, he jumped out of their station wagon, journal in hand, and hurried inside only to find Father Dennis exiting the confessional. He pleaded with him, even hinting at the severity of his sin, but Father Dennis said no, maybe after Mass. The problem there was that Damian needed to leave church immediately after Mass ended, lurching through the snow again to get to the gym on time. Scott, a lapsed Catholic, had no patience for religion, particularly if it interfered with Damian's training. Now his only hope was to catch Father Dennis later this morning, before the priest's infamous midday nap, when he and his mother would return to church.

The gym's clock showed fifteen minutes remained until this workout ended, but the second hand appeared stuck over the minute hand. He stared at the thin red line, trying to push it forward with his eyes, and began praying a Hail Mary, then, slowly but smoothly, the second hand emerged, mocking his panic, and he quit praying before Scott caught the pious look in his eye.

He shook himself, wiped the sweat from his brow, and tried to focus on his training. He inspected the platform from his seat, the middle of five platforms along the back wall. The plywood rectangle was chipped and dented at the far ends, where rubber plates had crashed for decades. The middle was rubbed smooth by lifters placing their feet.

Roy's Gym was located in what once had been a warehouse, and memberships were cheap. The ceiling was thirty feet high, corrugated metal, and strung with harsh white lights that illuminated the cinderblock walls and grey concrete floor. Free-weight equipment lined the left wall: three thick squat cages, three flat benches, an incline bench, and a rack of dumbbells. A row of stiff, rusty Nautilus equipment, which he, a provincial champion, never touched, ran parallel to the free weights. Stationary bicycles lined the right wall, and before them was a row of new treadmills—an effort by Roy to draw patrons from the public and not just cater to hardcore lifters. Damian found the treadmills distracting: spandex-clad women laughed, talked and—worst—bounced enticingly as *real* competitors trained.

Down the gym's middle an open aisle ended at the wall before him. The clock hung in the centre, directly above the front desk where the blond receptionist sat typing. She looked up from her computer and he traced her gaze to Scott, who was approaching her, banana peel dangling in hand. She reached under the desk and held out the trash can. He jogged toward it, pretending he was a basketball player, and skillfully shot the peel into the can. The receptionist waved the trash above her head before replacing it on the floor, and leaned back, smiling. Scott leaned into the desk to chat.

And he tells me to focus, Damian thought. Scott had been an altar boy before playing NCAA basketball at Gonzaga University, a Jesuit school, where, as he told it, he lost his faith. Damian wondered, during their many arguments about Catholicism, whether Scott ever considered becoming a priest, as Damian was considering now. And why had he left the Church? Damian often prayed to Saint Aloysius Gonzaga, a Jesuit seminarian who died at twenty having never entertained an impure thought, for Scott's reconversion. But today it was him who needed Saint Aloysius' intercession and example. And where was his mother? He wanted badly for her to return so he could end this workout, return to church, and confess to Father Dennis.

He craned his neck to better see through the tinted glass doors by the front desk out on to the street. Exhaust trailed the tops of cars, their tires blocked from view by the bank of road-cleared snow. Before taking his younger siblings home, his mother had dropped him off at the corner about an hour ago, at a gap between two waist-high slopes, and he walked half a block in the cold. Fresh snow had fallen since then and he tried to appreciate its purity now, but the tinted glass darkened the beauty of the white flakes.

How would he see his mom arrive? He'd have to watch for the top of their white station wagon shrouded in idling exhaust. Maybe she'd honk the horn. If she did, he might not hear because of the thumping speakers along the walls: another of Roy's recent additions. Another distraction. His mom's long skirt would prevent her from even trying to hop the snowbank—what if she fell, or got stuck, and exposed her legs? Too risky.

Scott returned, smiling. He shook his bald head, his crown reflecting the shine off the lights above, and chuckled as he leaned against the back wall. "That girl . . .

Craziest stories!"

Damian flushed and braced himself for crass details: he was in no mood to further endanger his soul.

Scott seemed to notice because he changed his tone and asked, "You going to Mass?"

"Already went," Damian said.

"This morning?"

"Yup."

"Then why is your mom picking you up early?"

"Going back to church."

"*Why?*"

Because I'm in danger of damnation, he thought, but then recalled that he had other, relatable reasons for returning to Canadian Martyrs. "I'm writing a saint's story for the parish bulletin. She's gonna pray and undecorate the church for Lent."

"I'm smelling incense again, Damian."

"I'm not thinking about—"

"You've been staring at the clock."

"I've been trying to concentrate—"

"Try harder. Look, I've got a hockey team coming in at ten, anyway. Keep your head in the gym until then."

"Okay," he said, trying to appear contrite. He appreciated all that Scott had done for him, giving him a chance when, four years ago, his mom had called the gym nearest Grandma Schiller's house and begged to speak with a weightlifting coach. Her one-hundred and sixty-pound thirteen-year-old son, anguished over his dad's recent death, had seen strongman competitions on TV and was now tilting up his grandmother's sofa with his siblings on it, hoisting stones in the alley, cleaning and jerking a coat rack (an exercise only possible to perform upstairs, since the basement ceiling was too low), and chinning himself in his mother's closet until, that morning, he'd pulled the bar from the aged drywall.

Scott, who'd answered her call, was intrigued by her story until she told him her payment limit was twenty dollars per month. He'd resisted, from what Damian had heard on his mother's side of the phone call, but when she'd mentioned that her late husband had been so strong he could lift broken water softeners—*without* draining them—from his clients' basements, loosen rusty pipes with his bare hands, and that now he was dead, his plumber's income gone with him, Scott had agreed to a trial workout to test Damian's strength.

He'd clean-and-jerked two hundred pounds that first workout, his technique understandably terrible, his potential, as Scott had said, limitless. He went on to win the 1995 Alberta Junior Championships the following year, the National Junior Championships the year after that, but his success had been hampered, as Scott often pointed out, by his Catholic faith: the Kurts' religious commitments often made Damian late or caused him to cut his workouts short, impeding a prodigy's progress. And while he cared more about sanctity than lifting awards, he depended on the sanctuary of his platform to deal with the stresses of his home life, which was why he wanted to keep Scott happy.

Scott was leaning against the gym's back wall, looking at his palm, picking at calluses. Damian took the opportunity to check the clock again: thirteen minutes to ten. He wanted to follow the second hand, ensuring its progress, but instead turned back to Scott. "I'm going for 242?"

"Yup," Scott replied. "Lemme see how it looks, and I'll decide where to go from there."

"All right," he said as he stood. He grabbed two 11-lb plates from a bar in a squat cage and carried one in each hand on his return to his platform. He loaded the plates, tightened the clamps, and chalked his hands before positioning his feet under the 242-lb bar. Pausing, he visualized himself standing quickly after racking the next lift.

"Pull it up and snap it out," Scott said from behind. Damian nodded, gripped the bar, and pulled: it reached his thighs and he wrenched upward, yanking it to his chest. He snapped under the weight and caught it with his thighs parallel to the floor. The knurling bit into his throat. He blew air like spray from a high-pressure hose as he stood. He straightened his legs with force to spare and the bar rose off his clavicle. Suspended a moment, it returned to his shoulders and he bent his knees to follow its momentum. When he'd dipped two inches, he reversed direction and drove it overhead. He split his legs as he straightened his arms under the weight. It felt light and he slid his right foot forward quickly—too quickly—tipping back and dropping the weight behind him.

"What the hell?" Scott yelled as the plates smacked the plywood and the bar rattled. Damian spun and grabbed the bar, settling it on the platform before it rolled off. He knew Scott would blame his faith.

"I rushed it," he said. "I know, I know. I'm sorry."

"Did your rosary catch on the bar again?" Scott said.

Several months ago, Damian had started wearing his rosary, even to the gym, where it'd caught on the bar and burst into beads that rolled off the platform, causing him to miss what would've been a personal best: 308lbs.

"No," he snapped, angry at Scott's accusation, but then, to avoid conflict with his coach, he said calmly: "Sorry—I'll be settled for the next lift."

"You better," Scott said. "Less than two months to provincials and you're dancing around like that!"

Damian stepped off the platform, but Scott stopped him. "This is your church when you're here—weights, not saints."

He wanted to protest, but instead nodded humbly and sat on the wood bench, hoping to gather his thoughts and focus as he leaned against the glass and let his breathing slow down. He shut his eyes and inhaled sweat, chalk, and lingering bleach. Just then the song that was playing changed, and he looked up at the stereo behind the front desk. The shiny dial reminded him of a trick Scott had taught him at his last weightlifting meet. The 1997 Alberta Junior Provincials had been held on a stage in a large, crowded auditorium, and he'd been distracted by women in the audience who were wearing tight shirts. Scott instructed him to find a fixed object—a fire alarm, an exit sign, a door handle—on the opposite wall to hone his focus. He stepped out onto the stage, positioned his feet under the bar, and then looked up to find a Canadian flag hanging from the second balcony. He concentrated on the maple leaf's tip and the attractive distractions melted away.

Now, in the grey gym, he focused on the dial. The gym went soft and hazy—Scott disappeared—as his eyes bore into the silver circle. It reminded him of his hours of adoration before the small white host, the centre of a gold monstrance on the altar, but he resisted these memories in favour of a blank, steady mind. He was just getting settled when a flash of light drew his attention back to the entrance doors where six or seven young women entered. The sunlight coming through the open doors illuminated their long hair. Damian couldn't distinguish the two blond girls from the dark-haired others until they approached the front desk. A tall girl with curly black hair, dark spandex pants, and a large duffle bag spoke to the receptionist, who pointed at him and Scott. The tall girl turned toward them, and Damian was already standing.

"Getting a drink" he said, stepping forward so quickly that his foot caught on his bar and he stumbled. He spread his feet to catch his fall, making a loud, embarrassing noise. He stared at his white-and-red shoes as he kept walking: were his steps always this heavy? He'd gained weight, and thereby strength, since living with Grandma Schiller, but he felt awkward and clumsy now.

A pink bum stamped with "Calgary Women's Hockey" in black letters blocked him at the fountain. He re-examined his scuffed shoes until the shapely bum moved out of eyesight. Then he stepped forward, stooped, and squirted himself in the eye. He quickly placed his mouth over the stream, but with his right eye blinking from the blast, he didn't see that the pink pants were now beside him. He nearly bumped her when he turned around.

"Where'd you get your lifting shoes?" she asked.

"Yup," he replied, and hurried to his platform, thinking: *Stupid, stupid answer! Why didn't I just say I mail ordered them from Germany?* But he quit chiding himself when he noticed the crowd of young women covering his sacred space and chatting with Scott. Damian tried signaling to him without drawing the girls' attention.

He waved his fingers and then made a shooing motion with his hand. Scott continued chatting. Damian stepped closer and waved his hand above his head in a quick arc, followed by the same sweeping motion as before. Giggling erupted and his heart stopped, but the girls were focused on Scott, who merely nodded and chuckled. Damian stepped forward again, his shoe touching his platform. No one moved. He tapped his shoe on the platform once, then again, then several times, until Scott stopped talking and looked in his direction. The girls parted and he stared directly at his coach, is voice cracking as he said, "I need my platform."

Scott smiled playfully. "Ladies, this is Damian Kurt, last year's Junior National Champion, and you are interfering with greatness—isn't that right, Damian?"

He spoke to his shoes: "I just need my space, here."

"Okay, okay," Scott said, laughing. "He means you need to move down to the next platform, ladies. Come on! Right over here. Right here! Let's give our champ his space."

He bent for his shoelaces, which were still tied, as the whispering girls receded to the next platform. He undid the laces, pulled them tighter, double knotted them, and then stood and stepped into a cloud of perfume. Lusty citrus and flowers polluted his space, his sanctuary, and he fanned the air as he approached Scott, who was now leaning against the glass and staring at the next platform down.

"Scott," he said. "How much should I—"

"Just pile your things along the mirror, ladies," Scott said. "And no outdoor shoes on the platforms! Ride the bikes and stretch until I'm done with Damian—we won't be long!"

"Scott," he said again, a little louder. "Scott?"

Scott didn't respond, still gazing at the girls. His blue eyes remained steady and intent to the point of embarrassment, in Damian's opinion. *Hypocrite,* he thought, but then stopped himself. He looked past Scott and saw a swirl of pink pants and curly hair in the mirror. He turned away and began to sit on his bench when a female voice shouted, "Look!"

Instinctively he looked up, along with everyone else, as the tall girl lifted the bottom of her sweater: vines curled around her belly button and entwined up her stomach. The tattoo appeared fresh, the green leaves and brown thorns still glistening beneath ointment. The image caught him, and he couldn't help staring as she pulled her sweater higher and inadvertently lifted her undershirt as well. When her arms straightened over her head, her black sports bra was momentarily visible.

"Not again!" he said, snapping his head down. Something stirred. The front of his pants tightened.

"What?" Scott asked. "What did you say?"

But Damian was already crossing his platform, forcing himself to notice how his frayed laces jumped and fell as his excitement passed. He grabbed two 22-lb plates, loaded his bar, and, as he placed his feet, shook his head to dispel the image of vines climbing smooth skin toward black-molded breasts. . .

"Saint Sebastian, pray for me," he said as he exhaled, then caught his breath and listened: a female voice rose in pitch, as though asking a question. Scott replied: "Mail order from Germany—size thirteen!"

They were talking about him, about his shoes, but

hadn't heard him pray. Four years ago, when he began weightlifting, his mother instructed him to preface every lift by invoking the patron saint of athletes. He'd done so until, at his first official meet three years ago, he walked out on stage, prayed aloud, and a judge had stopped the time clock, demanding to know what he said.

Grateful to have escaped Scott's certain reprimand today, he wrenched the bar up. His right hand soon slipped, however, and he barely whipped himself under it. He had to squat deeply to keep the bar racked, his buttocks nearly touching the platform before he slowly ascended. The bar began slipping down his chest. He forced his elbows forward as his legs, shaking, straightened. Finally, he stood. But he felt spent. The bar crushed his throat, making him lightheaded. Panicking, he dropped into a two-inch free fall before pushing with his legs, rolling up onto his toes. The bar rose and he pushed himself under it as he split his legs into a low stance. His right knee brushed the platform as his arms straightened. Keeping the weight overhead, he inched one foot back, then the other forward, until they finally met. His arms shook above his wobbling torso.

One Mississippi . . . Two Mississippi . . . Three Mississippi . . .

He collapsed forward, dumping the bar, which bounced into his heaving chest. He rolled onto his back, wheezing like a saw. His wet T-shirt sucked against the plywood as his breathing slowed. There—*if only dad had seen that!* He recalled his dad running after him the first time he rode a bike without help, praising him in his deep Kiwi accent. Now he heard that voice when he imagined arriving at Heaven's gates as a saint. *Well done,* it would say, *good and faithful servant*. What confirmation! And he'd be with his dad forever. . .

Where was Scott? That lift deserved some praise, even just a kind word. He was about to stand but decided to stay down to draw Scott's notice. He listened and heard his coach's voice, distant and directed away. He opened one eye and saw Scott's back. He opened both eyes, sat up, and saw that the tall girl was looking at *him* while Scott spoke to her. Her teeth were mysteriously white, like Granma Schiller's, though surely this girl didn't wear dentures. Scott paid him no attention, so Damian tucked his foot under himself and stood, twisting his neck back on the way up to check the time: ten o'clock. He smiled at the vertical minute hand and then turned back to Scott.

"Did you see?" he asked, trying to sound more winded than he was.

"I did," the tall girl replied, smiling.

"No—Scott," he said. "Did *you* see?"

Scott seemed to notice him only now. "Sure, Damian—nice lift. Do 308 and you're done."

"308?" he and the girl said together. He stared at her.

"Have you lifted that much before?" she asked.

"No—almost," he said. "I—my—"

"His rosary caught on the bar," Scott said, mortifying Damian. "He would've done it otherwise."

The girl tilted her head. *"Rosary?"*

"I can do it," Damian said, meaning the 308lbs and desperate to change the subject.

"Show me," she said.

Horrified, Damian examined her eyes, playful, glistening, green.

"This is Veronica," Scott said, and the girl extended her

hand. He looked at Scott, who nodded and arched his eyebrows. Getting the hint, he grasped her hand and felt slender bones compress in his grip.

"Wow," she said, "thanks for the chalk."

"Oh, God—" he said, "I mean, *gosh*. Sorry, I thought it'd already rubbed off."

Fluttering her fingers, Veronica pulled her hand from his. He felt like he'd released a baby bird. She wiggled her fingers beside her face, showing a few flecks of chalk, and then reached out and wiped her hand on his sleeve. "You're already covered."

"Oh, God," he repeated, flinching from her weak grip and then feeling embarrassed for doing so. He turned back to the clock: 10:02! Where was his mother? If he didn't return to Canadian Martyrs soon, he might miss his chance to confess.

He turned back to Scott. "I'll check for my mom."

"I don't see her," Scott said, looking toward the front desk. "Go check outside, but if she's not there then—"

"308," Damian called over his shoulder. He hurried across the gym, trying to see through the now-steamed entrance doors. As he approached, he could just make out the top of their white car. He opened the door and gasped at the cold. The car was bright white, a new sedan, the same height as his family's station wagon but otherwise unlike it. Traffic was moving by inches. His mom would be late, and he doubted Father Dennis would still be awake when they finally returned to church. *Maybe I'll just have to ring the rectory doorbell and wake him,* he thought, mindful of yesterday's pledge to become saintly within the year. His mom would arrive frustrated after all the traffic she'd sat through today, but hopefully she remembered to bring food, a need he was reminded of as a delivery truck stopped in front of the gym and fresh baking inside dispersed an invisible, aromatic enticement.

The front of his T-shirt had already frozen stiff to his chest. Shivering, he shut the door. The delivery truck had started his stomach grumbling again, so he hurried to the free weights. He slid a 22-lb plate off a weight tree and reached for the second plate, but then decided to carry them to his platform one at a time. If Scott inquired, he could say he was trying to warm up.

Veronica and Scott were still chatting behind his platform. He slowly added the 22-lb plate and leisurely tightened the clamp when Veronica said, "Wow."

Scott's voice followed hers: ". . . never seen a classroom in his life!"

He cringed, wishing Scott didn't know about his lifelong homeschooling. He was humiliated to have a pretty stranger like Veronica hear about his isolated life— and especially from Scott, whose ridiculing tone carried through the gym's noise. He stood, desperate to interrupt his coach, ask him to watch the next lift carefully, pose some question about technique, but then realized he needed the second plate. He got it hastily, glancing out the doors again and listening for the clomp of his mom's shoes on the way back to his platform, but the cacophony of music, girls laughing, and feet stamping the treadmills made it impossible to hear any one person's step. Once he reached his platform, Veronica's arms were crossed and she was nodding as though she'd realized something profound. He slid the second plate onto the bar, now 308lbs, and overheard her say, "In other countries— *maybe.*"

He was sure they were still talking about him and that she was referring to his many relatives living under one roof. His fingers squirmed around the clamp as he tightened it, and then he turned back to Scott (and Veronica) and asked, "Can you watch this one and make sure I fully extend my legs?"

Scott nodded. Veronica stared. Embarrassed, Damian turned to his gym bag under the bench and felt their eyes on him as he opened his journal to a blank page with one sentence at the bottom: *The arrows ended Sebastian's life, but could not weaken his perseverance—perseverance that earned him a martyr's crown.*

He planned to record the weights he'd already done, but—upon seeing Sebastian's example—shut his journal, dropped it into his bag, strode to the chalk bin, and thrust his hands inside. His fingers trembled as he chalked up. How saintly had he been recently? Had his life been worthy of recording for future readers, young Catholics to come? His journal bore yesterday's sin; he'd been ashamed when Scott told Veronica about his family and home life; and, only moments ago, he tried to avoid this last lift by carrying one plate at a time. Would Sebastian have deceived his coach—if he had one—thus?

He shook off the excess flakes, approached the bar, positioned his feet, and prayed silently. *With your help, Sebastian.* Then he inhaled deeply, wrapped his fingers around the knurling as he lowered his hips, and pulled on the bar. It felt bolted to the floor and bent as he dragged it up his shins and over his knees until he thrust his hips forward, shrugging with the bar, head snapping back. Now the bar reached his belly. He whipped himself under the weight and racked it firmly. From his low squat, he fixed his gaze on a ceiling light and began to stand. The blinding light distracted him during the agonizing climb. He forced his thighs straight and then stood with the wavering bar. At this point his back began to cramp up, so he bent his knees and gulped a breath on the way down. The weight forced him lower than his usual stance. After dipping some four inches, he reversed direction and exploded up onto his toes.

He drove the bar off his clavicle. Momentarily it met his eyes before he pushed himself underneath. He split his legs and straightened his arms but as his right foot shot back, he felt nothing. His right knee smacked the platform. His arms collapsed. The bar crashed to his head and slammed him down. A dent in the platform sped toward him. The plywood felt hard, and then it felt soft. And his world went black.

CHAPTER THREE
CALLED BY NAME

"Damian."

Damian woke to an unfamiliar female voice speaking his name. She sounded muffled, as though she spoke from behind a windowpane. He fell back asleep.

"Damian," the woman said again—he did not know how long since the first time. Something constrained his feet and he arched them upward to loosen the bind. The strain lifted his head from the pillow and he winced. His skull, seemingly larger than his body, felt raw and cratered at the back.

"Damian," she said again. "Look at me, Damian. There we go. Come on."

His eyelids flickered open. Through the window, a grey winter sky poured pale light into the hospital room. Orange blankets covered his legs, and he knew he was not at home. Small fingers grasped the left bedrail; a square emerald sparkled on a silver ring. A young woman in green scrubs adjusted an IV bag at his bedside. Her blond hair was pulled back tight, her eyes were oval like almonds but a darker shade of brown, her nose was sharp and turned down at the tip, and her lips sparkled around teeth that reminded him of Veronica. He marveled at the sight of her until the shame and guilt returned, and he tried to snap his head down as he usually did—but his neck was in a brace and pain tore down his skull. Stars exploded behind his eyes.

"Uh-oh," the nurse said. "Don't move your head."

He tried to focus on the far wall. The clock there showed the time was either 12:30 or 6:00, but he couldn't steady his focus long enough to distinguish which hand was which. The blurry numbers began to spin, and he vomited onto his chest.

"I can't leave you alone, can I?" she said, dabbing him with a tissue. She looked directly at him. "I'm Karen, and I need you to look at me. Steady, now. Having trouble focusing?"

Pinned, he gazed at Karen. Her face was so close that he took shallow breaths and pressed his head into his pillow until it hurt. More stars, and her pupils wouldn't stop moving. Still she continued to stare at him, and he forced himself to meet her gaze by holding his breath and wiggling his toes slightly. *This isn't so bad,* he thought, trying to repress his discomfort at being so close to a young woman. *After all, I could be looking at Satan, hearing him say, "Mine, all mine."* Then Karen broke their stare, allowing him to exhale, and she seemed to scan the perimeter of his rattled pupils.

The thought of losing his soul after all his efforts to sanctify it, along with being observed so closely, so carefully, made him feel pitiful.

"I dropped a bar on my head," he said, more to himself than to Karen as he swallowed back nausea.

"Good," Karen said, her voice moving to the far end of the bed.

"How is it good?"

"You know why you're here," she replied, and he knew she was smiling by the sound of her voice. "How much do you remember?"

"I was hanging out the front door, freezing, waiting for my mom, then I—then I went back to lift, and my foot slipped."

"Good. Your coach told the paramedics that your foot slipped—must have been a wet shoe, maybe from the snow outside—"

"No. I kept my shoes inside the door."

"Well, your foot slipped somehow, and you dropped the bar on your head. Then you got lucky."

"Lucky?" he asked. *Was she mocking him?* Karen was indeed smiling while she tucked the blankets back beneath his feet.

"Lucky because the bar pushed you down, but the weights hit the floor first and stopped the bar from crushing you—your coach said it was a miracle."

The word roused him. His sin had put his salvation at risk, but God had seen the state of his soul and saved him from early death and damnation.

"Thank God," he said, and slowly lifted his hand, which bore a white paper bracelet, to his bandaged head. He touched his ear and wanted to trace the bump on the back of his skull through the gauze but didn't—it was a sacred site. He brought his hand back to the bed, repeating, "Thank God."

"How much were you trying to lift?" Karen asked, raising a clipboard from the foot of the bed and writing on it.

"I—" he said, seeing Karen's pen in her fingers. "It was 308—I was going to write it in my journal. Hey, where's my gym bag?"

"Here." Karen lowered the clipboard and walked to the left of his bed where she pulled back the curtains to reveal the rest of the small, private room. Damian—forgetting his brace—turned to see what she was doing.

"God!—Gosh!" he said, reeling.

"Stop moving your head!"

He closed his eyes. Karen's steps receded, approached again, and then he felt his gym bag placed gently on his lap. He nearly threw up into it, barely holding back the bile that rose in his throat. Karen pulled the bag to his knees and said, "I'll look—just tell me what you need."

"Just my journal," he said. Her hands rummaged through his bag—looking past the knee wraps, belt, the rattling bottle of ibuprofen—had she not pulled the bag to his knees, he'd have felt violated. "I don't see a journal."

"What?"

"It's not here," she said, holding the bag toward him as he peeked inside. The possibility of someone seeing his sin worsened his nausea. "Look, I'll go ask at the front desk—they probably took it out to find your contact info."

"Can you hurry?" he asked. He couldn't rest until his journal was in his hands.

"I'll go ask *if* you stop moving and get some sleep." He nodded, winced, and then looked bashfully at Karen, who shook her head and whispered, "Keep still—sleep!"

"Okay," he whispered back. Karen shut the door, quietening and darkening the room. He shut his eyes and tried to relax. His journal would soon be tucked in his gym bag, unless cackling nurses were reading it, passing it around. He dispelled the thought: *No, Lord—you wouldn't let that happen.* But then he pictured himself crumpling beneath the plummeting barbell. What'd he done to deserve such punishment? His unconfessed sin?

He prayed: *My life is a miracle, Lord—You've worked a*

miracle. . . Thank You for saving me. I'll confess my sin as soon as I can, but please, please let me get my journal. Saint Sebastian, please! I want to be like you and die young when I'm ready for Heaven, but don't let anyone read about yesterday's sin. The embarrassment would be too much to bear. . .

"Damian."

Damian woke to his mom's voice. His head still ached. He shuddered before squinting. Snow was falling, illuminating the room through the window and softening the orange blankets that covered him. He thought of Karen and wondered why she hadn't brought him his journal.

From the corner of his eye, his mom approached, but he remembered not to move his head and waited for her to enter his view. The clock showed a quarter to one—he had only slept about five minutes. When she leaned in, there were wet spots on her shoulders from melted snowflakes. She wore the same dark-green, ankle-length wool coat as when they'd left the house that morning, the same white scarf she wrapped around her head like a nun and left on through Mass. A female voice on the intercom in the hallway loudly announced a floor number. His mom had not closed the door.

"Hi, Mom," he said, his voice so feeble it scared him.

"Hi, Honey," she said, placing her hands over his so he felt something hard and smooth in her grasp. His journal. Had she already looked inside? Part of him wanted that so she would see his frustration with living at Grandma Schiller's, sharing a bed with James, studying alone in the basement. But he also dreaded the embarrassment of having her read yesterday's private shame. *No!* She couldn't see how corrupt he was. He released his hands from hers and grabbed at the journal, but she lifted the blue, hard-covered volume and held it to her side.

"How do you feel?" she asked, appearing concerned but suspicious.

"Like a piano fell on my head."

"That's nearly the case."

He wanted to appear relaxed and maintain eye contact with his mom, but he couldn't take his gaze off the journal, his brace squeezing his Adam's apple. His skull throbbed each time he shifted his eyes and she followed them, all the way to the book.

"Got your journal" she said, holding it up and nearly sneering. "The nurse at the front desk said she was about to bring it to you—that you *really* wanted it."

"I guess. Thanks." He held out his hand.

"Seems important."

"Sort of," he said, subduing his voice and dropping his hand. He looked down his blankets and sighed weakly, hoping to persuade her to focus on his present plight. But, her manner brisk and deliberate, she pulled up a chair, sat, and opened the journal to where his pen hung over the page.

"Let's see what we have here," she said.

"No!" He rose toward her even as the pain split his head and shot down his neck. The rush of it was too much and he fell back on the pillow, blinded, and breathed heavily as his shoulders shrugged around his crackling skull.

After a few minutes, he felt better, and settled. He hadn't heard whatever reaction his mom had made, and now he opened his eyes slowly—half-expecting her to have run down the hall to fetch Karen. She hadn't moved. The journal still open on her lap. She frowned, scanning the information on the cover page, including the emergency contact that listed Father Dennis, not her. She did not look up. Did not speak. She flipped the page.

Damian buried his fingers beneath his blankets, where they made orange waves with their squirming. How could she do this? *She already knows my past,* he thought, *and my routine—she wants my dreams too, my faults and fears.* He kept gasping, each time as though to speak, but then he just exhaled and gasped again. He felt vulnerable, as when he presented Father Dennis his weekly saint's biography for the parish bulletin and waited for the priest's review. Or when his schoolwork returned in the mail, graded by his government markers. No, this was worse. This was like when he confessed to Father Dennis and the priest paused silently—saddened, it seemed—before giving him his penance.

Minutes passed. She didn't look up as she turned page after page, exposing his innermost thoughts.

"I don't believe this," she said finally. His fingers tore at the blankets. "You wrote this two days ago—"

The word "two" gave Damian momentary hope that yesterday's sin may still be kept hidden. She read aloud: *"Slept poorly again last night because Uncle Rick pounds on his keyboard, chatting online until two or three in the morning. Then I'd just dozed off when the phone rang—a new friend tonight, from what I heard, whom Rick affectionately called Fredrick. The usual followed: giggles and whispers till dawn."*

She lowered the journal and tilted her head. "He does that?"

"I guess—hand it over, Mom." He hated that he'd just unintentionally tattled on Uncle Rick, and he put his hand out for his journal, but she continued to read aloud:

"I can't sleep because I don't know what I'm going to do after I complete high school. I'm afraid of people because I know nothing but this routine—Mass, study, lift, try to sleep, repeat."

She paused and glared at him. "We live a Catholic family's routine. What's wrong with that?"

"Nothing," he said. "Just gimme the journal and we'll talk it over. *Please.*"

She returned her eyes to his entry and read aloud a third time: *"This shame—and my frustration at home—is so unsaintly. No one in Butler's would want to run away from—"*

His mom looked up. "Unsaintly? And you want to run away?"

"Give it!" His hand shot out from under the blanket, grasping air. How dare she so callously reveal his deepest desires? Whatever the state of his soul, his yearning for sanctity was sacred. And his desire to run away was so secret he barely admitted it to himself. But he was also panicked knowing that what she'd just read ended the page, that if she turned it, she'd come upon yesterday's shameful entry. He snatched at the journal, clamped it with his fingers, and pulled. A sheet tore out, crumpling in his hand. He looked at it, hopeful, but it was the page she had just read, and now yesterday's entry would be in plain sight. He screamed: "Give it to me!"

She leaned back in the chair, shocked, and held the journal against her chest. Then she set her teeth, clenching her jaw. Her foot came up against the side of the bed and she pushed herself back. The chair screeched against the floor, almost flipping back, but she kept the heel of her boot jammed against the bed and maintained her balance, glaring at him—a silent warning—and then returned to his journal.

She flipped the page and, interrupting his loud gasp that was meant as a final protest, said, "You wrote this yesterday—*It happened today. I knew it was coming—my thoughts, my dreams, have been of bodies and skin. What should—*"

"Stop!" Damian screamed. "Stop reading my *damn* journal!"

She gasped, looked up. He thought she would scold him for swearing and for the words she'd just read. Instead, she raised the journal before her face and yelled the remainder of his entry: "*—I do? Sins to confess to Fr. Dennis—looked at an impure ad, had sexual fantasies, resented my mom for pressuring me into the priesthood, masturbate—*"

Scott entered the room, holding flowers. She turned her head with her open mouth frozen, and then looked back at Damian. A silent moment of tension, held by the three of them, ensued. Then, slapping his journal shut, she threw it onto the floor and walked past Scott without acknowledging him. At the door, she turned back to face Damian. He'd turned in her direction and pain bloomed across his skull.

"God saved your life this morning!" she said. "You should be ashamed of yourself!"

He watched her leave and then, mortified, looked at Scott, whose blue eyes were wide, his brow high. Damian was too embarrassed to speak. He shifted back on his pillow as Scott approached.

"Thanks," Damian said, grasping the bright yellow flowers that clashed with the orange blankets, the white winter scene outside, the pale light in the room. "Would you—"

Scott grabbed the journal and passed it to him. Damian stuffed in the sheet he'd torn out and held the journal on his lap under the flowers.

"I just couldn't focus this morning." Damian said, wanting to divert attention from what his coach had just heard.

"Don't worry, don't worry," Scott said, sitting in the now-empty chair. "I'll just sit here. You rest."

Damian nodded, closed his eyes, and imagined the story he was supposed to have written at church today: *Sebastian lived in the second century and suffered Diocletian's persecution of Christians. At a young age he . . .* After the scene he had just endured, and with Scott beside him, narrating the story—even silently—was difficult at first, but then the tale acted as a lullaby, and his pity transferred from himself to the young martyr. Their similarities—young men persecuted by authority, suffering for sanctity—dissolved his anxiety so that he soon slept, pondering a heroic death, a spotless soul, and endless happiness in Heaven.

CHAPTER FOUR
OFFERING

Waking from a nightmare about Saint Sebastien burning at the stake, Damian pushed his cratered head into the hospital pillow. He relaxed his neck and pain rushed to the back of his skull. It felt shattered in his skin, like it would collapse into his brain, and he froze, praying for relief: *Take this pain away, Lord, please take it*. As the shards settled, he heard a familiar sound that reminded him of his father. *Was that? . . . no . . . yes*—choking!

In the bed beside him lay a man who resembled his father on his deathbed: the bulging arm, white paper bracelet, big knuckles on long fingers—it was him! No—not with that pale skin and thick, dark arm hair. But the choking was his father's.

And now he was thirteen years old again, hauling the hot water tank up the stairs when his father suddenly clutched his chest and collapsed. He fell down the stairs and the tank tipped back and would've crushed him if Damian hadn't, somehow, mustering all his strength, pushed it to the side so it landed inches from his dad's head. But still his dad writhed on the basement floor, clutching his chest like this old man did now. His dad had gasped and hacked in the same way, too—first on that basement floor, next in the ambulance, and then he'd continued fighting for breath in the emergency room of *this* hospital. Why hadn't Damian remembered yesterday—that his father died in this very building?

The old man must've been moved here last night. Damian leaned forward to see the man's face but saw only long legs and a round belly. The white curtain hid his head. He leaned further forward, but his jagged skull tore at his skin and the shards ached again. He eased back into the pillow, careful as with a vase, and watched the fingers in the bed beside him clutch rhythmically, forming a fist with bulging knuckles just as his father had grasped for a last cup of water.

After arriving at the hospital in the ambulance four years ago, Damian stayed at his father's side until an emergency-room doctor told him to go to the waiting room. Shortly after, his mother arrived and they waited together. Then the doctor reappeared and said they could come visit his dad, that he'd had a heart attack but was settled.

When they entered the curtained-off area where his father lay sleeping, they waited silently. His dad appeared dead but then suddenly hacked loudly, his eyes wide in panic. His mother ordered Damian to stay at his father's bedside and not to leave for any reason whatsoever as she ran to find a doctor. He obeyed, even ignoring his father's gasping plea for water moments before he died, his fist clutching at air before falling to the bed.

Now Damian plugged his ears and shut his eyes. He recalled going to work with his father as a child. The work van with grey seats that'd looked a mile up when standing on the street. His father would lift him into the passenger's seat, and from this lofty perch he dizzily surveyed the neighbourhood cars, lawns, and houses.

(The man in the next bed coughed; Damian shoved his fingers deeper into his ears.)

After buckling him in, his father hopped in the driver's side, slamming his door to send a wave of cologne across the cab. His brand never changed, which reinforced the cologne's comforting familiarity, its reliable assurance that his dad was near, thus the scent bonded them—something shared, yet exclusive.

Dad started the engine, always adding a wink and smile when its slow, steady chug rumbled to life: powerful and predictable. *What peace back then! Safe. Happy.* The van pulled away from the Kurts' house, and Damian would wave to his mother, holding Bernadette on the porch.

Down the street, safely out of his mother's earshot, his dad revved hard, and Damian beamed with pride because this deafening sound projected sheer power like his dad's brawn. As the engine surged, so did Damian's imagination: the van itself (by his boyish estimation) was surely strong enough to pull a train, yet his dad could easily push the van uphill, even while running if he chose. Or, gripping its front bumper, he could pull the van along like a laundry basket, on ice or in mud. Flip it like a toy.

As his dad steered, the rumbling van became a tank and Damian imagined vehicles flying and flipping in the wake of its power. Some motorists likely shook in awe, sensing the driver's might exuded by his van. Other witnesses trembled in terror: but, given the chance to meet his dad, intimidation would turn to easy comfort—even admiration for his serene gentleness. Indeed, their fear would fade, melt from his charm—just like with his clients.

(Suddenly Damian startled. Was that slurping? He peeked. A stocky, wrinkled nurse held a plastic cup and angled the straw into the old man's puckering lips. *So easy!* He shut his eyes tighter.)

What solace to relive those joyful dawns years ago! Damian recalled sitting tall to enjoy the windshield's broad view. And then, looking overhead, between the green leaves that hung over the street, the blue sky rolled past and turned brown in the tinted sunroof. When they braked, his feet—hanging off the seat—went numb, but the tingling passed when the light turned green and then he'd curl his toes and feel free.

"Socks in sandals," his father would say, *his voice* rumbling like the van. "A true Kiwi!"

Now the right side of Damian's hospital bed sunk; he opened his eyes and there sat a slim young doctor wearing wire-framed glasses and a grey tie against his blue, collared shirt. His cheeks stuck out like a frog as he read from a clipboard, his eyes intense. Damian unplugged his ears. The old man was still coughing. He had to escape. But how?

The doctor flipped pages and from beneath the clipboard removed X-rays that Damian vaguely recalled being taken yesterday after Scott had left. The doctor held one up. It wavered loudly.

"Your skull's chipped, but not fractured," the doctor said, his light, piercing voice punctuating the importance of the present. The X-ray showed a smoky, kidney-shaped oval.

"Where's the chip?" Damian asked.

"There." The doctor pointed to a pock, not a crater, and Damian's skull ached in anticipation of the poke. The pain certainly outweighed the tiny chip, which he could hardly see. What must saints have suffered when shot with arrows or stoned to death! He needed to toughen up, to strengthen his resolve, inflict penance upon himself, pray extra rosaries on his knees, fast, run through snow—anything as long as it was far away from this hospital and the old man beside him.

"No serious damage," the doctor said. "But why don't we keep you for another day or so, just to—"

The old man hacked violently. Damian and the doctor turned toward the sound. There, standing in the doorway, was his mother. She glared, still angry, or course, but he was happy to see her. She held his coat. Today was Sunday. *This* nightmare was about to end.

"No," she said, approaching the bed, holding out his coat. "Put this on. We're going to Mass."

She flipped down the bedrail as the doctor stood to face her. Damian pulled his journal from under his pillow and, blinking back the pain rushing to his head, swung his feet over the side of the bed. He took his coat and slowly slid his arms into the sleeves.

"You must be Mrs. Kurt," the doctor said.

"We're late for Sunday Mass," she replied.

"We have a chaplain."

"We're leaving."

"Hold on," the doctor said. "I want to run a few tests."

"No," she repeated, steady but fierce. She guided Damian's feet into his shoes. As she laced them, he stared at the old man's knuckles to prevent himself from fainting. They swirled in and out of focus, tanned skin to pale, past to present. "If he gets sick, I'll call you."

Nausea rose in his throat, but his mother, after shouldering his gym bag, leaned into him and helped him stand. Clutching his journal, he gripped her waist and took baby steps, following her lead.

He closed his eyes as they passed the speechless doctor. He would try to forget that froglike face. He was on a path to spiritual perfection: tests and a longer stay at this horrid hospital were merely disruptions.

He wanted to escape faster but swam in dizziness. They reached the door and entered the hallway. Damian anticipated hitting the floor with each step, each slow, head-jarring step that distanced him from the past, from that terrible day four years ago, he now fled.

The church aisle tilted. He swallowed hard, stumbling, and grabbed the pews for support as his mother mercilessly led him to the very front row. In his current state of distress, outright panic, could even the sacred Mass grant him solace? Holy Communion might, he desperately hoped, provide guidance, at least some solace—Christ as comforting companion to a battered, injured, despondent youth.

His mother sat, leaving space for him beside her. He was grateful to sit, but she sniffed when he did. Her head spun past him as he focused on her scowl, her puckering lips: he hadn't genuflected. She flipped the kneeler onto his shoe, and he pulled out just before she dropped onto her knees and crossed herself: *widely* so the congregants behind her could acknowledge her piety, and *briskly* to convey her anger at him.

On the way home she accelerated over potholes and speed bumps, merged by jerking the wheel. In the station wagon's rear-facing bench seat, he pressed his palms against the sides of the car until she stopped outside the house and rushed inside. His head throbbed at each step up the porch. Inside the foyer, Grandma Schiller squeezed his hand, and he wished her soft, wrinkled fingers could wrap around his head, his whole body.

Then, from the living room, he heard the voices of familiar biblical characters. Had the barbell dented his mind, leaving him to hallucinate? He listened carefully and recognized Abraham's voice: he was telling his son Isaac of the sacrifice they would make at the mountaintop. Isaac responded joyfully, unaware that *he* was the sacrifice.

Damian entered the living room and, on the TV screen, saw Abraham raise a knife above his head, about to plunge the blade into Isaac. At the last moment, a voice from above intervened and Isaac was spared.

Abraham praised the God who had commanded him to slay his son. Bernadette and Mary clapped their hands as they sat on the sofa, watching a Bible video.

"Praise the Lord!" Mary said. "And bless His holy name!"

"Oh my God," Damian mumbled as he walked past the TV.

"What's on your head?" Bernadette asked.

"A bandage," he replied. "I thought mom told you I dropped a bar on my—"

"You were smote!" Mary cried gleefully.

"Oh my God," he mumbled again.

"The Lord's name in vain!" his mother shouted from the kitchen. He went downstairs, opened the bedroom door, and stepped on the toy cars James was playing with. He lifted his foot, flinching in pain.

"Damn it!" he said. James looked up in horror, and then saw the bandages.

"What's on your head?" James asked.

"Go upstairs," Damian said. "The girls are watching

TV."

"This is my room too, you know."

"I know," he said, sighing. He shoved his gym bag under the bed because there was no room on the floor, and he lay down gently; the mattress springs squeaked. James continued playing, rumbling engine sounds, spitting explosions, squealing, and creaking as he raced and crashed his cars. Despite the noise, Damian thought he might sleep, but when he closed his eyes the plummeting barbell flashed through his mind.

"James!" his mother called. "Saint's life!"

James ran upstairs, rolling a toy ambulance along an invisible road and making rocket sounds as he went. Damian suspected she was too angry to call him, and now that he was home—away from the hospital and the horrible memories it triggered—he realized how much he wanted distance from her, too.

"Saint Dominic Savio, patron of young men," she read loudly upstairs. He waited for her to read the date, and when she didn't, he grew suspicious. He winced as he pulled his *Butler's Lives* from under the bed and checked today's saint. It was Winifred, patron of holiday travelers, not Dominic Savio, whose life she had obviously selected to inflict guilt for what she had read in his journal yesterday.

"Saint Savio," she continued, pronouncing each word with exaggerated clarity, "was born in Italy in 1842. One day, when he was four, he disappeared and his good mother went looking for him. She found the little fellow in a corner praying with his hands joined and his head bowed. . ."

A cowed, pious little boy, he thought, *is what she*

wanted to find in my journal—not a secret sinner.

Despite his fatigue, sleep was unattainable, so he grabbed his journal.

"When Dominic was seven," his mother read, even more loudly, "he received his First Holy Communion. On that solemn day, he chose the motto, 'death but not sin.'"

If only I had such resolve, Damian thought sadly. He shoved a tissue into his ears to muffle his mom's voice and opened to a blank page. He decided to compose a list that would ensure he got to Heaven, to his father:

Steps to Sanctity

(The first three steps were obvious, and he wrote them quickly.)

- *confess sin*
- *pray for purity*
- *gain distance from mom*

"And Saint Savio died young," she nearly yelled, the tissue no match for her volume, "having never sinned against purity!"

He knew she'd fabricated that last detail to make him feel even worse for Friday's sin: *Saint Aloysius Gonzaga* was the saint who remained perfectly innocent of unchaste thought until *his* early death. And now his siblings ·stomped to the dining table and pulled out their chairs.

"Keep it down out there!" Uncle Rick screamed from his room.

"Suffer the little children!" his mom replied.

How could he escape this crazy house? He had to find somewhere to live, somewhere far away. And suddenly Scott came to mind. Hadn't he often expressed frustration with the Kurts' home life? Their fasting, praying, and church attendance that he believed interfered with Damian's progress as a lifter? And wasn't he looking for a roommate to help pay his rent?

Living with Scott gained distance from his mother, and he could take his textbooks with him and complete his high school studies anywhere, really. But his job writing for the parish bulletin surely paid too little for his part of Scott's rent. What new, more lucrative job could he do? The priesthood was the sole career he'd considered seriously; the only lives he'd studied were saintly ones. He'd have to scour *Butler's Lives* for ideas of what holy men and women did before entering the monasteries and seminaries of old.

God would guide him. The saints would intercede. He added that final step:

- *read Butler's Lives for job ideas*

Upstairs his mother led grace before dinner: "Bless this meal, Lord, and help *each* of us do Your will."

More like your will, Mom, Damian thought.

That afternoon Damian sat up in bed and placed a pillow behind him for support. Despite his fatigue and desire to escape his mother, he wanted to work on a particularly important part of his dad's biography: his adolescent epiphany at the All Blacks' game. This crucial moment had inspired his dad to reform his base habits— or *habit*, more precisely, since youthful carousing comprised, to Damian's knowledge, his father's only instance of youthful depravity.

If Damian could fashion this pivotal moment so that it smacked of sanctity and projected piety, he'd establish religious motivation for his father—a prerequisite for canonization. And a truly *Christian* conversion in his dad's youth would ground the story wonderfully; it would also, in Damian's current distress, comfort him by confirming that his father was indeed in Heaven, that when earthly sufferings ended, they'd reunite, happy forever.

First, Damian skimmed his existing account:

One day George and his brothers attended a rugby match. . . Suddenly, in the sea of screaming fans at the stadium, he had a plan for his future. So, George slowed his drinking and, instead, practiced rugby on his family's station with his brothers. When they went to the bar, he ran laps around the fields, chinned himself on the barn's rafters, and did push ups with bags of feed on his back. . .

This version showed a decisive improvement from drinking to sobriety *and* disciplined training; this version also merely implied that his father's motivation was simply to become a professional rugby player. What could Damian do?

He scoured *Butlers* and considered possible approaches. Had his father, perhaps, sought to become a better man and skilled athlete *in order* to honour his family, country, and— ultimately—God Himself? *That might work!*

On a fresh page he wrote the new material that would hopefully improve his working draft:

Now George Kurt had not reformed his ways in order to directly spread the word of God by, say, founding a new order or going off to fight in crusades. Nor had he, after that fateful All Blacks match, explicitly renounced all sins of the flesh and entered monastic life, as had Saint Augustine, or abandoned earthly riches to rebuild a crumbling, persecuted Church, like Saint Francis of Assisi. But that was because George Kurt's talents lay elsewhere, in physical prowess and athletic ability. He honoured Heaven by rejecting the faults of his past so he could excel— to God's greater glory! —on the playing field.

These lines fixed the problem, but were they true? *Had* his father *actually* intended to thus glorify God? When he'd spoken about this part of his life, he'd never claimed that his ultimate goal lay in anything beyond wearing an All Blacks jersey one day. . .

Damian slowly shook his sore head. Had a professional athlete ever become a saint? He doubted it, and this worried him. He closed his journal, shut *Butlers*. He'd wanted so badly to plumb his father's youthful reform for saintly attributes, but none seemed inherent to the event as it'd actually occurred. So, success eluded him on such a dismal day, when it would've granted much needed comfort.

Hours later he woke from a hazy sleep. He'd been dreaming that his mother found The Bay's catalogue under his bed. Even though his head ached terribly, he leaned over and checked that it was still safely hidden. Once he recovered from his injury and ran away to Scott's house, he'd dispose of the catalogue—maybe in the dumpster behind Roy's Gym, which was too deep to reach into and retrieve it.

And what about his journal? He reached under the bed again and felt it, too, but he worried it was no longer safe there. Now that his mother knew he kept it in his gym bag, she might search for it while he was sleeping to update her knowledge of his secrets. If she discovered his escape plan, it'd be foiled; he needed a new hiding place. He considered stuffing the journal in the tower of National Catholic Registers, somewhere near the bottom, or sliding it into the dusty toaster oven that sat abandoned in the corner.

For now, James snored beside him and prevented him from falling back asleep. Their room was so dark he couldn't even see the outline of his desk or the crucifix on the wall. He closed his eyes and prayed for God to guide him when he left this home and ventured out into the frightening world. He was so lonely for his dad just now; his eyes moistened; his lips trembled.

Will I survive? He hoped he'd fare better at Scott's house, at a new job, than he had at the hospital. And then he heard a voice from above:

"What are you wearing?"

"Bandages," Damian replied tentatively. He wondered if this voice was celestial, maybe even divine; but, at the same time, something made him suspicious.

"What do ya wanna do?"

"Your will," Damian whispered, but he tilted his head; the voice's tone was undeniably lustful.

"Oh yeah? I'd like that, too," Uncle Rick—*of course* it was Uncle Rick—said. Damian felt stupid for not immediately recognizing his uncle on a chat line. Maybe the barbell really *had* scrambled his mind!

Uncle Rick continued for hours, his muffled questions, giggles, and moans complementing James' persistent snores. Damian kept his eyes open to avoid flashbacks of the plummeting bar, and slowly the sun rose, emitting dim light through the bedroom window. As the shadows lifted, he saw his reflection in the mirror on the wall: first his lumpy, bandaged head, then the stubble on his face, and last, the dark circles under his teary eyes.

His mother opened the door and flicked on the light. "James, go upstairs."

James blinked and scrambled from the room rubbing his eyes. Damian met his mother's glare.

"God saved you yesterday," she said.

"After dropping a barbell on me!"

"How dare you!"

"He did!"

"You should be grateful."

"I hate it here!"

"You owe God your life."

"What does that mean?"

"The priesthood."

"I hate church," he said, expecting a cock to crow. His mother approached him, lifting her hand threateningly. He pumped his palms at her and cowered. "Okay. Sorry."

"Give good example to your siblings."

"Fine."

"We'll discuss your future later," she said, hissing. And then she swept out of the room.

CHAPTER FIVE
SEVERANCE

On Saturday morning, one week after dropping the barbell on his head, Damian woke twenty minutes earlier than usual. He'd set his alarm for 6:10 a.m. the night before in order to give himself time to pack his bag and write a farewell note to his mother. After spending a nearly sleepless week in bed, surrounded by his family's activity and voices, he'd firmly decided to run away from home and live with Scott.

He sat up quickly; a wave of dizziness passed over him. For the past seven days he'd remained prostrate in bed, except for the occasional trip to the toilet assisted by James. He turned off the alarm and closed his eyes to prevent himself from falling over or vomiting. James snored. Damian didn't want to wake him, to receive any assistance, because he had to venture out on his own today, and he was determined to do so independently.

He inhaled deeply and opened his eyes then rose from the bed. His knees shook. The basement tilted as he made his way to the downstairs bathroom. He undressed. The floor tilted and swayed below him, a ship on a wavy sea. Head spinning. The drain spun between his feet in the shower. He placed his palm against the wall for support and turned the knob to Hot.

The water pressure lifted the caked gauze from his scalp, and the steam softened the bandages allowing them to peel off with ease. He opened the shower door to drop the clumped bandages into the trashcan. The sudden rush of cold air made him shiver and he wanted to return to the hot flow and sooth his tender scalp, but he forced himself to turn off the water and use one of Grandma Schiller's smoky towels to dry off. If he didn't keep moving, he might lose his resolve and decide that running away was too hard, too scary.

He shaved, removing all evidence that he couldn't grow a proper beard. His pupils twitched, as though the barbell had rattled his eyes, his face, his identity. *This is who I am. Wherever I end up, I am Damian Kurt, you, I—*

"Bernadette! Leave your sister alone!" his mother shouted from upstairs.

He sighed, then stumbled back to the bedroom, and found that James had already risen and gone upstairs. The room reeled as he struggled into slacks and an old T-shirt, but he clenched his teeth and prayed to his father for support. And because he didn't want to alert anyone to his running away after Mass, he'd decided to pack his belongings into his gym bag rather than a suitcase.

He lined the bottom of his bag with his government-issued textbooks—math, English, social studies, and—handling it with special reverence because his mother despised it—biology. Scott would not threaten to throw the text away, as his mother often had because of its chapter on evolution, and he looked forward to avoiding such conflicts in the future.

On top of the textbooks he placed his copy of *Butler's Lives of the Saints,* and then buried the books with sweatpants and T-shirts for the gym. He packed notebooks, pens, pencils, a ruler, an eraser, his razor, his toothbrush, and then, so they didn't rattle around when he carried his bag upstairs and into the car, he covered these items with underwear, socks, and his hated school-hours uniform.

"Damian!" his mother called from upstairs. "Let's go!"

"Coming," he replied, his voice still feeble. He packed his wallet, which held forty dollars from his last two biographies for the parish bulletin, and then retrieved his journal from the toaster oven and tore out a blank page. On it he wrote:

Mom,

Christ Himself told His Mother, 'I must be about My Father's business.' After publicly reading my most private thoughts last week, and this despite my begging you to stop, you now know that I want to become a saint to see dad again. I can't do that here. Not with you pressuring me into the seminary: your interference compromises the sincerity and authenticity of the religious vocation I may have.

I am leaving today.

Don't pick me up after my workout. You may guess where I've gone, but please don't try to contact me because I won't come back.

Damian

He folded the page, wrote "Mom" on the front, and left it on his pillow. Who'd find it first? If not his mother, James would discover it and take it directly to her.

He lugged his gym bag upstairs and passed Uncle Rick's room, but he couldn't even look at the door: the vile filth he'd heard his uncle speak over the past week disgusted him and fueled his desire to leave this house and never return, to survive out in the world and become completely unlike Uncle Rick.

Outside, his family was waiting in the car, their faces pressed against the window glass. They watched him exit the front door, and while his knees shook slightly down the porch stairs, no one seemed to suspect all he was carrying. The station wagon's rear door was wide open, waiting for him as it always was when they left for Mass. He got in, careful not to grunt or strain. His gym bag hit the rear seat heavily, bouncing the car, but he sat down quickly and slammed the door to blur the evidence of its weight.

Without a word, his mother pulled away from the curb.

"Bless me, Father," Damian said, wobbly on the narrow wooden kneeler in the dark confessional, "for I have sinned."

Dizzy, he suddenly found himself leaning to the left. He swung his torso in the opposite direction and almost fell through the confessional curtain and into the body of Canadian Martyrs. To steady himself he gripped the sides of the small, square window facing him. Through its diamond-pattern grating, Father Dennis slouched in a black cassock and purple stole. With his thick thumb and index finger, the priest pinched the ridge of his nose, raising his glasses to his forehead. Then he rubbed his eyes before resting his cheek on his fist. He seemed oblivious to Damian's flailing.

Damian was sweating now, and chilly, too; but he pressed on, driven by his fear of Hell. "It's been one week since my last confession. I am a sinner and these"— (he tipped again and gripped the grated window's frame tighter)— "are my sins."

He breathed deeply. He wanted to confess his masturbation along with looking at the underwear model in the catalogue, but it was his practice, when confessing acts of lust, to sandwich them between other, less embarrassing sins. Even in his current state, he found something to say before last Friday's shameful act.

"I'm running away," he said in an intentionally garbled whisper. He didn't want his pastor to recognize his voice because of what he had to confess next.

"You just got here," Father Dennis said. The priest pulled his hand away from his face and peered through the grating. Damian, smelling whiskey, leaned back into the dark confessional, hoping to conceal his identity in the shadows.

"No, no—" he stammered. "I—I left a note for my mom this morning and today I'm running away because she's pressuring me into the priesthood, and I can't stand it. So, I'm moving in with my weightlifting coach and I'll try to find a job and, and . . . And I'm never going back home."

He hadn't intended to reveal so much about his current plans, but, now that he had, he realized that what he was about to do—leave an emotionally abusive parent and venture out on his own—wasn't sinful. Or was it? Had his mother's control warped his conscience, so that any act she disliked now induced guilt? Considering what he'd just confessed, what'd instinctively sprung from his lips as though wrong and needing forgiveness, he realized how he *had to* escape her influence. He was grateful, and a little embarrassed, for what'd just happened.

"Right, well . . ." Father Dennis said, his whiskey

breath unbearable. The priest rubbed his temples. "Listen carefully to today's scriptures and pay close attention to my homily. You may be inspired to choose wisely in your future endeavours."

Father Dennis' advice in confession was always the same! Damian wished the priest had at least attempted to guide him. Never before had he described his home situation so honestly. But his present purpose, he reminded himself, was to confess his mortal sin, not to be advised. "And, last week, on Friday, I looked at a—"

"Was anyone behind you in line?" Father Dennis asked.

"No."

"Good. Well, pray three Hail Marys and be grateful for your lovely family."

"But I'm not done!" Damian's pulse rose.

"I've gotta say Mass. God forgives you."

And just as Damian opened his mouth to protest, Father Dennis slid the wood panel across the window, shutting him out, leaving him in darkness. Damian gnashed his teeth in frustration. Hadn't God seen his desire to confess?

In confusion, rather than the state of grace he'd so yearned for, he exited the confessional. Father Dennis was already lumbering down the aisle on his way to the sacristy; his corpulent form swayed with each step and masked, Damian realized, the alcohol's likely effect on his pastor's gait. Father Dennis passed the Kurts, sitting in the left side front row, as always. They'd confessed before Damian and had probably already prayed their penances. He envied their innocence.

He stepped forward to join them, but just then caught

a glimpse of his mother's satisfied expression as she knelt, head bowed, eyes closed, smiling. Beside her knelt little James, his arms wrapped around her waist. And to her right, at the end of the pew, was the usual space she left for *him*. The sight of that empty space suddenly enraged him, because to leave it empty and neglect praying his penance beside her would make him feel guilty, even though it wasn't wrong.

Before his mother opened her eyes, before Father Dennis emerged, vested, from the sacristy, and before he lost his nerve, he turned and walked out of the church.

An hour later, he turned a corner and saw Roy's Gym across the snowy street. He sighed in relief. His dizziness had cleared after the first few blocks, but now he was freezing, his dress shoes sopping, and his bag's strap cut into his shoulder: *like carrying the cross,* he thought, *the innocent man burdened with another's guilt, trudging the road to Calvary—I mean Calgary. . . .*

After abandoning his family in the front pew, he'd found the station wagon's rear door unlocked in the parish parking lot—a sign he was on the right path—and he grabbed his heavy gym bag, set his teeth, and began the cold trek across the city. Several times he thought he heard the family car coming up behind him, but it never had; and he'd tossed the catalogue in a deep back-alley dumpster— grateful to at least be rid of the *material* remnants of his sin.

Beside Roy's, a bakery displayed loaves, rolls, and pink cupcakes in its front window. They smelled delicious, and his stomach gurgled. He wanted to buy something, but the forty dollars in his wallet suddenly seemed small. Now that he was out in the world, cold and alone, how long would his meager funds last?

Humid air, suffused with bleach, sweat, and chalk, rushed out of the gym when he opened the front door, and it mercifully replaced the bakery's enticing aroma. Metal weights clanged, rubber plates slapped the platforms, and the radio played loud rock and roll. Across the crowded floor, Scott leaned against the mirrored back wall, chatting with Veronica and another, older girl Damian recognized from the hockey team.

"Hey," Scott said as Damian approached. "How's the head?"

"Better, thanks." He put his gym bag on the floor with a thump.

"You got a body in there?" Scott asked, smiling.

"Scott?" Damian said. Tears filled his eyes. He sobbed once, then put his hand to his mouth.

"You okay?" Scott asked. He approached and leaned in, sounded genuinely concerned.

"No." Damian's shoulders shook, mortified that the girls saw him cry.

"Ladies, just wait for me at the next platform," Scott said, and then he placed his hand on Damian's shoulder. "What's wrong, buddy?"

"Scott," Damian said between sobs. "Remember when you were looking for a roommate? Well, could I move in with you?"

"Um . . ."

"I, I can't live with my mom anymore and, and I don't know where to go, and . . ."

"Um . . ."

"I could pay and—"

"All right, all right." Scott looked at him intently and smiled. "Sure. Move in."

"Really?"

"I'm serious."

"Maybe just for a month or—"

"It's okay. As long as you need. I expected something like this, actually—with your mom and all."

"Yeah."

"You wanna just forget today's workout?"

"Really?" Damian was genuinely relieved. He couldn't have lifted in his present state anyway, upset as he was and still shaken from last week's injury.

"Yeah. Come on, buddy."

And Scott, an unbeliever but—at present—a saviour none the less, lifted the heavy gym bag to his shoulder. He waved at the girls, whom Damian couldn't acknowledge now, ashamed of his tears, and then led the way out of the gym.

"Here you go," Scott said, flicking on the basement bedroom's lights. Damian sighed in relief to see four clean white walls, a wood desk with a reading lamp and chair, and a mattress—*with* sheets—on the floor: he'd keep it just this tidy.

It was a small room, with a tiny window above the mattress, but it was still bigger than back at Grandma Schiller's *and* he didn't have to share.

"The dresser's in the closet," Scott said, dropping Damian's gym bag on the mattress.

"Thanks *so much.*"

"I'm happy you're here." Scott squeezed his shoulder, and Damian smiled. "I'll let you get unpacked."

Damian nodded, and Scott left the room. As soon as his coach shut the door, he had an overwhelming desire to drop onto the mattress and sleep, but he couldn't relax until he did something that he'd been waiting to do for a long time.

He unzipped his gym bag: there, on top of all he'd packed, was his uniform that'd symbolized his mother's hold on him while at home. The white dress shirt that constricted his breathing, the red cardigan that made him too hot, and the stiff grey dress pants that cut into his crotch and squished his thighs while he was trying to study. They'd all afflicted him too long.

First, he grabbed the cardigan, stood on it for leverage, and tore off the sleeves. He plucked off the buttons and snapped them between his fingers, like his father used to bend quarters as a trick to entertain his customers.

Now he laid hands on the dress shirt and tore it in half. Then he ripped the halves in half, shredding the pieces mercilessly until they were the size of stamps. He pulled his belt from its loops and, after biting it, threw it against the wall.

Finally, his hated pants. They had slipped between two textbooks as though they were hiding. He slowly pulled them from the bag and dangled them. Then he draped them around his shoulders, gripped the heel of each leg, and, as Sampson had torn down the pillars that he'd been tied to, he ripped the pants apart. They tore loudly. . .

He stuffed the remnants of his wrath into the trashcan, and finished unpacking. He lined up his textbooks on the desk and arranged his pens and notebooks in the drawer. *Butler's Lives* and his rosary went beside the reading lamp, and he folded his surviving clothes before placing them neatly into the dresser drawers.

Then he lay down, satisfied, to sleep in his new room.

CHAPTER SIX
COMFORTING THE SICK

The next morning, Scott stood at his kitchen island, appearing concerned as he silently mixed and poured pancake batter while Damian, sitting on the living room sofa, described his mother's religious hysteria, her pressuring him into the priesthood, her constantly demanding her own way.

"At least she busted me out of the hospital," he said. "The guy beside me reminded me of my dad—it brought on an awful flashback."

"Busted you out of the hospital?" Scott asked, flipping a pancake and then holding out the spatula accusingly. Scott's angry face worried him. In revealing all he had about his mother, he hoped he hadn't conveyed an unflattering version of his own piety because, after breakfast, he planned to convince Scott to drive him to Saint Joseph's Cathedral downtown—the only church in the city, as far as he knew, that offered confession on Sundays. He wanted to confess before the five o'clock Mass, which, perhaps, if he didn't anger him too much now, Scott might even attend with him.

"I recovered at home," he said, muttering to mollify his last statement.

"Did the doctors want you to stay longer?"

Damian hesitated longer than he should have.

"That means yes." Scott slapped the spatula against the counter and rolled his eyes. "Why am I not surprised?"

"What do you mean?" This conversation was souring quickly.

"Your mother thinks she owns the world—bossing everyone around. I should tell you about my first conversation with her, demanding I coach you after your dad died."

"Really?" He tried to sound intrigued, as though he hadn't heard her end of the conversation, successfully persuading Scott, whom she'd never met, to coach her son for a measly monthly payment. He *was* grateful for his mom's ability to manipulate people, as long as it wasn't him, and he wondered if he could now employ some of her skills to turn this conversation from his domineering parent to the possibility of arriving at church an hour early this afternoon. But, as he prepared his words, arranging them to sound offhand yet reasonable, Scott shovelled the browned pancakes onto a plate on the island, and pushed out a bar stool for Damian.

"Let's eat," Scott said.

"Awesome." He was really hungry, so he stood quickly, no longer dizzy, and sat at the island. The pancakes, with slices of hot banana in them, smelled delicious—entirely unlike the limp, thick-buttered toast and overcooked porridge that Grandma Schiller served at home.

"And don't bother saying grace," Scott said. He threw the pan and spatula into the sink and ran water over them. The pan, steaming, hissed.

"Why?"

"Because this," Scott said, pointing at the four walls of his house, "is a *faith-free* zone."

He wanted to plunge into the pancakes, but that last statement angered him: he had to say something. "It's not while I'm here."

"What do you mean?" Scott poured himself a cup of coffee and sat on the stool across the island. The morning sun coming through the living room window shone off his bald head. A thick vein that ran down his forehead showed clearly and appeared to pulsate. Damian recognized it from the gym, from the times he'd arrived late or let his lifting technique get sloppy. He had to be careful now.

"What I mean is—"

"You just got here, *Damian,*" Scott said. He helped himself to a pancake, slapping it down hard onto his plate. "Don't tell me what kind of house this is—it's mine, and *I* am letting *you* stay here."

"I know, I know," Damian said. "And I appreciate it *so* much. What I'm saying is that even though my mom pressures me into the priesthood, forces her ways on me, *I'm* still Catholic."

"*Why?*"

Damian paused. He tried to prepare a sincere answer, but Scott's angry face distracted him. He closed his eyes. Immediately the banana pancakes' aroma intensified. His hunger called to him, but he suppressed his stomach's desire by focusing on another, much deeper yearning: his father's smiling face blooming in his mind, and his goal—Heaven. Past his father's face, in the white-cloudy background, were the saints he knew well: their tonsured heads, clutched scrolls, and religious habits—brown, grey, and black—identified them easily, like characters in a favorite novel.

But then all that saintly imagery faded and what remained was his father's smile. His rough hands reached out and grabbed Damian's. They embraced, chest to chest, and he felt his father's heart beating again, against his. He opened his eyes, which were teary now, and forced himself to articulate what drove and defined him, what he often struggled to admit even to himself: "I miss my dad."

"I get that," Scott said. He appeared concerned again, had stopped chewing. His eyes were gentle once more. "But how does Catholicism bring him back?"

"I'll see him in..." he said, hesitantly uttering his deepest desire. The words, sacred to him, smoldered on his tongue; his voice petered into a whisper, "...Heaven."

Scott squeezed Damian's hand. "Okay. Be Catholic here."

"Thanks."

"Just don't bring me into it." Scott resumed chewing.

"But I need you to drive me to church this afternoon," he said, reluctant to push his luck but also unable to restrain his request.

"It's two blocks away—Saint Rita's. Mass is at, um, well, you'll figure it out. You're well enough to walk, aren't you?"

He nodded. He wanted to go along with this plan. Scott was already being very generous, but after imagining his father so vividly just now, his desire to confess had intensified again. The sin of masturbation burdened him heavily. "It's just, well, Saint Rita's doesn't have confession on—"

"I thought you went yesterday."

"I tried. It didn't work."

"Didn't work?"

"I—" But how to explain? A tear rolled down his cheek.

"I'm not falling for that," Scott said. "Your mom may not be here, but she's still controlling you."

"She's not!"

"She is! She sprung you out of the hospital against the doctor's advice. *You* should have stayed and *forced* yourself through that flashback."

"I know, I know. Just drive me this once and—"

"You even *sound* like your mom right now."

"No! She's . . ." He was nearly too angry to speak. "I'm not *forcing* you to do anything!"

"Sounds like you are."

"I just need . . ." he said, and then his frustration with trying to confess, unsuccessfully, returned. Damian stifled a sob by holding his fist to his mouth.

"Look," Scott said. He patted Damian's hand. "I wanna see you grow up while you're here—meet people, try new things, get a job. . . You *are* planning to work, right?"

"Yeah," he said, reminded that he had to find better-paying employment: an urgent problem, but secondary to restoring his innocence. "I'll start looking for something."

"Okay," Scott said. Damian nodded, smiled—he was waiting for Scott to agree to drive him to Saint Joseph's today. Scott seemed to understand and said, "And we can work something out with confession."

"Today?"

"Fine!" Scott threw his hands up.

Damian was sorry he'd angered his coach, but he was also pleased that he'd persuaded him.

"God! Just eat, and then we'll discuss some ground rules for living here."

Damian nodded, thinking, *And then confession.* He craved a spotless soul more than even the tastiest meal but helped himself to some pancakes, nonetheless. With Scott having agreed to drive him, he just had to review his confession list before arriving at church. Surely, by the end of the day, last week's sin would be forgiven.

The pancakes were as delicious as they smelled.

After breakfast Damian sat at his new desk downstairs. He needed to study extra diligently to compensate for last week's convalescence, but before he opened his textbooks he wanted to work on his father's biography. Doing so would help him establish good habits in these new quarters, habits that moved him towards his ultimate purpose and strengthened his resolve.

But he also wanted to just spend some time with his dad, recalling fond memories, silently chatting, praying to him. Damian opened his journal and imagined his father standing at his side, ready to guide his pen.

Leaving home had got Damian thinking about his father's emigration from New Zealand to Canada. He wanted to rewrite that brave journey so that his father appeared to be motivated by spiritual intentions. Damian would reveal the beginning of an inward journey toward sanctity that he believed *(or at least hoped!)* his dad had undertaken. But how to approach this revision puzzled him, so he thumbed through *Butler's* in search of inspiration.

Soon he found the life of Saint Francis Xavier, a Jesuit missionary who'd sailed to Mozambique, India, New Guinea, and Japan to spread the gospel. His evangelical efforts had succeeded despite many obstacles, but quickly it became apparent that his experiences were unlike George Kurt's.

First, his dad had initially come to Canada for a rugby tournament, not to win converts. Then on that first trip he'd met his future wife, and his infatuation with her brought him back permanently several months later, as Damian had described in his story, which he now read:

George moved to Calgary—his rugby career ended by a knee injury that some teammates suspected he had faked. After being baptized a Catholic, he married the young woman from the gas station and opened a plumbing business. And then the first of four children was born.

His dad had certainly acted out of love. Not the pious love for souls that motivated famous missionaries, but love for Damian's mother and, then, for the children they had together.

But he *had* (according to Mrs. Kurt) been baptized, and surely Damian could plumb *that* for religious motivation. Almost certainly his mother had encouraged his father to become Catholic, but in his planned revision he'd downplay her direct involvement. Instead, he'd describe his father's burning desire to embrace the Faith, and how the woman George had fallen for had so impressed him with her virtue and devotion, he'd abandoned his homeland and all worldly ambitions—namely his rugby career—to join her and grow together in Godly love. *That* was how Damian would refashion his father's journey!

He moved his pen towards the page, but then stopped. His father *wanted* to be baptized, didn't he? He hadn't simply agreed to his fiancée's desire, without taking the sacrament seriously. *No.* Yet Damian had just escaped his mother's wrathful manipulation. He knew her power and it frightened him.

He tried to recall his dad discussing his baptism, his becoming Catholic as an adult, but nothing immediately came to mind. He remembered his mother describing the event with pride, however, and suddenly Damian felt so uncomfortable he shut his journal, closed *Butler's*, and opened his math textbook. He stared at an equation to refocus his thoughts, to escape a deep doubt sprouting like a weed. . . Once, as a very young child, he'd knelt with his parents in the living room, praying the rosary. He'd looked up at his dad, who appeared to be daydreaming and barely mumbling the prayers until he saw Damian and winked.

He had only been distracted that day, as Damian himself was now by his recent conflict with his mother, by his new surroundings. Trying to write today was a mistake, something he'd try to forget. He just needed to confess.

Hours later, at about a quarter to four, Damian sat in the passenger-side front seat of Scott's Oldsmobile Cutlass. His eyes remained glued to his journal as he prepared to confess at Saint Joseph's Cathedral. On a fresh page he copied the list he'd written days earlier, the one he'd tried to use with Fr. Dennis, but since that attempt had been interrupted, he planned to confess each sin again this afternoon—beginning with the most serious offence to ensure its inclusion. And, having somewhat healed from his injury and thus thinking with a steadier, clearer head, he recounted the number of checkmarks allotted to each fault to ensure accuracy: "impure thoughts" five times, "resented my mother" three, "succumbed to despair" sixteen.

Then he looked up. Scott was pulling into the parking lot of Rocky Peak Hospital, the very place his mother had helped him escape last week, and he immediately opened the car door to run away.

"Wait!" Scott said, snatching Damian's journal.

"No!" Damian yelled. "You promised the cathedral, Scott!"

"Not yet!"

"Gimme my journal!"

"Wait!" Scott rolled down his window and pulled a ticket from the parking machine. The last two times Damian came here he arrived by ambulance. This was the first time he'd parked in the lot, the first time he'd arrived without bringing tragedy.

The yellow levered arm that blocked entrance to the parking lot lifted to let them pass. Its stiff, jerky movement frightened him: it was like a troll's arm, granting grim passage to those forced to enter because the hospital held their loved ones. But now no one he loved was within, so why come back? What was Scott up to?

"I'm not going inside," Damian said.

"You are," Scott replied.

"No."

"Or no confession."

"Scott!"

"I'm keeping your journal until you go in with me," Scott said, and he held it out his window as he drove down the parking lot's centre row. Damian closed his door and breathed heavily. Suddenly the car seemed to close in on him. His fingers shook. He looked at Scott. He could punch him in the face, so he dropped the journal on the ground, and then, as the car veered out of control, jump out, retrieve his private pages, and run. But where would he go?

Scott parked the car and placed the ticket on the dashboard. The hospital loomed before them. He still held

Damian's journal out the driver's side window.

"Okay," Scott said, sounding determined. He shut off the car, put the journal on his lap, rolled up his window, and gripped the steering wheel. Damian gazed up at the six-storied hospital. Its tan brick and green windows sickened him, as had the parking lot's yellow levered arm. Scott sighed and closed his eyes, preparing, as it seemed to Damian, to say something important. Finally, he said, "You need to heal."

"From?"

"You know what from. Losing your dad. Look at this." Scott held up the journal. "What have you been doing in the car?"

"Preparing my confession list."

"Yeah? How often do you do that?"

"Every day."

"Every day. And what do you do so wrong?"

"So much," Damian said, though he knew he should have answered differently for Scott.

"If I looked in here, I bet it'd be the usual for a guy your age—thinking about girls, sex, wanting to get laid."

Damian felt himself blush. He was embarrassed that Scott knew him so well, but also enraged that his coach trivialized such serious offenses against God. He remained silent and reconsidered punching Scott.

"The difference is, you think it's all life or death—"

"It is!"

"It isn't! This is life or death!" Scott pointed at the hospital with Damian's journal. "And whether people live or die, whether your dad did, it's not your fault."

Damian groaned as though he'd been hit. He shook his head.

"You need to come back here and help sick people. Be around them."

"No," Damian whispered. He didn't want to sound like he was crying again.

"Get out of your head. Reconnect with reality."

"I'll leave today." He wiped his eyes.

"Yeah? And go where? To your mom?"

Scott had him pinned, so Damian remained silent. He turned away and looked out his window. Beside them, a young couple got out of a minivan. The woman held balloons, the man a bag of Chinese takeout. They were smiling, chatting.

Hours before his heart attack, when he and Damian had set out in the van on that crisp spring morning four years ago, his father had promised Chinese food for lunch. Damian loved Chinese food, only had it a few times in his life, and he happily anticipated lunch that morning while driving to the house where his dearest parent would, hours later, collapse, clutching his chest.

Until now, he'd never recalled what occupied his mind in the hours, the moments, before his father's heart attack: delicious food, his father's company, lifting hot water tanks, looking out the van's window at the sunrise. His thoughts had been far from death and tragedy. No wonder that day's sudden loss had stunned him and that, quite honestly, he'd never—still never—recovered.

But he *had* changed since then, becoming more like his mother, really. He examined his conscience on his own now, whereas she'd guided him years ago, when he'd been a boy. And now he read saints' lives daily to nourish his soul, whether or not she told him to. Even though her pressuring him to enter a seminary enraged him, they wanted the same thing for his future: religious life, like in *Butler's Lives.*

The young couple chatted happily as they entered the hospital. What was their story? Would their loved one die, or would they be lucky enough to keep their smiles, to brush with death but then emerge victorious? Not everyone, perhaps, were as unlucky as his family had been.

"What job is it?" Damian asked.

"Porter."

Porter, Damian repeated silently. "What do they do?"

"Bring people things," Scott replied. Damian grew tense at this description, but then stifled the feeling.

"What things?" he asked.

"Whatever the nurses need. You help them, and the patients. You'll like it."

He looked up at the hospital. He couldn't imagine himself working in it, let alone doing so happily. But he *could* imagine himself walking out the hospital's front doors in a few months, high school complete and on his way to entering a seminary that'd accepted his application. On his last day as a porter, he'd say goodbye to his coworkers; it'd be the end of August, say, and he'd have his final paycheck in hand and have already confessed last week's sin months prior.

He counted the hospital floors, to the third row of green windows. His room from a week ago, number 317, faced this parking lot, and it'd been near the centre of the floor. When he thought he'd found room 317's window, he forced himself to stare at it. But then a face— (a porter's? a nurse's? a patient's? that old man from last week?) — seemed to form behind the green glass and Damian shut his eyes. Before he let fear take hold of him, he said quickly, "If you promise confession today, I'll go in and—"

"First you have to work for a month."

"A month!"

"Heal *this* way, then I'll take you."

Scott's offer was unacceptable, but Damian could always take the bus to the cathedral downtown or go to Saint Rita's after work. Scott would never know. "Okay."

"Good," Scott said. "Now let's go in."

Scott got out of the car, as did Damian. How was his coach so certain he could get him a job here? "Are you sure they'll hire me?"

"Yeah," Scott said. He shut his door after placing the journal on his seat. "Now, if I tell you this, you'll keep quiet, right?"

Damian felt nervous but said: "Yeah."

"Well, I'm dating one of the hockey players I'm coaching. Ellen. She's a nurse here. I called her this afternoon while you were in the shower. We talked about you. She remembered you from the gym and said they need porters. This is gonna work, buddy."

But suddenly Damian, was worried again. Roy didn't allow coaches at his gym to date athletes. Scott was blatantly breaking the rules. Was his desire that Damian work here a good one? Or was it contrary to God's plans?

He braced himself as the front doors slid apart with a whoosh. Just before he crossed this threshold, into Rocky Peak, he stopped supressing the memories he feared. When his father arrived here after his heart attack, with Damian sitting beside him in the ambulance, they'd wheeled him into the main-floor emergency room. He never left that room, not alive, anyway. The recollection was vivid and stark: glaring white walls, harsh humming lights, hard floors, white tiles, and the doctors and nurses darting around in masks and scrubs of blue, black, white. But maybe, after four years, and having largely recovered from last week's injury, he was now strong enough to face this place. To encounter the sick and suffering, not as one among them, but as an employee who had, in the past, experienced what they now endured. The thought cheered him, and he stepped into the hospital.

But once inside, the antiseptic smell—the one detail he'd forgotten from the day his father died—instantly enveloped him. Last week, dozy from the barbell's blow, he didn't notice the smell, or, if he had, the pain medication and stress blurred his recognizing it as he did now. It seemed like not a day had passed since four years ago. His father's body may even still be lying cold in the emergency room.

His heart raced. Scott waved at a young nurse, who waved back from the front desk. Damian recognized her from the gym. He nodded at her, breathed deeply, and walked further into the antiseptic smell, wondering: had he seen the old man from room 317, or perhaps his father's ghost—his spirit—a moment ago?

He'd find out soon enough. And he prayed that he was prepared to encounter what was waiting for him in these halls, smelling sterile as they always had, but perhaps not entirely scrubbed clean of the past.

CHAPTER SEVEN
WHEN I WAS THIRSTY, YOU FLED

On Friday of his second week as a porter, Damian lifted a tall stack of white towels from his delivery cart. The towels smelled fresh (like linen Grandma Schiller hung outside to dry on a flowery spring day) and provided a break from the relentless antiseptic odor that still bothered him every time he arrived at Rocky Peak. Other things bothered him, too, but by keeping busy he distracted himself from his surroundings and learned to cope.

He progressed in his lifting and studies over the last two weeks as well, despite his busy schedule. Judging by the rate at which he was mailing in his assignments to his government markers, he'd be prepared to write his final exams next month, in April—proctored by a recognized authority like Fr. Dennis—and graduate well before June. Twelve years of homeschooling would culminate with his high school diploma arriving by mail (at his new address). And though he'd never gone to a real school, his mother convinced of corrupting influences in any classroom, he was gaining valuable life lessons now, experience just before entering adulthood, by living with Scott.

Compared to life at Grandma Schiller's, he was happier now walking down the hall and depositing the towels in the supplies room. Only one major anxiety remained: he still hadn't confessed his sins. Saint Rita's, the parish nearest Scott's house, was no longer in operation. Last Friday he'd left work for the cathedral at four-thirty but arrived just as the old monsignor was exiting the confessional. He would've stayed longer, attending the afternoon Mass and then requesting confession after, but he had to be back at the hospital by five-thirty for Scott to pick him up.

He kept calm now as he pushed his empty cart towards the nurses' desk. He had a plan to leave work early today and arrive at the cathedral in time. He just had to convince his boss—Veronica, the beautiful girl from Roy's gym with big green eyes, long black hair, and a vine tattoo—to release him at four o'clock. Scott never mentioned that she worked here, but Damian was sure he'd known all along: when he'd come home after his first workday and told his coach who was supervising him, Scott repressed a smile and did a poor job of acting surprised. Damian liked Veronica and enjoyed having her as a boss. While she witnessed his accident, he was grateful she hadn't seen him bandaged and drugged on the third floor three weeks ago, because he wanted her to consider him capable, strong, active—a good employee. And, after correcting him several times during his first week, she *had* grown very sweet towards him lately, which he enjoyed but also worried about: he still had to progress spiritually despite living in the regular world.

Veronica looked up from her computer as Damian approached her desk. She smiled, crinkling the skin around her eyes and showing straight white teeth around plump, pink, glistening lips. He smiled, too, and then glanced nervously at his shoes. He really needed to get new footwear and be rid of every part of his past, his old life lived in a uniform he'd destroyed but for these ridiculous black shoes that clicked and clacked loudly.

"Hi," Veronica said. He nodded, grateful to stand still—and *silent*—before her desk. She smelled like flowers. Bashful, he pointed his thumb at his empty cart. She said, "Done?"

"Yup."

"That was fast."

"Yup."

"Excited about tonight?"

"Yup." What was tonight? *He* was on his way to confession.

"I can't wait to see the new building."

What was she talking about? He nodded again, like he knew what was going on. Maybe, acting casually, he could slip away. He said, "See you."

"I'm coming with you."

He laughed quietly. She was teasing him. "Okay."

"And Ellen. To Scott's place. Then he's driving us to the building where Roy's moving the gym. Didn't he tell you?"

She was serious. His jaw tightened. Roy was moving? He hadn't heard. And why hadn't Scott told him about tonight's plans? But then he certainly hadn't mentioned *his* plans to Scott.

Yet maybe he could still confess tonight. Scott wouldn't arrive to pick him up for another hour or so. He could run down to the bus stop in his scrubs and then pray that the bus traveled extra quickly to the cathedral. Then he could confess his sins, which, still without his journal, he'd memorized as best he could. He'd rush back here in time for Scott to pick him up with the girls, then go along and see the new site for the gym. He just had to get away from Veronica now.

"Yeah, tonight," he said. He tried to seem calm, in-the-know, but at the same time he didn't want to lie too badly. "I'm all done, so I'll just wait for Scott downstai—"

"Hold on," Veronica said. "You're delivering cups of water for the last hour."

"Cups of—" He couldn't finish the sentence. Suddenly this was a nightmare. Of all the tasks she could've asked him to perform, this was what he most feared: doing for others what he hadn't done for his own father. The dying request he'd failed to meet.

"Just park your cart in the hall and then get a tray. Fill enough cups for these rooms." Veronica slid a list of numbers across her desk. He glanced at it, counting how many times he had to perform the dreaded task. And as he counted the rooms—thirteen—he noticed that 317, his room from three weeks ago, the very one he'd shared with the old man and then escaped from, was among them. But surely that old, hacking patient had been discharged by now, hadn't he?

"I, I, I," he stammered. He fought off the memory of those bulging knuckles.

"Just get it done," she said, patting his hand. "And then we'll have fun tonight."

She winked; he could have cried. Veronica was unbearably attractive just now, and the prospect of spending the evening with her excited him and distressed him. She tempted his chastity and might prevent—or at least complicate—his becoming saintly within the year. Moreover, he was terrified of what he now had to do, and ashamed to show his fear. He nodded somberly and gripped the list with a sweaty hand. He pushed the cart slowly to the storage room; there he hoped to stall by searching for a tray, but a nurse saw the list he held and handed him one.

"Hurry to the third floor," she said. "They're waiting."

He tried to speak but had lost his voice. Even if he delivered the cups as rapidly as possible, he'd still miss confession. And tomorrow, Saturday, Scott typically brought him to the gym, where they stayed until evening since it was Scott's busiest day of the week. Would he ever get rid of his sin?

Depressed, he slid thirteen cups from the holder, filled them, and headed for the stairs. He was backing into the stairwell when another nurse walked by and said, "Take the elevator or you'll spill."

Up on the third floor, with room 317 before him, he tried to combat his fear by reminding himself how lucky he was to stand here, a healthy person who could serve the sick: had he not been crushed by tragedy just three weeks ago? And he was already well enough to walk, work, and help others. Even if the old man was there, still clutching his chest and gasping, well, surely Damian was now stronger emotionally. Wasn't he?

But then he heard that same coughing. It was *him*, unless his father's spirit had returned to haunt these halls. He checked his sheet for the name of the patient in room 317: Abe Shultz. *Abraham. Old Abe.* He silently repeated the name to distinguish this man from his father, but still he trembled. He couldn't flee, not again: God, and his father in Heaven, wanted him—were *calling* him—to conquer his fear right now. Why else had he been spared, his health restored, since he'd been a patient here? If his hands hadn't been full, he would've crossed himself before praying: *Dad, help me face this man.* He let his father's death unfold in his mind to prove to himself that he could acknowledge the past.

After his heart attack, while lying on a narrow bed in the emergency room, his dad had appeared dead. Damian and his mom sat beside him, praying rosaries, and Damian held his limp hand. Then his father's fingers suddenly closed into a fist, and his eyes opened. His mother sprang up to fetch a nurse, but before she left, she bent down and looked at Damian. Her face became an emblem of grief.

"You are not to leave him." Her words alarmed him; her tone dire. "Not for anything. I'll get help."

He nodded, promising to obey, and then she'd clacked loudly from the room with her thick-heeled shoes. The noise woke his father further, it seemed, but he couldn't speak. He saw Damian but didn't seem to recognize him. He began grasping rhythmically with his once-strong hands.

"Water," he'd said. He could barely whisper, but Damian heard him and understood. And yet he was nailed to his chair, paralyzed, praying for his mother to return.

"Water," his father repeated.

"Just hold on, Dad," he said.

"Water." That third time had been his father's final word. Damian remained totally still and silent so that his father couldn't detect him sitting there, seeming to ignore his request. Where was his mother? But then, why hadn't he just disobeyed her and gotten that drink? His father's knuckles bulged as he continued to grasp for the cup that never came. And then his hand dropped. Open. Empty. A last petering gasp and then nothing.

Without fully realizing it, Damian was now walking

quickly with his tray, forcing himself forward. He rounded the open door of room 317 with memories of his father still plaguing him. Abe Schultz—tall, bearded, his belly not quite so rotund—lay on the bed asleep, his large hands clasped across his chest.

Damian saw an empty space on the night table beside the bed and approached it with a cup. Just then Abe's eyes opened and he coughed. If only his father had coughed again before his mother returned! If only he hadn't died with Damian at his side, denying his thirst!

And now Abe reached for the water. Damian shook as he put it in his hand. Their fingers touched. Abe felt warm. The last time he touched his father's skin, several hours after he died, he was already cold. His heart stilled; the warmth of life gone.

Abe grasped the cup. Damian quickly retracted his hand. He was barely breathing. Then the cup fell to the floor and splashed up, sprinkling Abe's sheets. He yelped, and Damian dropped the tray. He ran from the room, raced down the hallway, and darted for the nearest stairwell. Abe moaned behind him.

He sprinted to the basement and changed out of his scrubs. Then he peeked around the corner for Veronica or anyone else who might recognize him. Abe had likely pressed the nurse's call button by now, and whoever came to help him had already seen the dumped tray, the discarded cups, the puddles of water. Counting the seconds, Damian exited the change room, slipped off his shoes, and crept up the stairwell. Whispers from a higher level stopped him.

"His shoes," a woman said. It was Ellen! She was talking about him!

"I don't hear anything," a man said. It sounded like Scott!

"Not here."

"Where then?"

"Staffroom."

Their steps descended. Damian backed down the stairs and ran to the elevator where he frantically pressed the button. The light for the main floor lit up: it would reach him momentarily, but still the wait was awful. The elevator opened and he threw himself inside, tapping the "door close" button. The door slid shut at the same time the stairwell door opened and two people ran across the hall. He pressed the button for the main floor and slipped on his shoes before the elevator stopped. Standing directly before him in a black wool coat and black hat, her arms crossed, was Veronica. She said, "There you are!"

"I ran and I—" he said, referring to Abe, but he couldn't finish the sentence for shame.

"You didn't have to run. You delivered all those cups?"

He shook his head. Veronica didn't know about the debacle on the third floor, so he began vaguely nodding instead.

"Yeah," he said, the lie burning his mouth. "I did."

"So fast!" Veronica said. "Scott got here early. Where is he?"

"With Ellen, I think."

"Where?"

"They're, um . . ."

"They're . . .?"

"Downstairs."

"Oh boy!" Veronica rolled her eyes and smiled. "Staffroom, probably. Ellen! I'll tease her forever for this."

Veronica took his arm. "Come on. While those two finish we'll warm up my car. Then you can show me the way to Scott's place."

They walked together, and he tried to ignore her perfume, her soft body beside him. But he was already headed for damnation. Unless his father intervened. Unless a miracle occurred. But what would that miracle look like? He was running out of places to hide, people to fool. And he was further from sanctity than ever.

The hospital doors opened, releasing him from the mess he'd made and the anti-sceptic odor that, like the past, still haunted him. He knew, deep down, that he couldn't mature into manhood until he overcame his fears. And he knew as well, more clearly than ever, that he was unprepared to do so.

Hours later he sat beside Veronica on Scott's couch. He was crushed by what he'd done to Abe and couldn't stop thinking about it. But if, as today had proved, he was unable to escape the memory of his father's dying request, how could he expect to already process—and somehow forget—such a dramatic failure from only hours ago?

Veronica hadn't left his side all evening, and now she cuddled closer into him, drinking beer. He'd slowly inched away from her as she pressed closer. Scott and Ellen sat on the love seat opposite them. Ellen spoke softly into Scott's ear. He smiled and sipped a gin and tonic. Ellen had pointed at Damian's shoes lying by the front door when she'd entered the house; then she whispered to Scott, who laughed and said, "Yeah. Lucky."

And now Damian suspected she was still whispering about him or about her encounter with his coach in the hospital basement that afternoon. He felt restless and awkward. He was ashamed of what happened, but unable to get away and consider his problems alone like he wanted. He also wanted to say something to silence Ellen, but the day's events had stunned him and he couldn't.

He stood to go the bathroom.

"Where ya going?" Veronica asked, slurring.

"Need something?" Damian replied, realizing he sounded cold, abrupt. He smiled to appear happy.

"Beer," Veronica said, drunk, smiling, beautiful. Her eyes were green grapes. Her lips painted pink like one of little Mary's dolls and her white skin appeared so soft, so comforting, he now regretted leaving her side.

He used the bathroom quickly and then took two beers from Scott's fridge: surely one drink wouldn't be a problem. Hadn't Christ turned water into wine at Cana? When he returned to the couch, he tried passing one to Veronica.

"Twist off the cap for me," she said. He did, and then handed her the bottle. "You're so strong!"

He raised his eyebrows and tilted his head, as though to agree but not wanting to make a big deal about it. At home he opened stubborn jars, shoveled Grandma Schiller's walkway, and moved furniture to accommodate his mother's lesson plans. He didn't miss his mother right now, not exactly, but he *did* miss serving his family as the largest and strongest male in the house. What were they doing without him?

They're probably suffering, he thought as he sat. Veronica immediately snuggled into him. He shifted on the couch so he didn't fall off, and his shoulder brushed her breast. He hardened and placed his beer bottle, which thankfully was cold, on his erection to hide it. She rested her head on his shoulder, sipping her beer, gripping his arm. Delighting in this moment, he became conflicted because her affection made him tense: he feared her allure.

"Comfortable?" she asked.

"Yeah," Damian lied.

"Here," she said, sliding down the couch but then dragging him to her. She lifted her lips to his ear and whispered, "I wanna ask you something."

"Okay," he whispered back, his heart racing. Her breath smelled delicious: clean, bitter, malty. He wanted to sip his beer, but it was still covering his crotch.

"About your dad."

He looked at her intently. Her face appeared serious, sincere.

"I lost my mom when I was young," she said.

"How do you know . . .?"

"Ellen."

Damian looked over at Ellen and Scott. Scott grinned. Ellen lifted her eyebrows. Damian scowled, embarrassed, but Veronica still focused on him with kind eyes.

"Do you want to talk about it?" she asked, placing her tiny, birdlike hand on his.

"Okay."

"But not here. Not with *them*." She moved her eyes to indicate Scott and Ellen, both still staring.

"Okay."

"Can we go somewhere else?"

"Downstairs," he whispered, and Veronica immediately stood and pulled him up from the couch. He kept his bottle at his crotch.

"Don't be long!" Ellen said. Damian winced.

"Call us when you're ready to go," Veronica replied, and then she and Damian descended the basement steps. His room was immaculately clean, something he was grateful for as she flicked on the light and flopped onto the mattress. He pulled the chair from the desk, sat, and awkwardly crossed his legs as he sipped his beer. He relaxed but reminded himself to be careful: God might test him now, even after such a hard day.

"My mom had breast cancer," she said. "How'd your dad die?"

"Heart attack."

"I'm sorry."

Damian nodded, looked down. He tried to think of something priestly to say, some solemn advice he'd surely received after years of weekly confession . . . but he couldn't. If only he'd confessed recently, something would've come to mind—maybe about the redemptive value of suffering or how God called some people to Heaven sooner than others. But he stayed silent.

"When did he die?" Veronica asked.

"Four years ago."

"How old were you?"

"Thirteen."

"I was eighteen when my mom died."

Veronica leaned against the wall, tucked her knees up. She patted the mattress, indicating that he should, once more, sit beside her, but he shook his head. He enjoyed sitting in the chair like this, discussing serious matters with someone of shared experience. He placed his now-empty bottle on the desk and picked up *Butler's Lives*. He hoped to find an inspirational passage, one that might convey his moral code to her—so she got no misguided ideas. And he wanted to keep his own thoughts chaste, too, because she looked very cute sitting on his bed.

"Did your mom remarry?"

He snorted at the thought.

"What?" Veronica asked, smiling now.

"She just wouldn't."

"My dad remarried. Helped him move on. Do you wanna get married?"

"No."

"Me neither."

"Why?"

"Wanna have fun, you know?"

Damian nodded, but also scowled to express disapproval of any fun that marriage disallowed. Veronica finished her beer and placed the empty bottle on the desk beside his. She picked up the rosary by his reading lamp and dangled it playfully. Then she leaned back against the wall and said, "So what *do* you wanna do?"

He looked up from *Butler's*. "What do you mean?"

"When you're older. A doctor?"

"No."

"I thought because you're working in a hospital, then maybe . . ."

"No. I work there 'cause it's near Scott's house, and..."

"And . . .?"

"To heal from losing my dad."

"Ah!" Veronica sounded wise. More priestly than he did. "I became a nurse to help sick people, people who've experienced what we have."

"Okay."

"So what then?" she asked. "When you're older?"

He hesitated because he was unsure how she'd respond to the truth, but he couldn't lie after just discussing his father, so he said, "A priest."

"*Priest!* Why?"

"I want . . ."

"What?"

"To become a saint, actually."

Veronica appeared stunned. Then she leaned forward and lifted *Butler's* in his hands to see the cover.

"You have to be a priest to become a saint?"

"Almost everyone in here," Damian said, pointing at *Butler's Lives,* "entered religious life at my age. Then they worked to save souls."

"Save souls," she repeated sarcastically.

"Yeah," Damian replied seriously. He resisted a grimace, however, at his own recent spiritual welfare. "But first I've got to save my own."

"To see your dad in Heaven."

He was surprised. Was he that transparent? "Yeah, actually."

She sat back, shaking her head. "No good."

"Why?"

"When my mom died, the minister at her funeral said we'd see her again in Heaven. Be with her forever. That she'd already know her way around up there, on a cloud, I guess, and be waiting to see us."

"So?"

"And now at the hospital, I hear the same thing from people who lose their parents, their kids—that they'll be waiting for them up above."

"It's true."

"Maybe. But seeing them as *souls? Resurrected* in the

sky, eternally ecstatic? . . . Even if that were true, it just won't be the same." This view struck Damian, held him in pensive concern. He hunched forward, scratched his forehead, and frowned—posturing to properly ponder this strange idea, what her proposal really meant and implied, but she prevented such a pause by saying: "Damian! Leave the past and enjoy today. Laugh, dream, have fun! Painful losses, well . . . we still have to live *our* lives."

"I am."

"Eager to enter the priesthood, keeping yourself pure and holy."

"Right."

"Well, what about love, other people?"

"What about them?"

"See? Your head's in the clouds!"

"I'm aiming for . . ." He was going to say eternity but stopped himself. He was a child, suddenly, before a grown woman. She smiled at him slyly.

"What if I told you you're very cute?" She leaned further forward, snatched *Butler's*, and tossed it on his desk. He lurched back to escape her, but she pressed herself into him, her breasts against his chest, and kissed him. Her mouth tasted like strawberries and beer. Her lips were warm and moist. His hands, instinctively, it seemed, since he'd never kissed a girl, wrapped around her tattooed waist and he wanted to squeeze her and pull her close. At the same time, recognizing what an opportunity this was to display his saintly resolve, he wanted to push her away and declare his commitment to chastity.

But just then she rose and grabbed his shirt, their lips compressed the entire time, and pushed him onto the mattress; his head was where his feet normally were, and she straddled him, kissed him more passionately. How could he stop her, stop himself? This was the most intense pleasure he'd ever experienced, and it terrified him. It was sinful. This embrace—on its own, even without his unconfessed sin—could easily land him in Hell.

Yet her mouth tasted so good, her hair smelled so clean, her skin so soft, he simply couldn't push her off. She'd likely doubt that he was serious about salvation, about seeing his father again, but he couldn't gather his thoughts, and now her tongue was in his mouth. She leaned over him, her hair dangling about his face; he was drowning in the moment. He gripped her tightly. He saw nothing but black curls when he blinked.

Then footsteps upstairs. Veronica raised her head and put her finger to her mouth.

"Who's ready to go?" Scott called downstairs.

"Come on, you two!" Ellen said.

Veronica grimaced, rolled her eyes.

"Okay!" she called and was about to climb off him when Ellen, as though recalling something, said to Scott upstairs: "Oh! I'll call Tori. She wants to see the new place, too."

And Damian heard her run to the office at the end of the hall, but Scott shouted:

"No!" He chased after Ellen. "Let's hit the road. Just us four. Nobody else. Remember?"

Veronica remained straddled on him and lifted her eyebrows, smiling at the conversation upstairs. He smiled, too, but felt embarrassed because certainly she could feel how hard he was. Shameful, guilty . . . and yet her body atop his thrilled him far more than any catalogue ever had.

"Just Tori," Ellen said. "She won't care about us."

"Don't call her!" Scott screamed. He sounded worried. Ellen must have lifted his office phone. Veronica tilted her head, intrigued. "You know I could get fired!"

"Is this how it's going to be?" Ellen screamed back. "Hiding, like we're having an affair?"

Veronica covered her mouth, stifling a giggle.

"Just for now!" Scott replied.

"I'm sick of this!" Ellen's voice sounded different, maybe because of the alcohol.

"Shut up!" Scott said. Then, more gently, he added, "Come on. You know the rules."

"That's it!" Ellen shouted. "We're through!"

Veronica's eyes widened. Her shoulders shook with laughter. Damian laughed too. The argument upstairs was so stupid. Ellen surely knew that if word spread about Scott dating an athlete while coaching her, his reputation would be ruined. But Scott should have known better from the start. It *was* kind of funny.

"Fine," Scott said. Ellen stomped down the hall and opened the front door.

"And tell your roommate," she yelled, "that I'll be sure to *hear* him at work next week!"

Then she slammed the door.

"Fuck!" Scott screamed, and then he marched to his bedroom and slammed *his* door. Damian considered what Ellen had said, about hearing him at work, and then realized she was referring to his shoes. He felt himself blush.

"It's okay," Veronica said, leaning over him and kissing his forehead. "I think your shoes are cute."

"I don't know. . ."

"They are." She *was* awfully kind. "Now we're alone."

His heart leapt into his mouth as she took his hand and slid it into her shirt. He—again instinctively—squeezed her breast. He wanted so badly to pull away, but her breast was soft and when he squeezed she moaned deliciously, so he did it again, apologizing to his father in Heaven all the while. She slid her hand down to his fly, but then felt the rosary beads in his pocket and stopped. She appeared puzzled, pulled them out, and looked at the other pair on the mattress.

"How many do you need?" she asked, and then threw the rosary behind her.

"Those beads are blesse—oh!"

She ran her fingers along his penis through his pants. He removed his hand from her breast to prevent himself from climaxing, but it didn't work. He moaned loudly, shut his eyes, and spread his arms as he clutched the bed sheets; stars covered Veronica's face when he opened his eyes, and she was smiling playfully when the stars dissolved. He gasped. Breathed again.

Then he felt something in his left hand. He wiggled his fingers: rosary beads. *Abomination!*

She smiled, satisfied, it seemed, as was he—but horrified, too.

"Get off me," he said.

"What?"

"Get off me!" He pushed her onto the floor, and then picked up the beads from the bed and those she'd tossed behind her; he kissed both rosaries and placed them in his pocket. Then he stood over her and pointed at the door. "Get out."

"I . . ."

"Get out!" He shrieked loudly. Scott opened his door

upstairs, likely startled to hear another argument, wondering what it was about, if he should be concerned, even intervene.

Veronica stood, tottering and teary. "I thought we could—"

"Just get out."

She was sobbing now, as was he. She walked to the door, but then turned back.

"You can't love because you're saving yourself for someone who's gone!"

And then she left. Damian stood, his skin prickling with tension as she climbed the stairs, mumbled something to Scott, gathered her things, and then—like Ellen moments before—left, slamming the front door. Swirling thoughts brought him to his knees. He felt sorry for Veronica, for Ellen and Scott, and for himself. He left home to pursue sanctity, to achieve independence from his mother, and he failed.

Right then his dad felt so far away. He could barely picture his face or recall his voice. He couldn't conjure the scenes from his father's final moments that'd haunted him this afternoon. He couldn't. Not now, not when he really needed his father, his family, anyone who understood him. He looked at the empty space above the desk, hoping to find the crucifix that hung above him for the past four years, but it was in Grandma Schiller's basement, above the desk he fled three weeks ago after a sin far less serious than what just happened.

Veronica! In a way he felt sorry for her. And for Abe. He couldn't return to his job at the hospital. And with no income, he couldn't continue to live with Scott. But if he left tonight, his weightlifting career, at least under Scott's watch, was also over.

He clutched his rosary. He was stuck.

CHAPTER EIGHT
PRODIGAL SON

Damian cringed as his keys slipped from his wet fingers. He hoped they'd hit one of his shoes, thereby muffling any sound, but instead they rattled loudly against the concrete between his feet. Suddenly he heard something from inside Grandma Schiller's foyer. The yellow lamp beside the window flicked on. Footsteps approached the front door, which swung open and there was his mother in a white nightgown, her face blurred behind the rain-streaked screen door. He considered jumping off the front porch and running away, but where could he go? He stared at her, speechless, wondering if she was angry or happy to see him.

But then she burst out the screen door, threw her arms around him, and buried her face into his chest. He hugged her, too, soaking her nightgown. He must have appeared like a vagrant seeking shelter. Tonight, the first rain of spring had begun just before he'd secretly left Scott's house, lugging his gym bag to the bus stop as the downpour melted the snow and warmed the air, but he was soaked and shivering badly. Holding his mother on the porch, in the rhythmic pattering of the rain, seconds passed before he realized she was sobbing.

"I'm sorry, Damian," she said. "I'm sorry I drove you away."

"Okay," he said. He wanted to say she would have to stop dominating him and pressuring him into the priesthood, because he'd firmly resolved on the bus ride home to tolerate no more abuse, but he also wanted to forgive her. Reconciliation would soothe him after today's failures and losses. And her crying sounded like a child. He patted her bony back, surprised at her slender body. Veronica was round and soft by comparison. But thinking of *her* while he held his mother disgusted him, and, ashamed, he dismissed Veronica's memory. "I just had to get away."

She didn't respond, so he added, "But I'm back now."

"You're back, you're back," she said, repeating the words as though to drive his arrival into her mind. She was now nearly as soaked as he was, and she shook more violently.

"Let's go inside, Mom. I'm freezing." He patted her again, slightly harder, and then abruptly removed his hand and stood erect to end their embrace. He must be firmer and more assertive with her now that he'd returned home.

"Okay. Oh, you're back." She sounded genuinely relieved. Her sorrow over his absence, and the guilt she seemed to feel for driving him away, granted him capital in establishing some new rules for his treatment. He planned to introduce these rules tomorrow but, since she greeted him at the door like this, he might have to do so tonight. Had she been waiting up, worrying nightly since he'd left? Part of him hoped so.

She stepped back to gaze at him. Her tear-drenched face and dripping hair made her look pitiful, but Damian kept a stern expression as he gathered his keys from the porch, picked up his gym bag and followed her inside.

"Wait here," she said as they stepped into the foyer.

"I'll get towels."

She clutched her soaked nightgown to her chest as she walked away. Her physical frailty, long concealed by stark attire and her rigid, dominating disposition, astonished him. He stared, though slightly embarrassed to see her body revealed, and almost, almost felt sorry for this vulnerable-looking woman whom he'd always feared. But perhaps that fear was dying now, would soon be overcome.

He sighed as he deposited his bag on the artificial turf that carpeted the foyer. The lamp's soft, yellow glow enhanced the colors of the holy cards on the walls: the red sores of Saint Francis of Assisi's stigmata, Saint Patrick's green shamrock, Saint Benedict's long white beard and black robes. Surrounded by such strange yet familiar company, he was relieved to be home.

He removed his shoes and slung his jacket over the radiator beside Grandma Schiller's chair, under which lay his departure note. A photo album and a brittle, browning letter in old-style type—neither of which he'd seen before— sat on her footstool, beside her always-full ashtray and pearl rosary beads. What a joy it would be to see her again!

His mother returned wearing a red cardigan over her nightgown. She'd wrapped a towel around her shoulders and held out another to him. He took it and wiped his face and head. When he removed the towel from his eyes, his departure note had vanished. Then she picked up the old letter and album and said, "Let's sit in the living room. I want to show you something."

Damian eased into the wide, mushy brown recliner in the living room, comforted by its familiar mouldy smell. His mother brought in Grandma Schiller's footstool.

"Lift your feet," she said. His arches hurt after walking from the bus stop, so he obeyed. Out of his shoes, off the cold, wet pavement, he stretched his feet on the small stool and they ached deliciously. He was happy to be home. So much so, in fact, that he *really* needed to be on guard against his mother's manipulation.

She sat on the floor, opened the album on his lap, and pointed to a weathered photograph. He stared several moments before recognizing his mother, a teenager, straddling her bicycle while Uncle Rick stood beside her.

"Look at my short shorts," she said, laughing.

"You were so pretty, Mom." Her youthful appearance entranced him. The way she tilted her head and gripped the handlebars . . . Who *was* this girl who'd somehow become his mother, this vibrant beauty with welcoming eyes and a sly grin? She was smiling in a way her face would no longer allow, her lips curled up in dimples, the pink tip of her tongue poked between her teeth. Veronica had smiled just so before kissing him tonight, and, even as he again dispelled *that* memory, he wondered: what had his mother experienced years ago, when she'd seemed lighthearted—the reverse of her current self?

"I *was* cute," she said, leaning in to admire the photograph. "Sixteen, I think. Almost your age."

"Probably more mature, though," he said, surprised she appeared so womanly at sixteen, even on a bicycle. And the sight of his adolescent uncle smiling peacefully, unaware of his dismal future, worried him. Considering *his* past two weeks, what horrors lay ahead? Surely he'd turn out like Uncle Rick, or worse. Panic tightened his chest. "Mom, I went to Scott's place and tried to work at the hospital, but then—"

"Shhh!" She held her finger to her lips and patted his leg. "Let's talk about me now, then you."

He nodded and stayed silent, at least for the moment, because his attempted confession had brought on tears.

"Look at me here," she said, pointing at the photo. "Don't I seem happy? Hair in a bob, and that big, sassy smile."

"You do look happy, Mom."

"I wasn't." Her tone flattened as she shook her head. "I was miserable over my dad. He was depressed, you know, after the war—"

"I know nothing about him—"

"That's why I'm telling you. He just lay in bed while your grandma worked the till and Rick pumped the gas. I'd come home from school, and my own *father* didn't even recognize me!"

"Really?"

"It crushed me. . ." She breathed deeply, but her voice still wavered as she continued: "Then, one day I met a boy."

Now Damian was fully alert; he hadn't heard *this* story before.

"He was a twelfth-grader who sold pot," she said. "One day he invited me to hang out at his apartment. I would've refused, but he looked at me so compassionately just then, like he somehow understood my problems, that I agreed."

She lowered her eyes and paused. "We got drunk that afternoon, slept at his place that night. And from then I didn't return home or go to school for over a year. Booze became my escape, and I worked at the grocery store under this boy's apartment, doing basically what I'd done back home, except for less pay."

Damian was speechless. *Drinking! And sleeping with that boy for a year!* Tonight's escapades with Veronica suddenly seemed trifling. But what disturbed him most was that he'd never really known his mother until now, and he felt deceived.

She appeared to detect his thoughts, however, because she rose to her knees, clutched his hands, and widened her eyes—preparing, it seemed, to divulge even more of her past. He braced himself. Was she revealing herself like this so they could finally relate as adults? He hoped so.

"One morning," she said, her voice rising in pitch, "the police came for me, a runaway minor, and took me to the station. Rick was already there, crying—they found dad dead in the bathtub, drenched in blood, his throat slit with scissors."

Her head dropped. Damian went numb. His grandfather! A suicide! No wonder his family never discussed him.

"Rick said that right after I'd left, Dad started asking about me. You see, he hadn't *seemed* to recognize me, but actually he knew when I was home or not." Her trembling voice had grown louder, and Damian worried his siblings might wake to hear this terrible tale. His mother bit her fist and tightly shut her eyes before continuing: "I just ran from the police station and kept going until I collapsed outside a church. Soon an old priest in a cassock opened the door. He brought me a blanket, let me lie down in a pew, and I felt safe and happy because he resembled my dad—yet was clear-eyed, healthy. A *priest,* Damian."

She looked up intently. He, though transfixed by the story, grew suspicious. "Mom, you can't pressure me to..."

"Hey—we're talking about *me,* remember?"

"Okay, but . . ."

"His name was Father Geraldo Viola, and he asked me about myself, made me tea. He heard my confession and then read the Parable of the Prodigal Son. He said to trust God and go home—that your grandma and Rick would forgive me because Dad had been sick. His suicide wasn't my fault!"

She smiled, though feebly: remnants of that terrible day were still visible on her troubled face. But now her eyes brightened. "Later that night I confessed everything—the boy, the booze, the running away—to Rick and your grandma—and *they forgave me.* Father Geraldo had been right!"

She sighed deeply and sat back on the floor, her hands resting in her lap. The towel around her shoulders drooped down her back like a shawl, but she let it sag. The events she'd just described relieved her still, it seemed, even after so many years, still absolved her of her father's death.

"Father Geraldo saved my life," she said, her voice steadier and quiet. "He got me to attend daily Mass, return to school, and quit drinking. He even visited our station in the afternoons to check on me. When I rounded the corner with my schoolbag, he waved and called in his Italian accent— 'Cyn-*thi*-a! Cyn-*thi*-a!' I can hear him still. Often, he stayed for dinner and helped with my homework. He became the loving dad I never really had."

Her pressuring the priesthood now made more sense. She probably imagined *his* ordination would vicariously allow her to repay a life-saving kindness from years ago. Were *he* to become *Father* Damian, he could rescue drowning souls—people that might appear beautiful, as she did in the photograph, yet were actually submerged in sadness.

But why she dominated him to the point of dictating his future and breaching his privacy remained unclear. "That's great, Mom. But you can't *force* me to become another Father Geraldo."

"I know," she said, "and I apologize for controlling you. It was wrong."

Damian, relieved, wanted to smile, but remained stern. "You have to stop!"

"I will! You'll see!" She clutched his hands again, as though to pledge her sincerity. "But my, . . . enthusiasm . . . well . . . Here—read this!"

She handed him the old letter. The crisp page felt like a dried rose petal pressed for decades between the pages of a heavy book. He held it on his open hand and read silently:

September 17, 1976

My dearest Cynthia,

Be peaceful, despite what I now tell you. I have cancer. My doctor says I will not survive for long. But rejoice! God is calling me to Heaven, our true home. And I am so grateful that before I pass into eternal life, I brought you the Faith.

Do likewise for others! And moreover, encourage young men to labour in His vineyard. Foster priestly vocations, so that as I touched your life, new priests may lead souls to God. Your efforts will be fruitful!

Geraldo Viola

Damian reread the letter, lowered it, and met his mother's expectant eyes; they worried him. Father Geraldo's assistance continued to influence her, and this commission to promote the priesthood clearly drove her still. Could he possibly pursue ordination *while* severing himself from her past?

"It's great, Mom, but—"

"He died a week later and—"

"Listen!" Damian said. "You don't have to make every young man around you a priest!"

"But don't you want to help others who—"

"I do!" he said. "But as *my* idea. Your pressure makes it false. Like I'm just—"

"Doing what *I* want," she said, finishing his sentence. She appeared to deflate and looked away. Her altered demeanor puzzled him, but he relaxed, relieved that she finally understood his recent frustration with her.

"Exactly," he said, sighing.

She nodded. "I should've learned my lesson, you know, with Rick. I pressu—encouraged him into religious life and, well . . ."

She pointed at Uncle Rick's room and shrugged. Damian nodded. He always suspected her of steering Uncle Rick into the monastery, but he left the issue for now to keep their focus on *his* priestly vocation. His mother shut the album, took back the letter, and folded it gingerly.

"I'm so embarrassed now," she said. "But I just wanted you to know who . . . who I was, and . . . since your dad died, all this has, well . . ."

Tears trickled into her trembling lips. Damian leaned forward. He grasped her face and gently tilted it to meet her eyes. "I'm so happy I know you better now, Mom—

your mistakes, everything. Through all that trouble, God led you back to Him. He'll lead me, too. *He* will. So, *let* Him."

"Okay," she whispered. She kissed his hands and then crumpled into his lap. She looked like the prodigal son, collapsed at his father's feet. Damian placed his hand on her head to comfort and pardon. He felt noble, even authoritative—wanting so badly to become a priest and maintain this sensation forever.

CHAPTER NINE
SPIRITUAL DIRECTION

After Mass at Canadian Martyrs the following morning, the Kurts parked outside Grandma Schiller's house and finished their rosary with Damian leading from the station wagon's third-row, rear-facing seat.

"Hail, Mary, full of grace," he said, finishing the first half of the prayer before his family responded with the second half. Failure occupied his mind as he prayed aloud. Surely Scott had found the basement room empty by now, his athlete and short-term roommate missing without having paid any rent. Could he find another coach, or did God want him to abandon lifting and pursue the priesthood exclusively? Veronica likely loathed him. He planned to call the hospital today to resign and ask someone at payroll to mail his check. Finally, Father Dennis hadn't heard confessions this morning, so his sins—worsened yesterday with Veronica—remained.

Distraught, he reined in his worries and tried to meditate on the Fifth Joyful Mystery. While traveling to Jerusalem for the Passover, Mary and Joseph lost the boy Jesus. They panicked, searched for him, and finally found him in the temple, debating the resident scholars. When Mary seized and scolded him, Jesus calmly replied: "Why did you seek me? Did you not know I must be about my father's business?"

Christ's answer gave Damian hope. After three weeks away, he returned home, his refuge—what Christ found in the temple. The familiar odor of his siblings' wet footwear made the station wagon feel safe and the bench seat comfortable as he stretched lengthwise. His mother yawned in the rear-view mirror. Damian loved James, Mary, and Bernadette, and after their conversation last night, he loved his mother more easily, too. But, like the young Christ, he felt called by *his* father in Heaven to leave his family's protective unit and make another attempt at independence, this time proceeding more prudently. Anyone his age, he knew, ought to feel likewise.

The difference was, while most young men went off to work, to pursue women, to pay rent and seek promotion and raise families, he was different. He also was called to dwell in the temple, the Church. If Scott, Veronica, or even Abe asked him where he'd gone, he could answer: "My life's path leads to the Church. Didn't you know I must be about the business of rejoining my father in Heaven?"

The Kurts concluded their rosary. Damian crossed himself with the crucifix, kissed Christ's pierced feet and hopped out the back. His family spilled out, slamming their doors. The sound, formerly so routine it'd become invisible, met his ears with comforting familiarity.

"The snow melted!" James ran up the front steps.

"Not here," Damian called to his brother, referring to the stubborn, exhaust-stained bank along the curb. The city's graters had left the hard-packed heap that grew higher every week when they plowed the streets. One spring rainfall lowered the range a few inches, but certainly wasn't enough to melt it entirely.

"Nothing to shovel, though," his mother said cheerily from the porch.

"Yeah," Damian replied. She smiled at him and he

smiled back. Then, she hustled his siblings through the front door. Cigarette smoke escaped as they entered the foyer because Grandma Schiller was there, of course—praying, experienced, wise.

Damian had almost approached Father Dennis after Mass this morning and simply told him he wanted to become a priest, but yesterday sensitized him to failure and made him cautious, which was why he waited outside now as his family cleared the foyer. He wanted to speak with Grandma Schiller privately, to gain her advice and direction.

As he waited, he gazed at the cracked sidewalk he shovelled on so many frigid mornings, often scraping the angled, uneven concrete blocks until his arms ached. He followed the spindly fractures in the concrete that always caught and dented the shovel's rusty edge All these lovable flaws were visible again after last night's rainfall, greeting him like the text in a familiar book.

No more sounds of stomping boots or slamming closet doors issued from the foyer, so he approached the house and leaned his still-damp dress shoes on the steps to dry in the sun. He'd replace them the day his paycheck arrived because they represented his past, and he wanted none of *that* clinging to who he was now, who he was becoming.

Inside the foyer dense smoke stung his eyes. He shut the front door and immediately wished he'd sucked a deep breath from outside before sealing himself inside this humid, airless space. He coughed, blinked, and—once his eyes adjusted—saw Grandma Schiller sitting at the helm of her house.

"Damian," she said affectionately. He knew she wouldn't ask about the last few weeks and he cherished how she respected his privacy. He sat on the well-worn turf and rested his back against the front door. Grandma Schiller's stumpy legs dangled from her chair. Her yellow stockings had probably once been white, and her ancient black shoes were brittle and thin.

"Smoke?" she asked. She blew a billowing stream from the side of her mouth and offered him her pack of Player's. He'd never smoked before, but he *was* changing, maturing. Why not? He took one, she lit it, and then he inhaled deeply—*too* deeply. He coughed and grew dizzy. Still, leaning back and steadying himself, he felt like an adult with his smoldering cigarette, ready to converse frankly, intimately. "Grandma?"

"Hmmmm?" she replied. She drew deeply, exhaling slowly. The smoke blurred her curly blond hair so it resembled a halo. Her cigarette's red ember dimmed and before his courage lost its glow, he said: "I want to enter a seminary."

"Hmmmm," she repeated, but now she sounded concerned. "Careful you no make mistake."

Her caution surprised him. Did she believe he didn't suit the priesthood, or that perhaps he was simply caving to his mother's former pressure? Or, most likely, was Uncle Rick's past causing her reluctance?

"Mistake?" he said. Grandma Schiller made no reply, so he took a chance and asked, "Like Uncle Rick?"

"Yah," she said immediately.

He nodded and yearned to know more, partly because he so feared becoming like Uncle Rick, yet he hesitated to inquire further because his family ignored his uncle, like a hidden source of shame and kept his personal history secret. But then Grandma Schiller, likely sensing Damian's curiosity, continued: "Ven your fater died, I wrote to Ricky in da monastery—his name vas Broter Minerad den—unt explaint vat had happened."

Damian listened intently even though his stomach churned. That first drag had nauseated him, but he was so intrigued by this conversation that he swallowed his sickness to avoid interruption.

"I sought he might write back, but no. Unt he vas forbotten to leave ze monastery—*even for funeral!*"

"No!"

As though nodding to confirm her statement, she waved her cigarette vertically, rattling her thin, tin bracelets. His nausea worsened and his gorge rose with a smoky aftertaste. He still hid his queasiness, however, in the hazy dark, and Grandma Schiller continued: "But zen, at ze funeral, a man at ze back of ze church sat vis his hat pulled low and head bowed, hiding—like dis."

She slumped forward, trying to appear guilty, but her kind face and placid blue eyes sabotaged her impression; he understood what she was trying to convey. Then Grandma Schiller sat upright again. "I sought he vas a customer of your fater's, unt I vent to ask dat he remove his hat."

She suddenly sounded sad and paused. Damian lowered his cigarette to the turf and slowly inhaled through his mouth to delay vomiting. Tears trickled down Grandma Schiller's cheeks. "It vas Ricky! He vas back, but—as it turned out—vis out his faith!"

She wept, and Damian managed to pat her hand despite his sickness. He suspected that Uncle Rick no longer practiced Catholicism. He never attended Mass, never prayed with the family, and then, curiously, he refused to contribute to his father's biography.

Had his father's death caused Uncle Rick to abandon his religious vocation *and* his faith? Had he been desolated, left hopeless, with God's blessing apparently removed as his life collapsed into its present state? Damian wanted to investigate, but he was about to vomit so he crushed his barely-smoked cigarette in the crystal ashtray and said: "Thanks, Grandma. I gotta go."

"Okay," she said, still crying. "Love you."

He sprinted—gagging—from the foyer. He wished he said he loved her too, but she already knew. He reached the bathroom and crumpled over the toilet, wondering—between heaves—if by becoming a priest he might compensate Grandma Schiller for Uncle Rick's lost faith. He'd then soothe the pain she obviously still suffered, while also avoiding his uncle's fate.

Twenty minutes later, after clutching the porcelain bowl when he could've been clutching Grandma Schiller, he rinsed his mouth in the sink and examined his pale face in the mirror.

Even after getting sick, his skin appeared darker than Grandma Schiller's fair European pallor, shared by her two children. Damian's Māori ancestry was apparent and displayed what he'd inherited from his father. For this reason, he loved his all-weather tan, a creamed-coffee hue that blended his diverse cultural ancestry. His darker complexion even likened him to Christ, who was middle eastern, after all.

He recalled sitting on the bathroom counter as a boy, watching his father's dark eyes peer into the mirror while his hands delicately handled the razor. The blade scraped with a smooth, grainy sound as it cleared away the white foam, and his father's aftershave—Kiwi Kool, imported from New Zealand—had smelled of oceans, ships, and adventure. And then, his Māori tan glowing, he'd gently lift Damian's chin and pretend to shave him, even adding foam and aftershave for effect.

He examined his own stubble. Those mock sessions had been his only instruction in the manly art of removing one's beard, as his dad had died before really teaching him how to shave.

"Oh yeah," Uncle Rick suddenly said, his voice travelling through the walls. "You know I like that."

Damian shook his head. He'd lost the ideal role model—a father noble yet nurturing, rugged but patient—for an unemployed uncle who constantly solicited phone sex.

Or was he judging too harshly? *He* hadn't lately exemplified adult independence either and Uncle Rick had lost a father tragically, too, only to then enter religious life, albeit for reasons unknown to Damian.

He planned to achieve sanctity through ordained ministry, while Uncle Rick abandoned his religious vocation for isolated indulgence. Yet, while repulsed by his uncle's current lifestyle, he'd nothing to lose by talking to him—and might even learn precisely what *not* to do as he planned his future. Besides, saints often conversed with sinners. After praying to his father for guidance, he knocked on Uncle Rick's door and then stepped back to avoid hearing any more antics.

"Settle down!" Uncle Rick yelled.

"It's Damian."

"Damian?"

"Yup."

"Hold on." Uncle Rick now bustled about his mysterious cell.

Damian hummed "Lord of All Hopefulness"—a hymn from this morning's Mass—but he still heard a phone cradled, a fly zipped, pages gathered, and other items stuffed into drawers that were slammed shut. Then Uncle Rick opened the door. His small, bald head was sweaty, his large, square glasses steamed, but he caught his breath and said, "What's up?"

"Not much," Damian said. He tried to ignore his uncle's stained V-neck t-shirt, his tight gym shorts, and the sensual way he stroked his narrow, crooked mustache. The blinds were down, but he could still see a balled-up blanket on a mattress, several chests of drawers with half-melted candles on them, and a night table covered with a sweater that partially hid various jars and a stack of magazines. Faded posters of Fleetwood Mac and Heart, tacked to the cracked plaster walls, curled at their corners. Incense lingered. "Dropped the bar on my head the other week—318 lbs."

"Jeepers." Uncle Rick cringed. "You okay?"

"Better."

His uncle nodded, and Damian, feeling awkward, said, "Yeah, and, um . . . can I ask you something?"

"Well . . ." Uncle Rick leaned forward, peering past Damian in the doorway. "What about?"

"Entering a seminary."

"Oh!" Uncle Rick sounded relieved as he leaned back in his chair and crossed his feet up on his computer desk. Beside his heels sat his greasy, black dial phone. "You joining an order or diocese?"

"Don't know, actually."

"I was a Trappist and—"

"Yeah, hmmm," Damian said, tilting his head. Somehow, he always envisioned himself joining his home diocese, even after reading about so many religious orders in *Butler's Lives*. Perhaps Uncle Rick's experience had subconsciously dissuaded him from considering an order, and he *had* only ever known parish priests.

"Don't join an order," Uncle Rick said flatly. He crossed his thin, pale arms.

"Why?" Damian asked, anticipating descriptions of the Trappists' fasting, coarse habits, and rigorous schedule, but instead Uncle Rick said, "Because you'd make a great parish priest."

"Really?" He was shocked. Uncle Rick had never complimented him—had barely ever acknowledged him, in fact. Optimism now replaced his nausea, and he wanted to continue chatting. "Did you like Father Viola?"

"I did," Uncle Rick said. "And you'd have made him proud."

Praise. *True* praise! "Why?"

"You're smart," Uncle Rick said, "and kind. You've stuck at weightlifting for years, just like Father Viola persevered in ministry. And you're helpful, shovelling snow, moving furniture."

"How do you know. . .?"

"About you?" Uncle Rick said, smiling. "You'd be surprised what I hear through these walls."

Tell me about it, Damian thought. He could've mentioned that sound travelled *out* of Uncle Rick's room as clearly as it traveled *in* but decided against souring the moment. "So, I'll ask Father Dennis, I guess, about the seminary?"

"Who?" Uncle Rick asked.

"Our pari—my parish priest."

"Do it," Uncle Rick said. But here a serious concern arose. In confession Damian had repeatedly described how his mother was pressuring him into the seminary, and now, if he declared priestly intentions, Father Dennis might doubt his sincerity.

"But what if . . ." Damian said, and now *he* looked around nervously, "I've already revealed certain things?"

"What *things?*" Uncle Rick asked, raising an eyebrow.

"In confession."

His uncle made a shooing motion. "You're clear."

"You sure?"

"Trust me. What I confessed at the monastery . . . unimaginable. They can't use it against you."

"It might influence him."

"No way."

Damian, relieved, leaned against the doorframe. He'd never been friendly (or even *personal*) with Uncle Rick before, and he was about to ask, as gently as possible, what had happened—why he hid in this cluttered chamber, mumbling lust and avoiding true relationships. But just then his uncle leaned in and said, "So what have you been up to, needing to confess?"

"What? Oh! Nothing like what you—you might, um . . ." Uncle Rick had been so kind, but was now leering repulsively. "Well, thanks. I gotta make a call."

"Me too," his uncle replied, smiling. Then he shut his door and loudly locked it as Damian ran downstairs, pulled his journal from under his bed, and updated his list:

Steps to the Seminary

- ~~*Talk to Uncle Rick*~~
- *Meet with Fr. Dennis*

CHAPTER TEN
OLDEST BOYS' CLUB AROUND

The hem of his robes swinging around his ankles, Father Dennis processed from the altar, past the Kurts in the front pew and down the centre aisle of Canadian Martyrs. As the congregation finished the closing hymn, "Immaculate Mary," Damian knelt to pray before meeting with his pastor.

Father Dennis sounded confused on the phone two days ago when Damian called after chatting with Uncle Rick and now Damian was anxious for this conversation to go smoothly so he could finally begin shaping a successful, independent future.

"I'll pick you up in an hour," his mother whispered. She hadn't asked the purpose of this morning's meeting, thus surprisingly maintaining the respectful distance she'd promised last Friday. Damian nodded and then shut his eyes.

Silence soon surrounded him. The solitude soothed. He'd never been alone in a church before but felt at home—not lonely. If today's meeting, and what hopefully followed it, succeeded, he'd likely often enjoy such quiet spaciousness. And then, after a life ministering to souls who filled pews like these, he could spend eternity with his father.

He imagined his father's smile, blew him a kiss before exiting the pew, and then approached the rectory, preparing to confidently articulate how the priesthood was *his* idea, *his* desire. He knocked on the rectory door and Father Dennis' heavy steps soon approached. Damian's heartbeat audibly as the lock clicked and the door opened. Whiskey, just like in the confessional several weeks ago, scented the air.

Father Dennis stood before him, flushed, apparently, from a quick shower. His thinning, light-brown hair was damp and uncombed, and water drops beaded his eyelashes. His blue eyes were bloodshot and dozy, and he blinked, seemingly trying to recognize Damian. He swayed in the doorway, his clerical garb exchanged for sandals, khakis, and a pink Hawaiian shirt. He appeared as though aboard a cruise—a plump retiree, older than the mid-forties Damian guessed him to be.

Stunned, Damian's prepared statements evaporated, and yet he spoke quickly, unthinkingly: "I've got something you need to hear."

"I don need your help," Father Dennis said, slurring. His eyes grew fierce. Damian wanted to flee but couldn't bear another failure, so he forced himself to continue: "I *want* to help, to serve."

"You don wanna get involved." Father Dennis' replies sounded well worn, as though he'd been thus defensive before.

"I do," Damian said firmly.

"Why?" Father Dennis was now angry.

Damian persevered and said: "I'd hoped to discuss that."

"Well . . ." Father Dennis said. He looked past Damian. "Is anyone else coming?"

"You mean my mom? Because this is *my* idea."

"Anyone!" Father Dennis shouted, and Damian

wondered at his pastor. Why bring others to this meeting? For spiritual support, to vouch for his pious character? *Or maybe for corroboration!* Father Dennis had obviously forgotten their phone conversation and he seemed to assume that Damian was now accusing or somehow confronting him; he needed to clarify why he was here.

"No others," Damian said. "Just us. To discuss entering—"

"Well." Father Dennis scratched his head, squinted, and then nodded. "Fine. Come in."

Damian entered the rectory and said, "So I'm considering the priestho—"

Father Dennis stumbled into the door as he closed it and Damian reached to grab him. Father Dennis caught his fall and promptly steadied himself before asking: "Are people talking? I mean, to the bishop or anything?"

"Father, I'm here to apply to the diocese," Damian said loudly. "To enter a seminary, if accepted."

"Oh!" Father Dennis staggered back and slapped his forehead. "I thought, you know, this was an interven—whew! *That's* good news!"

Damian stood silent, still stunned, yet grateful that his presence was finally understood. But was Father Dennis just relieved to have avoided an intervention, or actually happy about Damian's priestly intentions?

"Come on," Father Dennis said. He patted Damian's back, leading him down a hall. "Something before we chat. Whiskey?"

"Sure," he replied, wanting to please. But his conscience pricked him. His pastor's alcoholism had been undetectable at the altar only fifteen minutes ago and the congregation, including his family, regarded Father

Dennis as a religious leader and moral model. *What deception!*

But then he remembered, as he had with Uncle Rick two days ago, his own recent failures and tried not to judge. Here was a priest, what he wanted to become, who was flawed—just how *he'd* felt lately. So, in a way, Father Dennis' drinking was comforting. Priests could obviously be broken people—wounded, but still helpful.

As he followed his pastor into the rectory's wide living room and watched him pour amber into crystal glasses, he recalled his *true* purpose: sanctity. He craved perfection, not just priestly fellowship and mediocre ministry. God saw this desire, and still allowed his recent sins and failures to humble him and reveal humanity's flawed nature. His own mother had erred in her youth, and his father, the best man he'd ever known, had briefly floundered before reforming into a professional athlete and then a most loving parent.

In fact, even some celebrated saints had fallen spectacularly before exemplifying moral perfection. He just had to ensure, when his life was complete, that his devotion was palpable, his virtue unparalleled. Out of sheer mercy, *his* hagiographer ought to be spared the struggles *he'd* endured to capture his father's saintliness.

Father Dennis handed him his glass and sat, crossing his legs.

"All right," he said. "Now let's hear about your discernment, *how* you came to hear God's call."

Damian slowly leaned toward the coffee table, placed his glass on a coaster engraved with a cowboy lassoing a calf and then straightened himself in his chair. His priestly future depended upon the account he was about to give. While maintaining honesty, he'd avoid mentioning his mother's (former) control and his eagerness to escape his cramped home. Meanwhile, he ought to downplay his intense desire to become a saint, because *that* was a private endeavour and might sound selfish, even imbalanced—as it had to Scott and Veronica.   Also, whether he reunited with his father in Heaven was irrelevant to the spiritual welfare of his future parishioners.

Once prepared, he breathed deeply and met his pastor's gaze. His priestly vocation was God's will, so the Lord would guide him. "Well, Father, as you've probably noticed at daily Mass, I'm the eldest of four and . . ."

He confidently narrated how he'd come to hear God's call. He admitted that certain relative*s* had *suggested* his pursuing the priesthood, but that he'd only recently realized their advice was sound; he really did suit a Roman collar. He emphasized his undeniably unique upbringing, referencing, for example, his acquaintance with several volumes on Father Dennis' bookshelves.

After praising Grandma Schiller (and avoiding Uncle Rick), Damian grasped his glass, mumbled that his father supported his priestly aspirations, and then immediately asked what brand of whiskey this was; Father Dennis replied, and then, after nodding, Damian continued his narrative by revealing his great devotion to the rosary. Just like that, he avoided his father's death. He wondered why he'd done so, but then, as he heard himself talking, he abandoned this concern and grew excited. The crafty way he described his miserable life made it sound like something from *Butler's Lives*.

Father Dennis' eyes steadily widened and his brows rose with every detail; he was smiling broadly when he finally interrupted: "Stop, stop! Write all this down and I'll submit it to the bishop with your application. It's the best vocation story I've ever heard!"

"Vocation story?"

"How God led you to the priesthood."

"Write it out?"

"Please! And bring it to Mass tomorrow."

"Sure."

"Another thing—I'll become your spiritual director. We'll meet here weekly."

"Great," Damian said, and he meant it.

"And now I'm your sole confessor, too. Deal?"

"Well . . ." Damian replied hesitantly. After so impressing his pastor, he'd be embarrassed to admit—even in confession—what he'd just omitted from his vocation story: the catalogue, Veronica, his frustration at home, and his habitually harsh judgement of others—including Father Dennis himself. And how could he reveal despair over his father's death when he'd just implied that he was still alive? Though Father Dennis seemed to have forgotten past confessions, or was disallowing those forgiven sins from influencing him now, Damian's current confession list at least *seemed* to conflict with his just-given account. Indeed, Uncle Rick's assurances no longer applied. Thus concerned, he asked, "Why?"

"Because as your pastor, I'll oversee your vocation—especially your story." Father Dennis looked off, sipping and grinning. "The bishop'll be thrilled!"

He was obviously pleased, but Damian wasn't. He couldn't break his pastor's trust by confessing to another priest, so he'd have to withhold certain sins—a sin itself—until he entered the seminary and acquired a new confessor. And during that wait, he doubted Father Dennis could direct him spiritually because he seemed unstable, forgetful, and completely alcoholic.

Yet his pastor beamed so hopefully that Damian tried to quit fretting. Indeed, who was he to judge a priest? This first meeting had, ultimately, triumphed, and it certainly suggested future success. He brightened as Father Dennis smiled. And, perhaps more importantly, he felt valued and welcomed into the diocesan community he wanted to join—a clerical family of *surrogate* fathers.

He pictured the *other* list in his journal and imagined the satisfaction at crossing off the second step, of adding the third:

Steps to the Seminary

- ~~*Talk to Rick*~~
- ~~*Meet with Fr. Dennis*~~
- *Write Vocation Story*

"Another drink, Damian?"

"I'm good, Father."

CHAPTER ELEVEN

"THE FAMILY THAT PRAYS TOGETHER..."

Damian entered his bedroom later that morning—tipsy but enthused—and removed his journal from under his bed, sat at his desk, clicked his pen, and lowered the ball-point toward a fresh page.

But then he hesitated.

He still tasted the mouthwash Father Dennis gave him shortly before his mother picked him up and the lingering mint that successfully masked his boozy breath from her made him consider the veracity of the vocation story he was about to compose.

Father Dennis might forget much of what Damian had just related at the rectory, but he needed to retain those parts of his account that'd so visibly pleased his pastor. After all, his vocation story was now vital to his life's mission: he *needed* to impress the bishop and *ensure* acceptance into a seminary so he could become a priest, and then a saint.

Meanwhile, though, he could now rephrase in writing any inaccuracies he may have stated earlier today—adjust those details that could, in the future, suggest dishonesty. Doing so was ethical and would preserve the trust of his superiors—not just of his pastor, but of the bishop and seminary administrators who'd likely read his story as part of his application. And were his life ever investigated by, say, a diligent hagiographer working years after his death, major discrepancies wouldn't exist between his handwritten words and other, non-firsthand accounts of his early years.

Above all, God and his father knew the truth, and so, as he glanced at Christ crucified above his desk, he pledged honesty as he prepared to write well. . .

Writing his own account well would be much easier, he mused, than his struggles to capture his father's saintliness on the page. Now that *his* memory alone supplied the material, he could more easily shape the narrated experiences into a story that sounded, if not saintly, at least palpably pious. And if pious, then likely suited to the priesthood. Indeed, why not describe an *ideal* preparation for ordination? Had not his time at Grandma Schiller's been just that? And what valuable practice he'd gain if he now succeeded to be both honest *and* impressive. His next attempts at composing his father's biography would likely better match *Butler's*.

Solemn at the magnitude of his task, yet excited by its potential, he put pen tip to page:

"The Family that Prays Together"
by Damian Kurt
"The family that prays together, stays together." My family proves this statement true. We pray so much, we are always connected spiritually, and, growing up in a home that included extended family, we kept very close physical proximity, too. But not for long! Through the joyful din of voices filling my crowded home, I have heard God's call to labour in His vineyard—to join a seminary and pursue ordination.

But how did I hear God's call? A few months ago I had an experience like Saint Paul's on the road to Damascus.

While lifting weights at the gym, something I loved as much as Paul loved persecuting Christians, God literally struck me down by a force from above. When I awoke from this blow, I saw my life needed to change.

So, like Christ venturing into the desert, I went out into the world, alone and unsure where God would lead me, what I might find, who I'd encounter.

The lure of money, of paid employment, greeted me first, and though I tried to view my labours spiritually, to keep my thoughts on higher things while my hands worked busily, I soon realized I needed to flee my job—to cleanse my life of financial dealings much like Christ Himself cleansed the temple of the money changers and sellers.

No sooner had I escaped wealth's clutches, but doubt—expressed by those around me—attacked me to test the Faith I'd received at home and cultivated since boyhood. Though these worldly tempters craftily encouraged me to abandon my belief in God and Heaven, strength from those very two sources saw me through my trial.

Obviously frustrated that I hadn't fallen into his first two sinful traps, the Devil devised a sensuous snare that may have doomed my soul had not the rosary—those small but all-powerful beads—strengthened me to push off and dismiss this occasion of sin.

Thus, cleansed and experienced, I returned home a new man. One with his eyes set on a Godly path, indeed, the path to the priesthood. But I won't be home for long! As one who puts his hand to the plow when God calls him to, I, without looking back, will leave my earthly relatives and cleave to my new spouse, the Church!

But this forthcoming venture is not without bitterness that, I trust, will ripen into a sweetly fruitful priestly ministry. For I grew up in a truly loving nest and attended the Catholic school nearest my home. My mother administrated and ensured that only the True Faith was taught. From a young age, I cultivated my mind with study and pious reading. I also disciplined my body with rigorous exercise.

Damian scrutinized the last paragraph. He hadn't *lied* while describing his homeschooling, yet he'd avoided its embarrassing isolation. Any more transparency was unnecessary. Wasn't it?

He continued:

Like any good Catholic boy, I obeyed my parents, who encouraged me to study the lives of the saints, to pray the rosary, and to regularly examine my conscience.

Such praise matched what he read in *Butler's*—most saints came from pious parents—and Scripture gave much attention to lineage. Yet he also avoided emphasizing his mother's manipulation, as he had at the rectory. But what about his dad? When Damian finally completed his father's biography, thus familiarizing future readers with George Kurt's saintly life, wouldn't *they* wonder at his absence from his son's (and hagiographer's) own vocation story? He'd include a brief sketch:

My father, an immigrant, lived in service to others. His example of humility, hard work, and sacrifice struck many as saintly, and, because of him, my family's home included widows, orphans, and the poor.

The past tense implied the death he couldn't state explicitly, and now he mentioned other relatives so he didn't seem obsessed with his father:

My Grandmother guided us with her wisdom, and my siblings and I attended Mass every morning, where I watched our pious parish priest raise the host and chalice. In my heart, I would repeat the words of consecration he uttered, yearning to say them aloud one day!

Was the compliment to Father Dennis too blatant? He hadn't named him *specifically*, so he'd keep it and other clergy who might read this account would likely appreciate his nod to a local pastor's example.

After reading what he'd just composed, he decided to now focus on himself: to describe an ideal future—to clearly outline the saintly person he wanted to become. That way his goal would be set in his mind and in the minds of everyone who read this story. If he didn't achieve the ideal terms he was about to list, he'd be a fraud, which disqualified him from becoming a saint and thus provided the motivation he needed to attain his life's goal.

"The Family that Prays Together, Stays Together." I believe this statement is true. The saints have always taught that a prayerful family is the garden in which priestly seeds are planted. Now that I'm responding to God's call, the gift of a religious vocation is budding inside me and it must be transplanted to the fertile soil of a seminary!

Those last lines were a tad flowery, a bit boastful, perhaps, but he required momentum for a grand flourish to close triumphantly:

Now I will commit myself to seminary formation, to continuing the pious lessons I learned in my family's home.

Good. But he needed to be more specific. What was he working toward, exactly?

I will pray and study to hone my ability to save souls for Christ.

Great. But who was this document for? Who would

read it with the greatest interest? He needed to address his primary audience.

And I pledge my loyalty to the bishop and the hierarchy of the Roman Catholic Church.

Right. And now that he'd addressed the upper levels of his audience, why not acknowledge the common man and pledge to provide model behaviour?

And I will do my best to give good example to other young men, so they follow in my footsteps toward Christ's altar.

Poetic. Profound. Stirring, too. Very stirring. These were lofty hopes, but *his* hopes none the less. And after his recent failures and participating in the rather indulgent lifestyle exhibited by Father Dennis, he wanted to bind himself to a perfect, sinless, *priestly* lifestyle now—from the start. His future reputation would indeed depend upon adhering to the hopes he'd just expressed, on not slipping from his original purpose. This vocation story was a contract of sorts, at least one made between him and God. He'd know if he broke it.

Damian reviewed his story one last time: *A success!* He smiled, tore the pages from his journal to give to Fr. Dennis tomorrow, and then flipped back to his list to cross out the final item:

Steps to the Seminary

- ~~Talk to Uncle Rick~~
- ~~Talk to Fr. Dennis~~
- ~~Write Vocation Story~~

Satisfied, he pushed back his chair, and accidentally rammed the bed. The bed bumped the wall and the crucifix above his desk fell, face down, onto the pages of his story.

The whiskey's buzz had worn off during his efforts. His hand ached after holding the pen so tightly for so long. As he kissed the pierced feet and hung the crucifix back up, he stole a glance at Christ's face. It appeared sad.

But surely his eyes were already hazy from the beginning of a hangover. Christ was as happy as he was with his story. Surely.

After Mass one morning in March, Father Dennis approached Damian with the news: "You're in."

"Just like that?" Damian asked, wishing his mother hadn't been able to hear. He turned toward the priest to avoid her beaming face.

"Just like that," Father Dennis replied. "The bishop adored your vocation story—he photocopied it, so every parish has one. He instructed pastors to read it from the pulpit as a model for Catholic parents. With more families like yours, the seminaries will overflow!"

"He really liked it that much?"

"He did. His Excellency hopes that young fellas will follow your example."

"I doubt that."

"I don't. Kids these days are attracted to unique individuals, like Christ Himself or Saint Francis. And people want *authenticity*. That's what the bishop likes about you, Damian—you're the real deal."

Damian smiled, but a twinge of guilt cut the smile short.

"Well," Father Dennis continued, "we have to try something because times are tough for the Church. Most seminaries have about two-dozen men. That's why we need your kind."

"I'll do what I can," Damian said.

"Trust me. Your story's gonna' reel 'em in."

"Maybe."

"Have faith," Fr. Dennis said as he passed Damian a brochure. "And here, check out your new home. The bishop has already submitted your application to the Rector of Mt. Angelus Seminary. *He* loved your story more than anyone."

Damian took the brochure and gazed at the cover photo, which was an aerial shot of a small mountain with stately buildings and verdant grounds on its round, flat top. Before he could look at the seminary too closely, though, his mother approached Fr. Dennis and said: "I just want to thank you for inspiring Damian to the priesthood! He hasn't had a fath—"

"One second, Cynthia," Fr. Dennis said. "Damian, why don't you drop by this week for a little priestly fellowship? Friday night?"

"Sounds good, Father." Damian replied. "And I'll read this at home."

Fr. Dennis winked knowingly before Damian's mother resumed thanking the priest repeatedly, and then requested extra confession times at the parish.

That afternoon in his bedroom, Damian considered the bishop's reaction to his vocation story: *Will priests actually read it from the pulpit? Is anyone going to suspect me? Fr. Dennis doesn't, and he's heard my confessions. I wonder . . .*

But he was eager to read about the seminary, so he reigned in his worries for the moment. The brochure described a small mountain in the Okanagan Valley. Native tribes had revered this low yet lofty peak as a landing place for Heavenly spirits, or angels. When Europeans settled the area, they chose the name Mount Angel to Christianize these indigenous tales, and soon Catholic missionaries erected a chapel dedicated to Our Lady of the Angels atop the summit.

The aerial shot of the campus showed beautiful grounds: eight sandy-brick buildings encircled the mountaintop; a lawn and parking lot covered the center of the grounds.

The buildings were numbered in the photograph, and a legend identified each structure: the campus had a gym (Damian smiled), two dormitories, a library (he smiled again), a monastery for the monks, a cathedral church, a bell tower, and an underground chapel where the original chapel was built.

Damian lowered the brochure. The seminary, as described here, pleased him; from what he saw last month, Fr. Dennis' rectory pleased him, too—although hesitantly because he feared falling into his pastor's habits. *But surely God calls us to something that grants joy,* he thought. Just then Uncle Rick chuckled upstairs, and James burst through the bedroom door and dumped toy cars on the floor. A cloud of cigarette smoke followed him into the room.

Yes, Damian thought: *God's call grows louder by the day.*

He tucked the brochure into his journal and applied himself to his studies with renewed vigour. He had to graduate before he could escape into religious life, so completing high school was his next step.

And he studied hard, but, on Friday evenings when he visited his pastor, he drank even harder. Doing so bothered his conscience, but how else could he befriend Father Dennis? He'd never enjoyed alcohol before, but he did now and Father Dennis encouraged it, saying, "Celibates need fun too, you know."

"Yes, Father," Damian would reply as he sipped bourbon and beer and watched the priest barbecue. After his experience with Veronica in Scott's basement, the prospect of a lifetime of celibacy appealed to him all the more. His first sexual encounter had been so intense he could hardly shake it from his mind and the seductive lure of women scared him. The priesthood quelled this fear by simply ridding sex from his life and thus dispelling a possible hindrance to sanctity.

In terms of loneliness, he found a fairly good companion in his pastor. Father Dennis made him feel part of the larger, clerical family he now belonged to. The two enjoyed good conversations with their steaks and liquor. After this fun, though, Damian would have to call his mom for a ride because Father Dennis was invariably too drunk to drive and would, in fact, often be snoring in a lawn chair by the time Damian heard the station wagon pull up out front. He would run to the car, so his mom didn't see her pastor passed out. Were it not for his alcoholism, Damian often mused, Father Dennis may have proved to be a father figure. But with his pastor-turned-friend so often drunk, he found no substitute for his father in Heaven.

Damian's mother never suspected the heavy drinking at these soirees, happy for his acceptance into the clergy.

One night in late June, at their last dinner together, Father Dennis presented Damian with a gift. "Well, this is it, Damian. I'll miss our evenings together. I don't want you drying out at the seminary, though, so I got you something."

"Thanks, Father," Damian said, taking the gift. A flask with an etching of Christ emerged from the wrapping paper, on it, decorative lettering read: *"What Wouldn't Jesus Do?"*

"An inside joke," Fr. Dennis said. "Just between us."

"Yes, Father." Damian shook the flask, opened it, and smelled bourbon. "Thanks. I'll miss you too."

When he heard his mother arrive, Father Dennis now asleep on the chaise lounge, Damian slid the flask into his pants. This hiding place worked while seated in the car, but when he exited the station wagon at home, he faked a cramp in his thigh and kept his hand wrapped over the area. He limped up the porch steps, scared the flask would somehow slide from his grip and out his pant leg, but he made it downstairs undetected.

In his room, however, with James already snoring, he realized that the flask had just made him deceive his mother. And having bourbon hidden in the small container would put him at risk for excessive—or at least inappropriate— drinking. The etching of Christ and the slogan, too, were crass—irreverent, to say the least.

Father Dennis might find such indulgence, and such humour, acceptable—but he wasn't the kind of priest Damian wanted to become. And he hadn't turned out to be a great spiritual director, either. Damian kept true to his promise of not confessing to any other priest in the diocese, but neither had he confessed to Father Dennis. Since they'd become friends, and since Father Dennis continued to praise Damian as an ideal priestly candidate, he was too embarrassed to confess to his new companion. Whenever Father Dennis offered confession, Damian refused. He could've confessed just his non-embarrassing sins, meaning everything but masturbation and the Veronica incident, but that would've blasphemed the sacrament and simply added another blemish to his soul. He received communion reluctantly during this time, aware he wasn't in a state of grace.

Now Damian quietly pulled his journal from under the bed, careful not to wake James. In it, he had a copy of his vocation story. He reread it under his desk lamp, then took the flask to the downstairs toilet, emptied it, and discarded it under some used tissue in the trash.

His vocation story was working! At least on him. He decided to stop worrying about how it glossed over the truth, how it idealized not just the future but the past. He judged his story by its fruits, and just now it preserved his commitment to sanctity; to ensure that he kept this commitment when his new life began at Mount Angelus, he listed on a fresh page some spiritual exercises he planned to practice privately at the seminary. Nobody needed to know about the penance, fasting, and extra prayers he quietly committed to. They advanced him towards sanctity, as his story, gratefully, had tonight.

He thanked his father in Heaven.

The day after he threw out the flask, Damian returned to his journal to work on his father's biography for the first time since that troubling attempt in Scott's basement, about three months ago now. Since then he stifled the doubt that sprouted that day, but he also avoided writing about his father's life because he feared that doing so might actually weaken his conviction that his dad was a saint.

Now, sitting at his desk downstairs, he assured himself that such doubt came from Satan and was meant to discourage his efforts to see his dad again in Heaven. And the recent success of his vocation story—how enthusiastically it'd been received, and the positive effect it had on his behaviour yesterday—granted him new confidence as a writer. After turning his own miserable experiences into an ideal path to the priesthood, surely he could now, finally, refashion his father's life into a true tale of sanctity. He only needed to be more, well, factual than he'd been with his own life. . .

Today, he had a promising idea. This morning at Canadian Martyrs he'd summarized Saint Joseph's life for the parish bulletin, and Saint Joseph's example of the quiet carpenter supporting his family seemed highly adaptable to his dad's biography. So, he decided to present his father as the working man's saint, the humble plumber who, like Saint Joseph, used his daily employment as a means to holiness. Damian hadn't yet elaborated on his father's work, but there was plenty of material for him to do so.

He assisted his father many workdays and could clearly recall how personable he'd been with his clients. How, when they mistook his Kiwi accent as Australian, he feigned offense before laughing and revealing his true nationality; how also, when lifting hot-water tanks, he initially pretended he was too weak, grunting and straining to get the homeowner's attention but then, suddenly, effortlessly, hoisting the tank in a bear hug and walking it outside to the van with a smile, passing his gawking clients, he'd say, "See! No Sweat!"

His favourite trick had been to present a quarter to a client's kids and bet them he could bend it; if he couldn't, he promised to give the children the coin. Kneeling so they could see, he pressed the quarter between his thumb and index finger, shaking and grimacing as he again pretended to lack the strength. When his audience was certain he failed, and were extending their open palms for their prize, his dad folded the coin in half, acted surprised, and gave it to them anyway.

What happy days! He'd been so proud of his dad, and he recalled the homeowners' amazed faces as they watched this tall, tanned, musclebound Kiwi put on strongman shows in their houses *while* he fixed their pipes, drains, leaky taps. A true spectacle. . . And yet his father's audacity, though charming, better fit his former career as a professional athlete. As a plumber he worked hard while having fun, thus pleasing his clients, but didn't *Butler's* claim that Saint Joseph toiled in *silence* in his woodshop at home? The gnawing doubt Damian felt in Scott's basement, that deep weed, now sprouted again. Performing for his clients was something Saint Joseph would never do. Spectacles weren't saintly.

Other differences arose, too. Saint Joseph carefully constructed wood furniture, thus providing his customers with solid, permanent, and well-crafted wares to use and admire for generations. Saint Joseph's employment resembled his saintly reputation. Both rested upon the diligent, humble temper of a man whose product was of undeniable quality, whose character was fit to raise the

Son of God.

Damian's dad had been a capable plumber, but fixing toilets and unplugging drains somehow lacked the sense of dignity that seemed inherent in crafting quality furniture. And that his father had entertained while working divested his labours of the somber diligence that defined Saint Joseph.

Damian shut his journal, frustrated again. *Had a plumber ever been canonized? Had a strongman? What about a Kiwi?* He shook his head and, to cheer up, reread the seminary's brochure. Maybe his father's biography would blossom on Mount Angelus' peak.

He certainly hoped so.

The End of Part One

PART TWO

CHAPTER TWELVE
TRAVELLING COMPANION

One morning in late August, Damian sat in the basement on an old bus bench holding Grandma Schiller's dusty, green, dial phone as he discussed travel plans to Mount Angelus with Calgary's other seminarian, Theodore Messier. Although the two had never met in person—they lived at opposite ends of the city—Father Dennis had suggested they drive out together because Damian didn't own a vehicle while Theodore had a massive panel van from his days as a welder.

"I guess I should call you *Saint* Damian," Theodore suddenly blurted sarcastically.

"Um . . ." Damian replied. Theodore's tone frightened him.

"I mean your vocation story. *My* pastor read it from the pulpit! *Your* story!"

"Oh," Damian said, feeling unexpected guilt and nearly apologizing even though he'd known his story was to follow Sunday sermons at *all* of Calgary's parishes; such publicity had gladdened him, yet now he was very uncomfortable to have taken attention from Theodore at his own parish, and he felt like he'd been exposed as a fraud.

"I guess I'm just lucky to be talking to the real thing," Theodore said, his tone playful but still bitter.

"Ha!" Damian said before his fake laugh petered out.

Silence passed for several slow, awkward moments as Damian sat tensed, unsure what course this conversation would take. Then, just as quickly as his tone had soured, Theodore's normal voice returned. "But we'll have a good drive out there, eh?"

"Yup," Damian said, relieved to change the subject.

"When should I pick you up?"

Damian imagined Theodore entering Grandma Schiller's house. What if he saw their poverty, that the widow and orphans described in his vocation story weren't those brought in off the streets, but in fact the Kurts themselves?

What if he saw the tiny desks upstairs in a row, the crooked blackboard on the wall? What if he saw the room that Damian shared with James, his textbooks sitting on the small wood desk where he'd studied so diligently, completing high school in June? His vocation story gave the impression he'd actually *gone* to school, a school where his mother taught. If Theodore entered the Kurts' home and saw this tiny desk crammed into a basement corner, with toys scattered and clothes strewn about, he might detect the truth. And Damian might not be able to deny it, either.

"Let's get an early start on that drive," Damian said. "Why not four-thirty?"

"In the morning?"

"Sure."

"It'll still be dark out."

"Fine with me," Damian said.

On the morning he was to leave for the seminary, Damian stepped onto Grandma Schiller's porch and shut the door: it gave him goose bumps to think he wouldn't return for months. Grandma Schiller had cooked a huge dinner the night before, and even Uncle Rick had come out to eat with the family and wish him well.

Now the stars were still out, the city—and Grandma Schiller's house—shrouded in darkness. Damian dropped his packed gym bag on the sidewalk near the street and turned back to the house. He planned to spy Theodore's van while it was still blocks away, and his method would ensure he was standing, ready, at the street corner to meet his travelling companion, who'd have no time to examine Grandma Schiller's house. *He was going to climb onto the roof to wait, watch, and listen.* He'd have to do so quietly so he didn't wake his family, but he was confident he could. Even though he hadn't climbed onto a roof for probably ten years, he'd done so many times as a child.

At seven or eight years old, he'd complete his school day by copying out the spelling words his mother had assigned, generally formal nouns from the Hebrew Bible like "Moab," "Gideon," and, if he'd been bad, "Nebuchadnezzar." These were followed by catechetical terminology like "atonement," "purgation," and "redemption."

He had a knack for language and would race through the words. Then, having presented his work to his mother and corrected any mistakes, he was permitted to quit for the day. He'd run to his room, remove his hated school-hours uniform, change into play clothes, grab his dad's old rugby skin, and climb the lattice at the back of the house to get onto the roof. There, he tossed the skin a few inches in the air and listened for the deep chug of his dad's rumbling work van, announcing his return from blocks away. When Damian heard it, he'd scamper down the lattice and run to the front yard just as his dad parked the van, *Kurt's Courtesy Plumbing* stenciled in broad blue letters along the side.

Now Damian stood on Grandma Schiller's porch, the cherished rugby skin packed tightly in his valise so both his hands were free to climb. He inhaled deeply to steady himself so he could move quietly. He reached up and held onto the eavestrough as he placed his foot in the porch railing's wrought-iron lattice and climbed it. The railing wavered and groaned under his bulk, but Damian maintained his balance and swung his right leg onto the roof. Then, pushing off the railing with his left foot, and thus nearly tearing it out of the concrete, he heaved himself up, wriggling across the shingles. When his whole body was on the gently-sloping, quietly creaking roof, he rolled onto his broad back and gazed at the stars. His proximity to the heavens—a star-punctured canopy burning brightly, despite the frigid morning air—made him feel closer to his dad, to the gaze he longed to see and that he could now almost imagine looking back at him through twinkling pupils.

"Dad," he whispered. A particularly bright star twinkled back at him and he reached up with his finger, as though he could touch it, when a deep chug came down the street.

That chug. Exactly like his dad's work van! He quickly sat up and saw a white van rolling towards the house. He inched his massive frame down the roof, desperate to meet this vehicle—if indeed it was Theodore Messier's—at the corner. But as he neared the edge, he gathered speed: the shingles were dewy and slick. His foot caught the edge as he slid from the roof tearing off the eavestrough as he went. He barely landed on his feet in the front yard. The eavestrough hung loose now and had made a loud noise— a noise that could wake his family when he needed them tucked away, asleep in their beds and out of sight.

The van pulled up to the curb. Damian sprinted to grab his gym bag and opened the passenger-side door just as the van stopped. A short, bald man in his mid-twenties was at the wheel. He looked more like a mechanic than a seminarian, and Damian was surprised at his appearance. The young man, too, appeared surprised.

"Did you just fall off the roo—" the young man said.

"Theodore?" Damian asked, interrupting so he didn't have to explain himself.

"Yup," Theodore answered.

"Damian," Damian said, and Theodore stuck out his hand just as Damian heard the front door of Grandma Schiller's house open. He threw in his gym bag, slammed the door, and said, "Let's go! Quick!"

Theodore appeared bewildered, retracted his offered hand, and stepped on the gas. The van chugged away, and Damian's reputation was safe. For now.

"Wow," Theodore said minutes later.

Damian realized that falling off the roof, frantically stuffing himself in the passenger seat, and demanding that they leave immediately—without time to even shake hands—had made for an odd introduction, and he worried about what his travelling companion thought of him. An interior light above the front seats, the type that usually shut off when the doors close, still flickered. In its glow, Damian tried to assess Theodore's expression: bemused, pondering. Theodore was not much more than five feet tall but stocky and muscular; he had a beard, and his head was shaved bald.

"What?" Damian asked.

"Why were you on the roof?"

"Wanted to be ready for you, to waste no time."

"Jeez," Theodore replied. "You're so eager to get there, just like I thought you'd be."

Damian nodded. Their introduction had actually *added* to his saintly reputation. But at what cost? Who'd opened the front door as they'd pulled away? He tried not to think about it as he and Theodore reached the city limit just as the sun rose.

He'd never been outside the city. The rolling foothills were sprinkled with round hay bales the size of his family's station wagon. In the distance the Rocky Mountains appeared in profile; their jagged peaks and massive bases seemed impassable, but, based on the saints' lives he'd read, he knew that if he and Theodore were determined to cross the mountain range, God would strengthen them to do so.

As the van whizzed past farms, Damian noted the red and white barns that could've been taken right out of a child's picture book. Indeed, they appeared ideal. Theodore, as though reading Damian's thoughts, said: "Them barns look nice, but they ain't too comfy."

"What?"

"Inside. They're cold and full of mice."

"How do you know?"

"Born in one."

"Actually?" Damian tried not to laugh at his new friend.

"I'm telling you," Theodore said. "A barn in Quebec. Since my dad was on the run from the law, and my mom didn't want to go to a hospital."

"Wow," Damian said. He was enthralled as Theodore shared his life story—a criminal father, a mentally ill mother, and life in a trailer park in Edmonton. In its authenticity and share of suffering, Theodore's life was saintlier than Damian's, but he, of course, couldn't say so.

Theodore continued speaking, sharing stories about his brief engagement to a stripper, how he worked as a welder before starting his own used car business, but then he heard the Lord's call one day when his father, finally caught and imprisoned, repented of his former sins and asked his son to spend his life undoing the wrongs he'd committed. It was a great story that, in its raw detail, was also honest, personal, transparent.

"So that's me," Theodore said. "And I already know about you—Mr. Perfect! On your way to becoming pope!"

Damian turned and looked out the window. The Rocky Mountains scraped the sky with their sharp peaks. The day was beautiful, the sky blue. He was leaving his past behind—the cramped quarters, the poverty, the loneliness.

Grandma Schiller's house had been less than perfect, but he wished he'd thanked her for his time there. He wished he hadn't damaged the roof and then left, vandalizing and fleeing the house he'd called home for the past four years. Guilt threatened to taint the sunny drive through the Rockies, and so he shook his head and turned back to Theodore. Damian wondered at Theodore's work experience, his encounters with women. He looked forward to further conversations.

But what could he reveal about himself? The lingering

fear of being discovered prevented him from sharing anything about his own life, so he gazed up at the peaks they passed, in awe of the massive mountains. They appeared eternal. Solid. Permanent. If only the reputation being spread by his vocation story shared these qualities.

So peaceful was the remainder of the trip, with the rhythmic rolling of the tires and the setting sun, that Damian fell asleep. He awoke when the van heaved up a gentle slope and chugged more deeply.

He rubbed his eyes. Pine trees lined the road winding up and up and then levelling out at the top: yellow streetlights glowed before the line of beautiful brick buildings that he recognized from the brochure. He couldn't wait to explore tomorrow, after a good sleep.

Theodore parked. Damian was so tired he didn't speak, and Theodore appeared in a similar state. They hauled their luggage through the humidity to the dormitory, the only building with lights on inside. As they opened the door, the cool air inside smelled of ancient wood and old carpets. On a small table in the foyer sat two envelopes, *Damian Kurt* written on one, *Theodore Messier* on the other. Inside Damian's envelope was a key with a blue tag that read: *Room 301.*

Past the foyer lay a broad hallway with white marble floors that shone below chandeliers. An ornate staircase in the middle, with polished wood railings and red carpet branched up to left and right.

Theodore and Damian climbed the stairs and, at the top of the third flight, Damian saw his room; it was right across the hall from Theodore's. He was suddenly wide awake as he inserted his key, opened the door, flicked on the lights, and stepped inside. He gasped.

This is mine, he thought. A white-walled room with hardwood floors—polished, reddish brown and undented—stretched out before him. Damian stepped carefully, then, realizing he had no toy cars or plastic soldiers or brothers to avoid, he removed his shoes and slid across the smooth wood surface. The walls were white plaster, old but spotless and freshly painted; indeed, the air smelled faintly of paint, but that lingering odor only helped contrast this clean, fresh room with the stale, smoky one he'd left behind.

Two tall windows encased in brick filled the far wall. An old-fashioned radiator, also freshly painted white, sat between the windows. Along the right wall, a metal-frame bed with a thick mattress *and* box spring was neatly made with white sheets, white pillows, and a blue blanket. No chomping Tyrannosaurus Rex twisting up the blanket. No smoke stains on the sheets. Damian let the door close behind him. He could lock it: no one else needed to come in. Not here. Not tonight.

Along the left wall was a large oak desk with drawers and a comfortable-looking black chair with a cushioned seat and arm rests. The desk was three times the size of the one he'd left in Grandma Schiller's basement.

Mine, he thought. Tears filled his eyes. This room was better than what he'd had at Scott's, but it held another advantage, too: not only did the door lock, but here he wouldn't be visited by seductive nurses, by unbelievers—by any temptation whatsoever. He cried but smiled.

Only mine, he repeated. He'd find a priest and confess tomorrow, so his soul would soon be white like the walls to either side of him, walls he couldn't touch with both hands at once when he stuck out his arms and tried. He sighed. The bed didn't even squeak when he collapsed onto it.

Handcuffed in front of Grandma Schiller's house. Night. Through the darkness the eavestrough hung from the roof. On the porch huddled his family, wet, shivering— even Uncle Rick. Sorrowful stares.

Tied to a post, hands bound behind him. Couldn't move. From the front lawn smoke suddenly curled up into a black-hooded figure who pointed at him, pointed at the eavestrough, and then pointed down, at Hell—this grim judge's home.

So ashamed for what he'd done, but he couldn't stop staring at the pointing figure and at his family's sad eyes. Then—horrible! An erection! His mother began to cry. The hooded judge shook his head and approached; Damian squirmed and tried to escape as a bony hand emerged from the judge's dark sleeve and reached out for him. . .

Knocking at his door woke him from his nightmare. When he first opened his eyes, he forgot where he was: where was James? Why did the air smell so clean? Then he remembered and wondered if he'd dreamt the knocking, but then he heard it again. He jumped out of bed and threw on clothes and shoes before opening the door, thinking how nice it was to finally have one that locked.

A tall priest in his mid-fifties stood before him. He wore a long, black cassock, had large, black, square glasses and a mustache. He was balding at the very top of his head, which made him look like he had a monk's tonsure.

"Good morning, Mr. Kurt," he said.

"Good morning, Father," Damian replied. Theodore

stood behind the priest, lifting his eyebrows as though something important was going on.

"I'm Father Rector," the priest said. "And I'd like to welcome you and Mr. Messier to Mount Angelus Seminary."

"Thanks," Damian said.

"Since you two are our new men, I'd—"

"We're the only new guys?" Damian asked.

"Yes," the Rector replied. "Numbers are, well . . . I'd like to take you on a tour of the seminary."

"Sure." Damian let the door close behind him. He and Theodore walked at the Rector's sides, but, as they descended the staircase, Damian found he was stiff after yesterday's drive and he struggled to keep up with the Rector's long strides. He forced himself to walk fast, though, because he wanted to request confession; this desire—denied for so long—burned within him.

The Rector stopped before a large, stained-glass window midway down the staircase, and Damian was grateful to rest his legs while the Rector spoke: "This, gentlemen, is Saint John Vianney, patron of parish priests. He'll intercede for you if you pray to him."

The window was beautiful. Saint John's curly grey hair, purple stole, and white, ruffled vestments were vibrant as the sun shone through them. Damian prayed to the saint for the grace to confess his sins soon, preferably at the end of this tour.

The Rector showed Damian and Theodore all of the buildings that were featured in the brochure, but those pages failed to convey the lush lawns, tall trees, and rich red brick. Also, the brochure's aerial shots hadn't shown the truly majestic view of the Okanagan Valley that the seminary afforded: between two rows of mountains that formed a deep V-shape, a river wound for miles through vineyards and orchards.

The fresh smell of pines gave the grounds an alpine ambience, and behind the cathedral a round pond with a pebble shore sparkled in the sun. Below the cathedral, which was used for Sunday Mass and feasts, was a low-ceilinged underground chapel called "the crypt" that served for daily Mass, communal prayer, and weekly assemblies.

Damian enjoyed all he saw, but his stiff legs continued to ache. He lamented the distraction of his lingering sins as he tried to appreciate such splendid beauty around him, and he couldn't wait to gaze at the Okanagan again when he was in a state of grace: he was sure a spotless soul would allow him to better concentrate on the splendor of God's creation, spread before him like a banquet. So, he was certainly grateful to hear the Rector say that the next stop, the seminary's museum, was the last on their tour.

"Now for something strange," the Rector said. "And its presence here on the hilltop was decided by earlier rectors, though I keep it because it's popular. What we have next is a museum of death—a *memento mori,* a reminder that you will die. The idea was that seminarians shouldn't get distracted from their true purpose—which is to prepare themselves, and one day their parishioners, for death and hence eternal life."

At this description, Damian anxiously remembered his nightmare from that morning. Were he to die right now, he'd likely face a demonic, hooded judge as he had earlier, and that judge would have good reason to direct him below. He wanted to interrupt the Rector and confess on the lawn immediately, but he managed to contain himself as they neared the museum. It was a small, square building about thirty feet down the hillside and approachable by a rickety wood staircase. The Rector opened the door, and Damian and Theodore reluctantly followed him in. The air was stale. The museum was dark, and in the first room was an old electric chair with a buzzing yellow light bulb above it.

"We got this from the fine state of Montana," the Rector said. "Their last electric chair. See the cap that fit the skull? And the straps that held your wrists and ankles in place? I heard this chair killed over a hundred men."

Theodore's jaw hung open. Damian took quick, shallow breaths. He seemed to *feel* the mortal sins on his soul; they pinched like twisted muscles in his back. *Straight to Hell,* he told himself. *If I die, straight to Hell.* He promised himself he'd start praying more, would perform severe penance to strengthen his will and avoid future sin. Just then the door they'd entered through slammed shut, its hinges squealing like demons. The museum was thrown into total darkness but for the display lights showing various objects that, from what Damian could tell, all related to death.

Beside the electric chair, a noose hung from gallows that stood about ten feet high and was made of thick wood beams. Spindles extended from the white rope. His neck itched and he began to sweat. His sin made him fearful. He was spiritually soft and definitely needed to chastise himself with physical mortification, perhaps with the spindly cord he'd packed in his bag. Better to embrace temporary discomfort on earth than to suffer torments eternal in Hell.

In the next room were taxidermied animals: a wolf, foxes, a possum, and a bear. Beside the bear a hairy scalp hung in a display case.

"What's this, Father?" Theodore asked, pointing to the scalp.

"Hunter brought it here years ago," the Rector replied. "Claimed it came from a Sasquatch. Looks an awful lot like bear fur, though, don't you think?"

The adjacent room was brighter, but the light only revealed worse horrors: paintings of martyrs having their eyes plucked out, being boiled in oil, burned at the stake. On the opposite wall were portraits of mothers holding pale, pale babies.

"Victorian fad," the Rector said. "Families photographed their stillborns."

"Is there a lower floor?" Theodore asked.

"Yup," the Rector said. "Weapons room."

"I'm gonna check it out," Theodore said. "These photos are too much."

He ran downstairs, leaving Damian alone with the Rector. They both smiled. The Rector seemed friendly, if not a little awkward.

"Many of these items came from small mission parishes and mining towns that were scattered up in the mountains," the Rector said, as though the strange collection required some explanation. "The buildings are likely still up there, but the towns are abandoned, the parishes closed long ago. The bishop asked us to collect and preserve the old items, so we do. You should see our vaults below the cathedral! Every year they're packed with more clerical antiques—chalices, vestments, and such. I just wish we attracted new recruits like we do these old oddities! Anyway . . ."

Damian nodded. He could tell the Rector wanted him to ask about the vaults, but he didn't want to get distracted from confessing. The Rector looked at him intently.

"You know, Mr. Kurt, anytime you need me, I'm here for you. If you have worries this year, if studies seem overwhelming, if you miss home—even if you miss your parents, I'm here."

"Actually, Father, there is something."

"Anything."

"May I confess?"

"Right now?"

"Um, yeah."

"Why don't we go up to the chapel?"

Damian wanted to acquiesce, but images of Hell, of torture, streamed through his mind, and the lights around him seemed to buzz threateningly. He couldn't wait any longer. "It's just a few sins."

"Go quickly," the Rector said, and Damian, with one ear listening for Theodore to come up the stairs, knelt before the Rector and finally confessed the catalogue and Veronica, along with several other sins. The Rector listened, and then, for his penance, told Damian to trust God throughout the school year; he then gave absolution: "And I forgive you in the name of the Father, Son, and Holy Spirit."

Damian, his head bowed, felt fifty pounds lighter. "Thanks, Father."

The Rector nodded. "All right. Maybe stand up now, in case anyone—"

Just then, Theodore yelled, "Damian! Look!"

Damian stood and turned to go downstairs, but the

Rector caught his arm. "I'll see you men for the general assembly tonight—just a few announcements to start the year. You explore and unpack this afternoon. Good to have you with us."

"Okay. And thanks again, Father," Damian said, and then he ran downstairs. Another dark space with pistols, muskets, swords, and bows and arrows on the walls. But in the centre of the room was an empty glass case, its display light still shining above it.

"Look," Theodore said. He pointed at a small card taped to the glass, and Damian approached.

"Display missing," the card read, as though whatever the case had housed had simply disappeared, evaporated—just like Damian's guilt and fear of damnation.

"My pastor told me there was an incorrupt hand down here when he was a seminarian," Theodore said. Damian lifted his eyebrows at Theodore, who was very excited. "It's like it walked away—on its fingers!"

Damian shrugged and nodded. He felt relaxed now, even with such violent displays around him, and he realized that his stiffness was gone, along with his sin.

At the general assembly that night, Fr. Rector described daily life at Mount Angelus: prayer, Mass, study, pious reading, recreation, sports, and ministering to the poor, sick, and elderly. The routine sounded ideal, and, for the first time in years, Damian anticipated a happy, placid future. His only surprise had been how few seminarians Mount Angelus had, about thirty in all, and considering these men came from dioceses across Canada and abroad, the number seemed meager indeed.

After the assembly, he exited the underground chapel

and strolled to his dormitory with Theodore beside him. Far from any city lights, the stars twinkled brilliantly. Damian was so content—his future as bright as the stars, his soul pure white like their light—that he and his diocesan brother walked in comfortable silence. When they reached their rooms, they bid goodnight by a simple nod.

He entered his fresh, orderly room and flicked on the light. This afternoon he'd opened his gym bag to unpack and had found—folded neatly atop all he'd brought—his father's All Blacks jersey and several championship medals. His mother must have kept them all these years, and then, when he'd been asleep last night, placed them neatly in his bag, knowing how much he'd cherish them. Especially the skin his father kept from his last professional game, the smell of aged, worn leather and thick stitching that grew ever fainter each time he'd smelled it.

Now the jersey hung above his bed, his father's number—33—showing proudly. The medals hung in horizontal rows on either side. On his dresser he'd placed the old rugby skin he and his dad used to toss in the yard. It bore George Kurt's now-faint signature along with swirls of every other teammates signed name. The old leather smelled musky and rich, like his dad's aftershave, in a way. And the skin, dented and scarred, made him imagine his dad still living, bearing blisters and bruises incurred from his daily work, his feats of strength.

Right above the skin he'd tacked the photo of his father he'd formerly kept in his journal. Now his room had the proper theme, and he felt secure he wouldn't forget his true purpose in coming to Mount Angelus.

He turned to his desk, where his journal lay at the centre of the wide wood surface. In it his father's biography awaited completion. After today's tour of the museum of death, Damian had a daring plan for how to re-approach his precious project. He would, as was his habit when writing for the parish bulletin back home, compose the very last line of the story and then work backwards. When summarizing the lives of other saints, he'd found that if he began with the final flourish, the concluding sentence that encapsulated what made that saint great, he could then add, in reverse chronology, the details that led to the grand conclusion.

Employing this method now seemed hopeful, but it presented a problem, too. The last sentence of his father's biography, and the material immediately preceding it, would necessarily describe his death—which Damian had never been able to write about. That is, perhaps, until now.

He sat quickly and before he could consider what he was writing, he pushed his pen across the bottom of a page. One sentence—his initial goal—led to another, and soon he had a paragraph but no more space. Thrilled to be writing so quickly, and eager to maintain this momentum, he flipped the page and scrawled another half-dozen lines.

He leaned back in his chair, closed his eyes, and breathed deeply. He'd composed, he realized now, not his father's death—not exactly—but his funeral: the open casket, his father's muscular corpse stuffed into a small, unfamiliar grey suit and his stolid face caked with orange makeup that covered his once-glowing tan. Damian had wanted to kiss away that awful orange, or wash it off with his tears, but he had to sit still just a few feet away, in a hard pew, forcing—feigning—composure.

Beside him, huddling in support, sat his family, the pitiful audience to the tragedy before them. The other pews had held embarrassingly few attendants, and then Uncle Rick had been disguised at the back. None of his father's former clients came, nor any relatives from New Zealand, who claimed, suspiciously and lamely, that their sheep needed shearing and, besides, the airfare was just too expensive. So, grieving by themselves, the five remaining Kurts sniffled and sobbed—but softly because they were in church.

The memory was as black as the suit Damian had worn that day. He glanced at the words on the page, too scared to actually read them. He wanted to tear the page out, shred it, burn it and abolish forever the images of his father's funeral—but he didn't.

Instead he shut his journal and slid it into his desk drawer.

For the first time in months he successfully added to his father's biography and though it'd been excruciating, perhaps his best approach in the future was to thus catch himself off guard—to burst into his room between classes, or immediately upon rising before he fully awoke—and, working backwards from the funeral, write about his dad's death, even if he could only manage one line per session.

Doing so would hurt. But his dad was worth it.

CHAPTER THIRTEEN
TOLLE LEGE

The classroom door burst open and Dr. Harold Baker House, the seminary's literature professor, entered with a book under each arm and a cup of coffee in each hand. As always, he'd prefaced kicking open the door by yelling *"Tolle Lege!"* so that seminarians standing near were warned of his arrival.

Dr. House's messy blond hair shot forward, as though a tremendous gust of wind had blasted him from behind, ushering him into the room. His wire-rimmed glasses also felt the gust, it seemed, for they tottered at the end of his narrow nose. And hanging unevenly from his hunched shoulders was the black turtleneck he'd knitted himself, as he'd proudly related on the first day of class, which had been three weeks ago now. Apparently, he'd also shorn the sweater's wool from the sheep he raised with his adolescent son on their nearby farm.

Damian opened his book and binder in front of him, already comfortable with his new life at Mount Angelus. The seminary's routine satisfied him, as he'd anticipated it would, but he'd also supplemented the community's schedule of Mass and prayers with his own, *extra* spiritual commitments. He fasted by eating half portions and no meat on Wednesdays and Fridays, said a second rosary on his knees before bed, read from *Butler's* and the Bible daily, and, as penance for past sins of the flesh, he cinched the spindly old rope around his waist each morning. He'd found the rope while packing in the summer, and it still stank like the damp burlap sacks that'd been burying it in Grandma Schiller's garage. It itched and pinched, and he worried that his behaviour was extreme, unbalanced, but, at the same time, many saints had flogged themselves and slept on thorns, so, in a way, the rope's biting rash assured him that he was on track to Heaven and his dad.

Academically, Dr. House's class, Spiritual Autobiography, was by far the most stimulating of his courses. The assigned texts—autobiographies by saints and other spiritual writers, but memoirs by secular authors, too—included Saint Augustine's *Confessions*, Montaigne's *Essays*, Saint Teresa of Avila's reflections, John Bunyan's *Grace Abounding*, Henry David Thoreau's *Walden*, and the autobiographies of Harriet Jacobs, Ghandi and Gertrude Stein.

Upon seeing the eight texts listed on the syllabus as required reading for the upcoming, four-month fall semester—meaning an entire book to read, discuss, and write about every two weeks—the class had groaned, but not Damian. He was thrilled to read the lives of (likely) interesting strangers, or to finally learn about famous authors he (as yet) personally knew little about. Indeed, even as he strove for holiness, he yearned to broaden his knowledge beyond *Butler's*.

The other seminarians, though, had vociferously protested the books proposed in the syllabus, even objecting (on vaguely stated moral grounds) to the non-Catholic writers. Dr. House, seeming to assume that these complaints stemmed from laziness he'd encountered before, assured the class they'd benefit from diverse spiritual traditions and be grateful, come Christmas, that they'd read about these lives of great merit. Damian already found this true, as the first assigned text—Saint Augustine's *Confessions*—inspired ideas for improving his father's biography.

His other courses—Old Testament, Early Church History, Foundations of Theology, and Canon Law—were interesting, too, but the elderly, indistinguishable monks who taught them simply lectured from ragged textbooks—written in stilted English and sprinkled with Hebrew, Greek, and Latin terms—while the seminarians stooped sleepily over their desks and scribbled notes. Damian wondered if these greying, scholarly clerics had simply lost their former zest for the material.

"*Tolle Lege,* gentlemen!" Dr. House repeated as he reached the podium.

"Take and read!" the class responded lustily, translating the Latin phrase from Saint Augustine's *Confessions*. They'd quickly abandoned their initial complaints about the class, indeed, Dr. House had already won them over as literary converts.

"Now you've all finished the *Confessions* and written essays on how reading drove Augustine to conversion—and you *have* finished your assignments, I'm *sure.*" Dr. House, tilting his head, looked at his students inquiringly. "Evidence, please! Show me your essays, gentlemen! Wave them in the air!"

Damian eagerly waved the four pages he'd printed and stapled last night in the seminary's computer lab. Other pages fluttered around him. Dr. House smiled.

"Very good, gentlemen—very good! You took and read and wrote something, too. Just lovely. Now, who can tell me, where does our famous phrase figure into Augustine's conversion?"

Anxious to impress his already-favourite professor, Damian raised his hand. He'd anticipated Dr. House addressing this climactic incident in the book, which he loved and read in a single sitting, and he had an answer ready.

"Damian!" Dr. House said. "Your hand was up before I finished my question. Yes, what happens?"

"Augustine collapses in a garden," Damian said, "weary after years of searching for the truth. He hears children playing in a nearby yard, and they keep calling 'Take and read, take and read.'"

"Yes, yes—he overhears them but takes their words for himself," Dr. House said, nodding.

"Right," Damian replied. "So, he interprets those words as a sign, then looks up and finds a Bible on a bench. He opens it at random and finds—"

"And finds Saint Paul's words!" Dr. House shouted. Damian smiled and gazed admiringly at his professor. Dr. House's enthusiasm for literature was contagious. "And what does poor old Augustine read?"

Damian assumed the question was directed at him, so he quickly opened his book to the page he marked when writing his essay. "Here it is. He reads Saint Paul's injunction to the Romans— 'Let us behave decently, as in the daytime, not in carousing and drunkenness, not in sexual immorality and debauchery, not in dissension and jealousy. Rather, clothe yourselves with the Lord Jesus Christ, and do not think about how to gratify the desires of the flesh.' And Augustine applies those words to his life, deciding to reform right there!"

"Lovely summary," Dr. House said. "I look forward to

your essay. Now I want to continue our discussion from last class, about the vision of Heaven that Augustine and his mother behold after his conversion. And today I'll emphasize a particular detail of that vision, so if I can just find it here . . ."

As Dr. House flipped through his book *while* sipping coffee *and* scratching his ankle with his other foot, Theodore turned back, grinning, and winked knowingly at Damian—who'd almost forgotten he had classmates while he'd been discussing Augustine's *Confessions*. Damian nodded at his fellow Albertan and smiled. Dr. House was indeed eccentric, truly a sight to behold. *But*, as the seminarians had quickly discovered, their literature professor easily wandered off topic, discoursing at length about private obsessions and a specific, well-timed question could elicit one of these disquisitions. Theodore's wink, Damian knew, was his cue to pose such an inquiry.

"Dr. House," he said, "would you say televangelists and computer screens, are, well, perhaps interfering with true learning—like, from *reading*?"

"Televangelists!" Dr. House dropped his book and shook, spilling coffee on his shoe. He slapped his forehead as though showing how passionately he felt about Damian's question. And as he clasped his hands behind his back, pacing from the podium, he was obviously about to elucidate his opinions. Satisfied, Theodore nodded, smiled, and turned around in his seat to get comfortable.

"Televangelists! Screens are the whole problem, gentlemen. When you're ordained, preach against screens until you're draped over the pulpit, breathless!

"Why . . ." Dr. House approached the class, scratching his head. "Why, screens are the eyes of Satan and I defy the man who disagrees! They blunt the brain! When I was a boy—and from this very window, gentlemen, I can see the farm where I grew up! From atop our peak, I can see the fields my father ploughed so that I could study, so I could use my mind instead of my hands. And look at me now—I don't even use my hands to open the door! Ha, ha!

"But screens! My father ploughed those fields in this, the Okanagan Valley—where pioneers arrived after suffering and sacrificing to travel across our beautiful country. My father said we disgraced their trials by idling away the day, and that's why I studied so hard!

"And my father lived to see me graduate from Stanford and receive my Rhodes scholarship, but he passed away while I was overseas. When I came back for his funeral, my mother and I chose *Ora et Labora* for his gravestone— 'Work and Prayer'— for that was the credo by which he lived.

"But I chose *Tolle Lege* as my maxim." Dr. House paced past the desks, his hands still behind his back, his brow furrowed. He would stop talking, Damian guessed, only when the seminary's tower-top bell rang, announcing the hour's end. "'*Take and read,*' because, as you all know, I believe books are the jewels of civilization, the prizes won by the labours of history's greatest minds.

"For this reason, gentlemen, my son will never watch an imitation of life on a television screen—never! He'll live a life of the mind, as I have, and as I hope you will, too. Now, do you suppose the Oxford dons approved of television? Of course not! Why, once . . ."

Theodore leaned back in his desk, as did other seminarians. Many closed their eyes. Dr. House's voice dipped and peaked, modulating to match the meaning of his words, and though Damian let his eyes wander to the window, where he admired the dips and peaks of the Okanagan Valley, he still followed the gist of his professor's rambles. These rambles continued steadily as the minute hand traveled a complete circle around the clock at the front of the classroom.

With the hour nearly passed, Damian stared at the clock, waiting for the final minute to elapse. Dr. House, oblivious to time, still discoursed with unflagging vigour: ". . . then who should I see walking out of the library but Isaiah Berlin—smoking his pipe as always! So, I stopped him and said, Professor Ber—oh!"

The bell rang. Dr. House had spent another hour of Damian's favourite class—*Spiritual Autobiography*—discussing everything from television's evils to philosophers he'd met years ago. Yet his digressions had, again, been delightful. Dr. House pursued daunting endeavours, succeeded in so much, experienced diverse cultures, and visited many foreign cities. He'd met such amazing *characters*—some that he collected through reading, others that he caught with his attractive personality—so that his personal history, indeed, was richly peopled.

His classroom ramblings themselves, then, provided an autobiography of sorts, and these satisfied Damian's longing for an articulate acquaintance who shared his love for language. And while Dr. House generally neglected to address the assigned texts in class, Damian compensated for this by visiting him during office hours to vigorously discuss the readings—which had not only already influenced his father's biography—but had also begun to expand, even *alter*, his own spiritual outlook, but these personal matters he'd so far kept secret.

"That's all the time we have, gentlemen. It seems I got sidetracked somewhat, but so it is when discussing such interesting subjects. Delightful, delightful."

Dr. House walked to the podium and picked up the second book he'd brought today.

"Please read the first chapter of Thoreau's *Walden* for next class. If you can read more, do so, but be sure to attend to Henry David's beautiful descriptions of his beloved pond. Beautiful! Makes you want to jump right in and swim about." Dr. House performed a paddling motion and puffed up his cheeks. "*Tolle Lege,* gentlemen. And won't you, please, hand me your essays on the way out."

The class rose to leave, but then Dr. House gasped—apparently recalling something important. "*Oh!—* I want you to begin planning this semester's major assignment. You are to pick a life you admire, one you believe exemplifies virtue and honour, and write about it—*descriptively*. Ten pages, double spaced."

Damian, of course, immediately thought about his father's biography, but could he share his beloved pages with Dr. House, and possibly the entire class? He'd have to show them publicly some time, since ultimately his goal was to spread the story of his father's life and, also, he even considered submitting the biography to the Vatican one day as part of an application for canonization. Were his dad officially declared a saint, Damian's years of writing and revising would certainly receive ample reward. His dad would be known, *doubtlessly,* to dwell above with the company described in *Butler's*!

"But," Dr. House continued, "you'll need to supply sources, gentlemen—articles on that life, chapters of books, and so on."

Damian's heart sank. He had no sources, but his family's memories given verbally in Grandma Schiller's living room. He raised his hand and Dr. House nodded at him. "But what if we write about someone unknown, with nothing published about him yet?"

"Perfect!" Dr. House replied with gusto. "Just find letters, journals, photos—sources that corroborate your claims. Okay?"

"Okay," Damian said. He wondered what his family could send him. His father had kept a training journal from when he was trying to make the All Blacks. That might help to bolster the assignment's bibliography, but he'd already scoured it, finding only lists of exercises performed, calories consumed, descriptions of plays made on the field. He'd ask his family to send it anyway.

But letters? He never heard of any, though he certainly asked after his dad's death. He'd inquire again, however— something might've been overlooked, or perhaps buried beneath the bulk crammed into Grandma Schiller's house. He'd pray that some new information about his dad would be discovered, and suddenly this assignment *really* excited him. Now he'd be *forced* to complete the biography, and soon!

He handed his Augustine essay to Dr. House, who winked and said, "See you soon."

"See you," Damian replied, realizing Dr. House expected him for office hours later that day. But even so, as he left the classroom, he was sorry to leave the comfort of his professor's voice.

CHAPTER FOURTEEN
BAPTISM

Damian silenced his beeping clock as it displayed 4:00 a.m. in red digits. Today was the first time in over a month he'd woken to his alarm, and he felt sleepy but excited. Since arriving at Mount Angelus, he developed the habit of rising with the seminary's bells, which clanged at 5:00 a.m.

But now, as he flicked on his bedside lamp, dispelling the pre-dawn darkness, he saw his two reasons for waking early: *first,* Thoreau's *Walden* lay on his desk—its lyricism and rebellion still flowing through his mind as they had since he finished the book yesterday.

Walden tantalized him because it questioned common assumptions, as though Thoreau had discovered life anew. In plain, memorable language he brazenly challenged authority *and* organized religion, which had initially shocked Damian, but he'd also been intrigued by this secular yet spiritual hermit, and therefore kept him company late into last night. And when Thoreau stated why he moved into a solitary forest shack, explaining that most people are confused about life *"and have somewhat hastily concluded that it is the chief end of man here to 'glorify God and enjoy him forever,'"* Damian guiltily savoured such rhetorical flourish and pondered his own beliefs, past and present. To glorify God *so he could be with his dad in Heaven,* thus enjoying *his company* forever, was certainly still his life's purpose; and he'd recalled his pledge—already seven months ago!—to become saintly within the year.

But that catechetical phrase Thoreau quoted was familiar for another, agitating reason, too: Damian's mother had forced him to recite it in his youth, entrenching it in his mind. At first, he found the exercise boringly easy, but then he hated, and *still* hated, actually, how she continued to endorse this slogan—life's entire purpose reduced to a line—*even after his dad had died.*

He resented her having done so because, by taking his dad away, God had made Himself *harder* to glorify, had made eternity with Him *less* appealing and, though he harboured such blasphemy at fourteen, he'd been afraid to even silently admit it until reading *Walden* yesterday. And still, had he actually expressed these feelings in his own words now—either in writing or by speaking them aloud— he would be terrified, guilty, confused.

Walden, he realized last night, could act as a guidebook for how to sever himself from his past: because his past, excluding the early years with his dad, seemed increasingly stale—stale like those smoky old sheets he shuddered to recall as he rose from his fresh bed now. He stood in his spacious, clean room and stretched by lifting himself onto his toes, raising his arms above his head, and extending his fingers towards the ceiling, which was *several* feet out of reach. Doing so felt luxurious after years of his head brushing the drooping panels at Grandma Schiller's.

But now he abandoned such constriction—his former *life of quiet desperation*—and henceforth he took full advantage of the personal freedoms granted by the seminary, which were admittedly limited, but compared to life back home, provided a veritable paradise. Here no voices traveled through the walls. He could go to bed when he wanted or wander down the hill to explore the town below and eat only those foods that appealed to him in the cafeteria's buffet.

And though he still fasted regularly, prayed *some* extra rosaries, and—of course—read *Butler's* daily while trying to revise his dad's biography, he also conformed to the seminary's routine more closely over the past few weeks. He'd discarded the rope that burned around his waist and sometimes even replaced his Scriptural reflections with studies, socializing (especially with Theodore), and—best of all—staying up late to read and reread the assigned texts for Spiritual Autobiography.

Tempering his initial zeal and pious rigour didn't bother his conscience, though, because he felt spiritually nourished by his theological studies, the hilltop's clerical atmosphere, and the seminary's schedule of prayer and sacraments. Also, those extra devotions—especially the tortuous rope—had distracted him from his proper, present duties—namely, his academic endeavours. God, he believed, now wanted him to just humbly submit to Mount Angelus' proffered formation program and avoid excessive, secret ascetic stunts. Overall, his lifestyle finally seemed balanced, healthy, relaxed.

And to christen his new, unburdened existence, this morning he planned to re-enact a stirring scene from *Walden*: Thoreau's *nude* ablutions in the pond. Since this devotional exercise required *privacy*, however, Damian had to hurry before anyone else rose.

This morning's swim would involve the *second* reason he'd woken unusually early: his cassock, the black, ankle-length robe worn by seminarians and priests on campus, had arrived yesterday, and now it hung on a hanger from a hook in his door. It came at the perfect time, because following this morning's ablutions—or *baptism*, a rebirth to new life—he planned to ceremoniously don this clerical attire on the pond's shore while reciting a line from *Walden*: *"Perhaps we should never procure a new suit, however ragged or dirty the old, until we have so conducted, so enterprised or sailed in some way, that we feel like new men in the old, and that to retain it would be like keeping new wine in old bottles."* That phrase would replace the now-arid catechetical line forced upon him years ago—*for he was new wine*, a *man* severed from his mother's influence, from his constricted past, and thus more independent. In *this* way, at least, he was saintlier now than last February. Surely he was ready for his very own cassock, worn by many saints on Grandma Schiller's holy cards. Indeed, this fresh uniform would mark the symbolic rebirth he was about to perform.

Eager to get to the water, he threw on the clothes he'd been wearing since shredding his homeschooling uniform in Scott's basement—an act he recalled with pride, for though it marked his first, *failed* attempt at independence, he'd at least been brave enough to try. And while the hand-me-down slacks from Uncle Rick were tight and *truly ragged*, and his *dirty old* T-shirt persistently reeked of cigarettes and mothballs, he wore them lightheartedly because today was their last.

He solemnly lifted his cassock from the hook, then tossed the hanger on his unmade bed—no time to smooth the sheets and position the pillows as he usually did upon rising. He was already striding down the hall as he draped the cassock over his forearm, covering his breviary *and* his copy of *Walden* to maintain the privacy of his present endeavour. He walked rapidly but was careful not to step too heavily. No slits of light appeared under the dorm room doors, meaning his fellow seminarians were likely still sleeping—and he wanted them to remain so a little longer.

But once at the marble steps that didn't creak, he descended by stomping leaps and then exited the dormitory into the late-September air—brisk, but mercifully mild. He sprinted down the sidewalk, excited to try some transcendentalism, his first non-Catholic spirituality. The sun was not yet visible itself, but it already brightened the eastern horizon, so he hurriedly rounded the monastery and descended the short, wooded slope to the small pond shrouded in mist.

He wanted to saunter along the pebbly shore and sit on a log to read, but the sun would soon scale the sky. Priests and seminarians would then begin filing from the dormitory to the chapel to prepare for Morning Prayer at 5:15 a.m., and while the path they'd take granted but a sliver-width view of the pond, he couldn't risk being seen. So, after scanning the area to ensure he was alone, he placed his books and cassock on a large rock on the shore, and then stripped bare. Resisting the urge to cover his crotch, he stood tall with his arms at his sides and approached the water's edge. There he closed his eyes and imagined Henry David plunging into cool, clear Walden Pond.

Damian's first step into the water stung, but then it felt warmer as he waded in further. When the water reached his knees, he dove in—producing an enormous splash—

and glided above the pond's bottom. He opened his eyes when he emerged from the waist-deep centre, wiping his hair back and spitting out a few grainy drops. The mist had cleared, and he stood on the rocky bottom as the rising dawn streaked across the east.

I have a good half-hour, he thought, and fell back into the water, floating. He gazed at the grey-blue sky and the tips of the pine trees that bordered the shore. Calm yet invigorated, he was ready to live independently—but *saintly,* of course, too.

He pondered Dr. House's assignment. Where might he find objective sources about his dad that he hadn't already searched for years ago? Could he contact his relatives in New Zealand? His mom had ceased communicating with them after they curiously failed to attend his dad's funeral. In fact, Damian could only surmise that his paternal grandparents were still alive as he hadn't heard otherwise. But perhaps he could reconcile with his dad's family now, since he was no longer bound to his mother.

Whether he did or not, he'd call Grandma Schiller's today, finally apologize for damaging her eavestrough, and then ask *her* to borrow family photos, his dad's training journal, and anything else—*if anything else existed.* New material excited him, as did the prospect of finally completing his dad's biography. Yet the project rested more buoyantly in his mind: it nagged less. . .

As he kicked up water, paddling backwards, Thoreau again came to mind: though he urged his readers to transcend everyday experience and follow their intuition towards *spiritual* enlightenment, *Walden* was the first overtly non-religious book he'd ever read—other than Grandma Schiller's aged encyclopaedias and his government-issued high school textbooks. Thoreau's courageous individualism, his revelling in nature's beauty, and his skepticism of hackneyed beliefs rendered *Walden* a bracing tonic—like the pond's water.

Damian was fully awake now and recalled Thoreau's injunction to *keep* awake *"by an infinite expectation of the dawn."* This *infinite expectation* was, to Damian's understanding, a perpetual readiness to re-approach life, adjust one's worldview, and to daringly alter how you spent your days. Also, to ever hope afresh, to never dampen one's outlook by adopting dull, outmoded, and conventional beliefs. Ultimately, to retain, as Christ had enjoined his followers, a childlike awe for nature's beauty, for life's flowing spring of surprises.

And since today was just about to fully dawn, he waded to shore where, chilly and dripping, he realized he'd forgotten a towel and fresh underwear. If he dried himself with his old clothes, his stale, smelly past would cling to him just when he was about to sail forth into a fresh future!

He paused. *What would Thoreau do?* Immediately he knew. Thoreau would never blur a properly abandoned past with a symbolic rebirth, so Damian confidently dried himself with his hands and then shook off the remaining drops. The autumn wind gently blew, as though assisting him, and he was barely damp as he approached his cassock.

Even draped over a rock, the garment appeared noble.

He'd been measured for it soon after arriving on campus. That day Father Rector had said he ought to charge Damian's diocese double considering how much material his cassock would require but then Father Rector had closely observed Theodore being measured, and joked that the meagre material needed for *him* would compensate for the amount required to outfit Damian. The other seminarians laughed, but Theodore grimaced, which had worried Damian. Then, after stating that Calgary's bill would ultimately balance out despite the disparate sizes of the diocese's two seminarians, Father Rector had thankfully stopped comparing him to Theodore.

Now, anxious that it might not fit given his massive bulk (*and* pained history with crotch-biting uniform pants and Uncle Rick's tight slacks), he quickly un-clasped the cassock's top two snaps, stuck his head through the neck hole, and pushed his arms through the long, black sleeves—which, *thank Heaven!*—met his wrists. He let the long skirts fall to his ankles as the garment hugged his body *comfortably*.

He approached the pond, now restored to a still surface, to see his reflection and recite Thoreau's line about *procuring a new suit*, but just then came a sound— like footsteps nearby!

He turned and saw Father Rector stepping out from behind a tree. The priest appeared terrified, as though he'd been caught stealing, but then quickly frowned and stomped down the slope towards Damian—who grew terrified himself.

"What's going on here, Mr. Kurt?" Father Rector, in *his* cassock, stopped about two feet away on the shore—fists on his hips, breviary in hand.

Damian opened his mouth to reply but was gagged by fear as he faced Father Rector. Embarrassment prickled him.

"I—" Damian said, forcing himself to speak, "swam."

"Swam," Father Rector repeated in a demeaning tone, tilting his head and lifting an eyebrow. Damian wondered what he'd done wrong. And how long had Father Rector been watching? He felt vaguely guilty. "I see your cassock fits nicely."

"Yeah," Damian replied, trying to sound pleased. Father Rector still seemed angry. Damian looked down at the handsome robe and smoothed it against his sides. Did Father Rector know he was naked underneath? He *had* been hiding behind the tree. . . "I'm sorry I was naked. I'd just—"

Father Rector raised his palm and shook his head, silencing Damian. "Are the pews dusted?"

"What?" Damian was confused. "The *pews?"*

"Your responsibility, yes?"

"Yes."

"Well?"

"I should dust them *now?"* Damian asked.

"Morning prayer's in half an hour," Father Rector said, as though Damian was late performing his weekly chore. He normally dusted the cathedral's pews some afternoons after class, and he'd never been told he had to complete them by a specific time of day. But, as though growing increasingly impatient, Father Rector widened his eyes and tilted his head towards the cathedral.

Damian nodded and keeping his eyes down, walked around Father Rector to the large rock where he slipped on his socks and dress shoes while wrapping his old clothes around his breviary and *Walden.* He felt the priest's stare from the water's edge, and, eager to escape, he ascended the wooded incline. He was about halfway up when Father Rector called: "And Damian!"

Damian slowly turned around expecting the priest to demand that he go to his room to put something on under his cassock, or to reveal what book he was holding other than his breviary. "Yes, Father?"

"I called Father Dennis the other day, to discuss you and Theodore." Damian's heart raced. He swallowed hard. "And we've, that is, *I've* decided to show your vocation story to our seminarians—to launch an initiative here at Mount Angelus like your bishop did, sending the others to give their testimonies in local parishes, but using yours as a model."

Damian just stared. He didn't know what to think or how to respond. Father Rector then spoke slowly, as though Damian was too dense to understand: "I'm photocopying and distributing your vocation story as a template, *all right?*"

A twinge of anger pricked Damian, but he was still so embarrassed—and so shocked that his story would now be touring parishes *in another province*—that he just nodded again. The Rector nodded back, once, and then Damian turned and climbed the hill.

He passed some seminarians, also in cassocks, sleepily descending the concrete stairs to the underground chapel where the community prayed psalms from their breviaries every morning, noon, and evening. Damian angrily proceeded to the cathedral. He suspected that Father Rector had been watching *for a while* from behind the tree. Also, Damian resented being bullied into offering *himself*— at least as he'd presented himself in his story—to the entire seminary as a model of what *they* should be.

As he pushed open the cathedral doors and passed through the dark foyer into the church proper, he fumed at how he'd been randomly *commanded* to dust the pews *now*—when he should be at Morning Prayer. On the very day he planned to celebrate the *freedoms* granted by Mount Angelus, he was being *doubly used*: as an errand boy *and* as an ideal type, which would likely stir jealousy and compromise his friendships on the hilltop—particularly, he guessed, with Theodore.

The cool, still air that encased the cathedral's marble walls calmed Damian *somewhat* as he briskly passed the pews. His new dress shoes—which had arrived last week, allowing him to finally discard his old footwear, the final remnant of his former life—clicked against the smooth stone floor and echoed in the massive hollow space. His cassock swished deliciously as he strode. Reaching around the sacristy door, incense lingered from yesterday's Mass as he felt for the switches and threw them up. The cathedral's lights snapped on behind him, and leagues of darkness instantly drained from the body of the church.

He left the sacristy and passed the brass tabernacle, which shone but didn't sparkle. He'd remind Theodore to polish it later this week—*if* his story hadn't already been distributed by then and their friendship thus ended, silenced.

He walked to the front centre of the cathedral, still holding his books balled up in his smelly old clothes and gazed at the huge hollow innards. They resembled a carcass, with the pews spaced like ribs against the ground. The peaked, wooden supports along the ceiling looked like a spine.

He glanced at the first row of pews, *gleaming*—they needed no dusting, not for several days at least. The real problem was that they were *empty*: empty before him and increasingly so in churches everywhere. And below him, in the chapel, not even a quarter of the chairs would be filled by seminarians for Morning Prayer, which was about to begin.

He shook his head. He was at the mercy of a dwindling Church, represented by Father Dennis swaying drunk in his doorway, by Father Rector peeping from behind a tree, and by *him*—or at least his vocation story's inflated, embellished persona—now to be spread even further as a cure for the dying clergy.

He turned off the lights and walked back through the dark cathedral, his shoes echoing again. He suddenly wished he could silence them, as he wished he could somehow silence the story he'd already bound himself to and that seemed to echo further and farther afield. As the claims of his vocation story would spread and multiply, he'd feel constricted again (like back at Grandma Schiller's) by the false impression he created in a desperate attempt to escape his former life.

And after this morning, *escaping the seminary* rather than celebrating the liberation he'd hoped it provided, seemed quite obviously, and disturbingly, the deliberate course for his future: what Thoreau would surely recommend.

CHAPTER FIFTEEN
PRIESTLY PATTERN

The classroom door opened, but the other seminarians just kept chatting and didn't seem to notice Dr. House until he reached the podium. Where was his usual battle cry— *Tolle Lege!*—and his booting open the door? Where were his two cups of coffee?

Rather than enter with books under both arms, Dr. House placed his briefcase on the table behind the podium and slowly removed his tattered copy of *Walden* and a stack of pages. He wiped his red, teary eyes before turning towards the class. While his hair was always messy, today it was different—sweaty and matted.

"*Tolle Lege*, gentlemen," Dr. House said feebly. Damian barely recognized his voice. The other seminarians worriedly glanced around, and they didn't repeat the Latin phrase in English as they habitually did. "I'm sorry I'm late. I'm never late, but . . . Let's just begin, shall we?"

Dr. House stood still, staring at the ground, his glasses hanging from their cord around his neck. Then he startled, as though recollecting where he was. "But I'm—why don't I just return last week's assignments. And no haggling over grades, please. I haven't the pluck to debate whether a three-page essay on Thoreau's admiration for the train deserves any better than a *B*."

Dr. House sighed as he lifted the stack of assignments and squinted at the top page.

"Theodore—here, son." Dr. House handed Theodore his essay. "Please write your lovely, Godly name on future assignments. I know this is yours, though, because of the consistent francophone misspellings. Perhaps Damian can help you. All right, there you are.

"Wally. Wally, dear, you haven't any idea what you're doing with commas." Dr. House shook his head as he approached Wally's desk. "You splatter them across your pages like Jackson Pollock splatters paint, son, and I prefer Raphael's *School at Athens*—everything in its proper place. No one can help your punctuation but me, and possibly God. Meet me for office hours or I'll see you for Spiritual Autobiography again next year. All right, there we are.

"But, *Damian*." Here Dr. House paused, gazing at Damian from across the classroom. "How did you achieve such verisimilitude when describing Thoreau's ablutions as a failed attempt to escape the corrupt dominance of paternal authorities? You write, dear boy, as though you yourself jumped into the cool waters of Walden Pond, and yet were still faced with a ruler's frown."

Normally Damian would be eager to relate to Dr. House, when they were alone, of course, how indeed his essay *was* inspired by actual events. Furthermore, he wanted to share with his professor what'd actually happened at the pond—*at least* what Fr. Rector planned to do with his vocation story, if not his hiding behind the tree.

So far he'd kept the pond incident secret—even though he almost told Uncle Rick about it when *he* answered Grandma Schiller's phone last week. Damian had never called her house before, and therefore needed to refer to his journal's personal information page, where he'd recorded her number years ago. Though initially surprised to hear his uncle's voice, he then recalled how Uncle Rick *certainly used the phone more than anyone else in the home.*

They bantered until Damian mentioned his assignment and his need for sources on his father: at this point Uncle Rick had grown awkward and sounded anxious. Damian hoped his uncle would just offer to ask the rest of the family about any stored-away sources, or to even search himself, because then Damian could've revealed the embarrassing swim—which had been troubling him. But when Uncle Rick fell silent, they'd quickly said goodbye and hung up.

With Uncle Rick seemingly unfit as either confidant or adviser on the shameful matter, Damian also considered mentioning the pond to Theodore, but hadn't because of his friend's apparent jealousy over the attention already given to Damian's vocation story. Theodore indeed seemed resentful when the story, circulating their diocese, had been proclaimed from *his* pastor's pulpit—so how might he react when he discovered that it'd also soon be touring the parishes surrounding Mount Angelus? Damian already considered Theodore a close acquaintance and likely a future friend, but didn't want him privy to any embarrassing, personal information. Might he try to tarnish Damian's pristine reputation? To somehow skew the pond incident and spread it as slander? Their relationship was promising, but left much uncertainty, too.

Now Damian's thoughts returned to the present—to his slumped mentor, the classroom, the graded papers—as Dr. House passed him his essay and said, "Here you are. Well done."

On the top right corner of the first page was the *A* Damian always looked for, but today the letter *A* was not pressed firmly as usual, with its sharp peak indenting the paper to render the grade permanent and doubtlessly merited. Rather, it was feebly scratched and lacked the robust swirling circles that normally enclosed it. Yet *how* his *A* had been marked concerned him far less than Dr. House's trembling hand.

"Thanks," Damian said, taking his pages. He leaned forward and met Dr. House's eyes—raw, damp, sad—but still his professor smiled weakly before dropping his gaze, and his expression drooped again. Dr. House then looked at the next essay.

Damian pretended to peruse his assignment, while really observing his professor, his dear friend, as Dr. House walked away, his shoulders slumped in a lower hunch than usual. He shuffled slowly like a very old man. Damian would have to wait until after class to ask what was wrong, *then,* perhaps, after Dr. House had revealed what was troubling him, and if Damian wasn't too embarrassed, he could mention the pond.

So, for now, he opened his essay and actually read it: Dr. House's normally tight cursive was slanted and sloppy in the margins, and there were fewer comments than in weeks prior. In fact, mostly he'd just check-marked beside the paragraphs and sentences he seemed to have enjoyed.

"Daniel!" Dr. House said with slightly rising vigour as he waved some pages. "Daniel, do you or do you not understand why we *paragraph* our writing, son? Did you simply start speaking as a toddler and continue without pause or structure to your language? Do you hear—"

Suddenly his voice petered into a sob. Tears streamed

down his cheeks and almost hit the remaining essays he held. Dr. House turned and staggered toward the front of the classroom briefly raising the essays above his head, indicating where they'd be, before placing them on the table. Pale and sweaty, he wheezed as he gathered his copy of *Walden* and his briefcase, turned to face the class, opened his mouth as though to speak, but then just slouched away without closing the door behind him. The seminarians were silent, staring ahead, stone-still in their desks as Dr. House's steps receded down the hall.

The urge to follow his friend nearly lifted Damian from his seat, yet he was reluctant to single himself out from the others. Until Theodore turned in his desk in the front row and motioned with his thumb that Damian ought to check on their professor. Damian nodded and folded his essay into his binder and exited the class.

There, at the end of the hall, slumped before his office door, was Dr. House. He held *Walden* under his left arm, his briefcase in his left hand, and with his right, fumbled with his keys. He was better at kicking doors open than unlocking them.

"Dr. House," Damian said. "What's wro—um . . . are you sick?"

"Damian." Dr. House looked up just as the lock opened with its familiar click. "No, son. No. Come in, won't you?"

Damian followed him into the office and closed the door, so they were surrounded—protected—by the rows of books that encased the room. Normally this was the most comforting place on the hilltop. He loved the high-ceilinged study because, like Dr. House's rambling tales, it was familiar *and* exotic—predictably revealing. At every visit, some new, intriguing artifact like a stone pipe from

Scotland or a bamboo spear from Burma sat atop the collected works of Shakespeare.

The thick, soft carpet was deep-sea blue. A large, red-oak desk filled the left portion of the long room, which ended in a wall-sized window overlooking the Okanagan Valley: until recently a panorama of lush orchards and green vineyards, but, over the past week, it'd become a snow-covered canopy—frigid and withering.

A globe stood on a dark-wood stand. It could spin on its vertical axis, but so many pins stuck out from its surface, Damian was reluctant to touch it. He envied the clumps of pins, however—testimony to vast travels *he* could only imagine.

The ceiling, Dr. House had related with pride, he'd painted with his fourteen-year-old son, Eden, to resemble the night sky: tin-foil stars scattered across the suspended surface, an un-lacquered charcoal that suggested infinity.

Dr. House's personal library filled the towering shelves. The tomes—short and tall, thin and thick, cloth and leather, old and new—together emitted a vaguely-salty, aged, woody aroma that Damian somehow affiliated with seaports. Perhaps the books had been carried in crates or casks on ships, and, while travelling the globe as cargo, their porous pages had absorbed the spices, styles, flavours, and flairs of disparate peoples and places. Gathered here, they combined into the single scent of the world, producing an oddly familiar ambience, something shared by everyone on earth.

Since the window light was pale grey, leaving the room shadowy, Damian pulled the cord on the lamp they habitually lit when he came to chat. It sat beside Dr. House's writing pad on his desk, and he'd said it was very old: a Spanish ship captain's lamp that'd sailed with its owner to the West Coast. Dr. House had inherited the ornate, molded-iron base, then he ran wires through it and collected beach glass that he melted into a sphere-shaped shade—a mosaic of illuminated blue and green shards. Damian loved the way it glowed, casting aqua green onto the already colourful room. Somehow the hue satisfied his eyes, just as gazing at a photograph of Earth did, taken from space.

But that particular pleasure Damian sensed within this room—a dreamy, rocking comfort—snapped away as Dr. House dumped his briefcase onto the carpet, ditched his book beside the lamp, and sat, dropping his forehead to the desk with a thud, then lifting his face and burying it in his hands. Tears squeezed through his fingers.

"Oh, Damian," Dr. House said. "Eden has cancer."

"What?" Damian gasped as he spoke. He lost his voice and—feeling suddenly numb—dropped into the chair that faced the desk. He closed his mouth, and struggled to appear calm, for poor Dr. House's sake. He tried to think of something to say, something relevant, something that avoided false sentimentality—what people had expressed when his father had died. "What kind of cancer?"

"He—thank you for not apologizing." Dr. House looked up, intently, making eye contact through his tears. "People apologize like his ailment is their fault. It's leukemia. Eden's likely-lethal cancer dwells—*growing*, in fact—within his bone marrow."

"When was he diagnosed?"

"Three days ago. But he's been weak and tired for about a month. I'd have taken him to a doctor, but I thought it'd pass! You know, I was forty-five when he was

born, worried I might die when he was still a young m—"
Dr. House sobbed. "Oh, Damian."

"Cry," Damian said. "And don't apologize for it, either.
Sometimes crying's best."

"All right," Dr. House said through his hands. He
wiped his eyes.

Damian grasped Dr. House's teary hands: his fingers
were thick, but frail compared to Damian's father's, which
had been calloused, taut, and strong even on his deathbed.
Damian had failed to fetch him that last glass of water, but
he could make amends here, in a way, just by listening—
by finally supplying a sufferer's need. He tightened his grip
and nodded to indicate that he was ready to listen. Dr.
House's countenance expressed relief—recognition that
here he could unburden the shock and sadness that'd
suddenly befallen him like the snowfall burying the
recently-verdant valley. Dr. House's crinkled brow,
wrinkled eyes, fading blue pupils, his drooping cheeks and
hanging throat together enlivened, it seemed—lost their
aged sag—as his noble and articulate voice returned.

"He's already in the hospital," Dr. House said, "and his
chemotherapy begins today. I'm just so scared that . . ."

He continued to describe his anguish and sense of
futility. Damian knew these emotions well, but kept them,
and his father's death, silent for now so he could be
available for his friend. As Dr. House spoke, the solitary
lamp illuminated their clenched hands, locked gaze, and
stooped shoulders: united in concern, the world
surrounding them receded, faded away, forgotten. . .

"Maybe the barbell scrambled your brain," Dr. House
said hours later, smiling now as he referred to Damian's

accident last year; the two still clutched hands under the lamplight.

Dr. House had lovingly described Eden's childhood, his brilliant mind, and his interest in astronomy that—given Eden's precociousness—was best cultivated through homeschooling. Then he'd candidly related the severity of Eden's current condition, his four-month life expectancy, and his very poor chances of a full recovery. Dr. House also discussed his wife leaving him for a younger man about three years ago, how that loss had affected Eden—how the boy had grown suddenly anxious and quiet several months after—and then Dr. House had disclosed other personal information, too.

Apparently wanting to change the subject but retain Damian's company, Dr. House had asked him how he'd discerned a priestly vocation. Grateful for the chance to be honest (contra his increasingly popular persona), Damian had told his whole life story, even his father's death, without embellishment. Still, though, he kept secret his plan to reunite with his dad in Heaven.

But now he wanted to reveal what he'd written in his vocation story and what his diocese had done with it. Then he could disclose Father Rector's plan and, perhaps, mention the pond incident, too.

"Scrambled my brain?" Damian asked, smiling to show he wasn't offended.

"It's just, well, your path to the seminary has been—and no offence—*unusual*," Dr. House said. "With losing your father and then considering your recent domestic conditions, I can see why you wanted to venture off, but . . ."

Suddenly Damian was concerned and felt defensive.

Dr. House seemed to be implying that his vocational discernment had been an escape. An exercise in self-interest and convenience? Damian tilted his head, hoping for clarification.

"I'm just being frank here, Damian, but are you certain you want to devote your life to ordained, pastoral ministry? I mean, and it's not my place to say, perhaps, but I see your real strength in writing, your real love for literature and reading."

This unexpected appraisal discomfited Damian. He retracted his hands, sat upright. He needed to defend himself. "I'm striving to become a saint, you know."

Dr. House leaned back, surprised. "A saint?"

"Well, yes." The declaration, pronounced so abruptly, so definitely, seemed awkward for the first time—even archaic.

Nodding slowly, Dr. House raised his eyebrows and polished his glasses. "I can't argue with that, I guess. Very noble. Noble and lofty, indeed."

"Well, yeah. And, I thought, you know, after studying *Butler's*, this would be the best place to become one."

"And now having been here a month, do you believe you were right?"

Damian pondered the question. But then he recalled Father Rector's guilty face peeking from behind the tree, and formulating an answer proved elusive. "Well, I guess it's better than—"

Just then the tower-top bell rang.

"Oh!" Damian said, standing as he remembered the assembly that Father Rector had scheduled for 11:30 a.m. It'd been announced that morning on a posting tacked to the Twenty-Four-Hour Board, and Damian suspected it concerned the recruitment initiative featuring his vocation story.

"What's wrong?" Dr. House asked.

"The assembly—I'm late." The wall clock showed noon, confirming the clanging bell.

"You'd better run," Dr. House said. Damian nodded and then, just before dashing off, squeezed Dr. House's hand again, which had now steadied. He smiled with an expression of deep gratitude, thus assuring Damian that he'd assuaged his professor's new-befallen anguish: that particularly piercing agony caused by empathy, when you vicariously endure what a beloved father, a cherished son, suffers. Then, too, of course, was the added frustration of yearning to assist when you couldn't, could not ease your cherished one's pain.

But today Damian had comforted another, acted like a true *friend*, sharing candid details, establishing easy intimacy, assured trust, mutual concern. Indeed, he already considered Dr. House a mentor and unexpected confidant—someone fascinating and fatherly, who provided enjoyable—yet *profound*—company. A great improvement, at least thus far, over drinking with Father Dennis, though admitting this comparison felt selfish, uncharitable.

"I'd appreciate it so much," Dr. House said, holding onto Damian's hand, "*Eden*, I believe, would enjoy it so very much if you'd visit him in the hospital. Homeschooling leaves him few friends—as *you* may know."

Damian nodded again. And, out of his affection for Dr. House, he stifled his phobia of hospitals . . . at least for now.

"Would you?" Dr. House asked. "Say, once a week? I'll ask the Rector's permission, if you don't mind."

"I'd love to," Damian said, and he meant it.

"I'll assure Eden that you're simply a young student, and not a priest. He's got a . . . a strange aversion to priests, to Catholicism, too, actually. Befuddling—I just don't understand it."

"Really?" Damian was intrigued. "Well now I want to meet him even more. *I've* become weary of certain clerg—um . . . I bet we'll get along."

"Wonderful" Dr. House said. "But now—run!"

"Okay." Damian said as he strode across the room with his book and binder; but, at the door, he turned to face his friend. "I can't wait to meet Eden, and for us to chat again. Try to hope."

"Thank you," Dr. House said, and then made a shooing motion. Damian smiled before sprinting down the hall.

By now he'd missed much of the assembly that might concern *his* story. His glaring absence would thus certainly be awkward for Father Rector. Damian forced himself to run faster, fighting his apprehension of creeping into the crypt chapel half an hour late with Father Rector's eyes on him—*again*. He'd grown to fear the Rector since their pond-side confrontation two weeks ago, and this fear had driven him to ask other seminarians about their stern superior.

As Damian exited the building, the bell's twelfth toll rang. He shivered against the cold, which cut through his cassock, and glanced at the now-frozen pond. He imagined Father Rector's sharp stare through those thick, black, square glasses. The Rector's reputation seemed to scare some seminarians. When asked about him, many hesitated, looked away. . . Damian had heard a rumour that the Rector, Father Bernard Anthony Bunyan Jr., was issued those glasses when he'd been an army chaplain. They were the same boxy style *his* father—also a military man—wore in the portrait hanging in the Rector's office: Bernard Bunyan *Sr.*, standing proudly before the provincial legislature as British Columbia's first conservative premier, glared from that portrait as his son had glared at Damian on the pond's shore and would likely glare at him again now.

Applause rose as Damian—trembling not only from the wind but from dread, too—descended the narrow, concrete staircase to the crypt. He quietly opened the door at the back. Just as he entered and then shut the door carefully, the applause died so the latch clicked crisply in the silence. From his lectern at the front centre of the chapel, Father Rector looked up as the seminarians turned back in their seats. Damian's already-numb fingers tingled and his pulse beat in his ears as he, briefly meeting the Rector's glare, hurried into the back row. If only the chapel—a quarter full—had been more crowded, he might've somehow snuck in unnoticed.

He anticipated the Rector publicly scolding his tardiness, but he didn't, so Damian stared at his shoes to avoid the eyes behind those boxy glasses. He was tense, waiting for the others to turn around, for the Rector to speak. Finally, he did.

"As I've already told you," the Rector said, sounding exasperated. The seminarians faced their superior again, "this isn't my vocation story, so stop clapping. It's Damian Kurt's—*whose presence we are now so grateful for. . .* Now, why might I want you to use his story?"

Damian hesitantly looked up. Theodore was beside him. Damian rolled his eyes to make light of the situation: to indicate that he'd neither desired nor planned this initiative. He tapped Theodore's knee to get his attention so that he could then shake his head and grimace. But Theodore stared straight ahead, stony. He frowned; arms crossed. Damian's heart sank. He suspected their friendship—just blossoming—had already soured. Or even expired. Theodore's simmering jealousy that'd burst through their first phone conversation months ago now appeared like a poisonous resentment.

Damian looked away, hurt and lonely. At least he had Dr. House. Unless his vocation story and this initiative tainted that much deeper relationship. . . He shuddered to imagine the pain of losing his beloved professor friend. He'd soon explain the situation to Dr. House and justify why he'd embellished his vocation story, before Dr. House heard about the initiative from others, like Theodore, or— worse—read the story himself and compared it to the factual account Damian just gave in his office.

Several rows ahead, a slim, silver-haired seminarian raised his hand.

"Yes, Derrick," the Rector said.

"I'm offended," Derrick said as he stood, sweeping his cassock behind him with long, thin fingers. He shook a sheet of paper at the Rector. "I mean, Damian's story is obviously the traditional ideal—what stuffy, narrow-minded parishioners want to hear. But the reality for me, and most everyone here, is that tomorrow's priests will be older, or immigrants, or guys who've tried mainstream life but chosen ministry as an alternative. Why should we rewrite our personal histories to match Damian's Bing

Crosby archetype and—"

"Derrick, Derrick," the Rector said. "My hands are tied. Bishop Spur's panicked. Church attendance is dwindling, and parishes are closing. *Our* numbers are the lowest in forty years—we're not earning enough in tuition to keep this place viable. You want to go all the way to *Rome* to study theology?"

"Yes, actually," Derrick replied. "I'd quite enjoy a little European flavour."

"Forget it," Father Rector said. "The founding purpose of Mount Angelus—the whole reason we exist—is to provide *local* theological training. Now some of you *are* from overseas, but that's just because your local seminaries already closed. *So*—we need to attract *local guys* to sustain the Church in Canada. And how else can we do that if you men don't drum up interest? Young fellas in nearby parishes need to hear about you—and be *inspired!*"

"But that's just it!" Derrick said. "Parishioners won't hear about *us*. We're simply substitutes for Damian—going around, delivering his vocation story as though it's ours. Won't people suspect my grey hair when I claim I just left my family home and Catholic high school?"

"You're not listening," Father Rector replied. "I said borrow and adjust *some* elements of Damian's story. The bishop wants *young, local* guys. We have no problem recruiting ESL retirees. Just look around!"

Derrick shook his head, defeated. He sighed and sat. Damian felt guilty—personally responsible, in a way—for Father's Rector's communal insult. He sensed Theodore's resentment spreading through the crypt, infecting the others.

"Now," Father Rector said, walking forward from the podium and holding up a typed page, obviously Damian's vocation story. Some lines were marked in yellow, "look at what I've highlighted, boys."

Theodore sighed loudly as pages lifted from every lap but Damian's. He, however, glanced at his story in Theodore's hands and noticed that his name had been whited out. He felt stuck. He'd privately composed this false account out of (admittedly) prideful enthusiasm and a desperate attempt to escape Grandma Schiller's, but now it'd multiplied—like the Gospel story's loaves and fish—to sustain and spread the lie, feeding this crowd's dislike for him—for this false, fabricated version of himself, which would likely never be distinguished from who he really was.

"So," the Rector continued, "when preparing your stories, add details that could basically apply to you. Maybe say your home life was like Damian's—very loving and devout. Or that you're happy to offer your best years to Christ. Now in your case, Derrick, gloss over your decades at the flower shop and, instead, emphasize how your mother prayed for a vocation and then, one day, you finally heard God's call."

The Rector walked further down the centre aisle, reading aloud the portions of Damian's story that'd he'd highlighted—those he'd deemed potentially most applicable to the others, the most generic, seemingly. "The point is, guys, Bishop Spur wants *ideal candidates*—like Damian. Transfer some details from his life to yours, anything that young guys from pious homes will recognize."

"But what if such men are virtually extinct?" Derrick asked, and then he glowered at Damian, who bit his lip.

Theodore sighed even louder and nodded, apparently agreeing with Derrick.

"Damian exists, doesn't he?" Father Rector said. "We just need more like him. Compose your stories and expect your parish assignments by next week. All right, men—lunchtime. Our Lady of Priests . . ."

"Pray for us," the chapel responded feebly. Seminarians exited the crypt, while Damian avoided eye contact with them. Theodore sat, still staring ahead. Damian remained beside him and tried to think of a joke.

"Well," he said finally, but then fell silent.

"Well I guess you're famous," Theodore suddenly said, turning to him. "Where's your copy? Oh, right. I guess *you* don't need one."

Damian sheepishly extended his hand for the page and caught it when Theodore tossed it at him.

"I can't believe this!" Damian said, scanning his story. The Rector had highlighted every second sentence and crossed out others before photocopying it. Damian wanted to carefully examine the changes, but before he could, Theodore said:

"Neither can I!" Then he leaned back, eyeing Damian. "Are you nervous?"

"No." But the sheet wavered under Theodore's glare.

"What?" Theodore asked, tilting his head.

That people will discover my lie, Damian thought, but instead said, "Well, you know, it's just my story sounds a bit, um, boastful—maybe unbelievable, too. . . I don't know."

"*You* exist, don't you?" Theodore said sarcastically. He snatched back the page. "It's like Father Rector said—we just need more guys. *Guys like you.*"

Theodore stood but Damian, scared and shameful, remained seated, silent. Already he mourned the loss of Theodore's once-cordial company. *Mourning*: precisely what he'd hoped the seminary would drain from his life, how Mount Angelus would heal his memory, marred by loss. But for now, he mentally scrambled to make amends with Theodore and salvage the friendship.

"I can't eat lunch," Theodore said as he passed by. "I'm going to the flower shop."

Damian watched his (former?) friend leave, off to get drunk. The flower shop was seminary code for the local liquor store. He'd never been because booze only figured into the lamented pasts of the saints he'd read about. Drinking hadn't assisted their ascents to holiness.

But as Theodore walked away, he wanted so badly—even just this once—to come along. To stay pals. And as a prayer answered, Theodore stopped and turned at the stairs. "You coming?"

Damian launched from his seat. "You bet."

And though drinking at midday was definitely unsaintly—something Father Dennis might do but *not* him—he was just so happy to ascend from the crypt with a friend.

CHAPTER SIXTEEN
WALK ON WATER

Half an hour later, bottles tucked up their coat sleeves and ancient skates slung by frayed laces over their shoulders, Damian and Theodore surveyed the seminary's frozen pond from its pebbly shore.

Pines encircled the space, bordering the shore's outer edge, where the pebbles quit about ten feet from the water. The pines—fragrant poles tightly packed like a stockade—enclosed in privacy the pond's circular clearing, scenting and stilling the air for a peaceful ambience. More pertinent, however, to Damian, who worried about getting caught, the pine wall protected, or at least conveyed a feeling of safety, against witnesses who might secretly spy on the boozy skating, soon to occur. Worse, these spectators would probably report to seminary administrators—*and on the very day he'd been showcased as the model candidate!*

For now, though, sensing the security and serenity within this enclosure, Damian relaxed and almost, *almost*—by exerting mental effort—dispelled the memory of Fr. Rector spying on him at this very spot. . .

Theodore motioned for Damian to follow him onto the pond, and Damian was grateful to accompany his friend, thus returning his attention to the present and, at least temporarily, abandoning the past.

They tiptoed onto the ice, but once out a few feet, cracks splintered from under their shoes. Damian instinctively retreated to shore, but Theodore ventured out further, obviously deterred by neither the spindly cracks nor the bubbles beneath the thin ice. In fact, the creaks his stomps produced seemed to satisfy his appetite for rebellion, his desire to dare limits and shuck off the constraints imposed upon him in chapel today. Damian, tense on his friend's behalf, nevertheless wished that he'd stayed at Theodore's side, while Theodore now leapt directly on the pond's centre—likely the thinnest, weakest point.

Fearful that Theodore's stomping might cause an accident, or, worse, draw attention from others on the hilltop, Damian—who wanted to appear nonchalant—felt compelled to say, "You're sure Father Rector's gone?"

The question palpably arrested Theodore's attention. He stood still and stared directly, silently, at Damian. His stern gaze indicated that he'd detected the underlying fear in Damian's voice, in his inquiry. Theodore strolled back to shore, sat on a log, and unlaced his shoes.

"You missed him talk about it," he said, shoving on a skate. "He's spending the weekend with Bishop Spur to present the new vocations initiative—*you.*"

Damian wanted to change the subject, to be cheerful, but still he craved assurance. "And no one will see me drinking? You know the underage policy is—"

"Look!" Theodore said, clearly annoyed. "Just keep the bottle up your sleeve. And stop worrying!"

"Okay," Damian said. He sat beside Theodore, praying silently: *Forgive me, Father, for what I'm about to do!* He didn't want to lose his friend, to be the ideal seminarian on the page while an outcast among the men on the hilltop. . . *I could just pretend to sip from the bottle,* he thought.

He loosened the powdery, threadbare laces on his skates, pulling gingerly because they felt frail. He and Theodore had borrowed the skates from the seminary's sports closet—a tomb-like space burrowed deep into their dormitory's cavernous basement. This closet sealed in stale, stagnant air that poorly preserved the Victorian-era athletic gear, held within. Cracked, brown-leather goalie pads piled waste-high in one corner and in the opposite slumped a dusty black punching bag that bulged, rotund, around its bottom—the effect of having been suspended for decades. Aa bundle of lacrosse sticks, their torn nets intertwined with spiders' webs, had filled the centre of the room. This aged equipment could have stocked an entire antique shop, Damian had thought, and he'd been barely able to fit his corpulent figure into the cramped, cluttered space.

And yet their exploration had succeeded for within that musty, dusty, arid room—smelling even more morbid than the Museum Mortis—had sat crisp leather baseball gloves and stiff catchers' mitts—in *rigor mortis*, it'd seemed—that'd been heaped upon the ancient white-and-red leather skates that surprisingly fit his and Theodore's disparate sizes.

But that aroma of extinction, Damian now mused as he gazed at the pond, that sense of obsolescence, that antique ambience of the sports closet—it pervaded the hilltop. In terms of atmosphere, the seminary was like a sarcophagus, suffused with a grim sense of death. Mount Angelus sat atop a hill, yet in truth it was sinking into oblivion, barely able to support or sustain itself.

And this decline, this sense of defeat, was more than just an unsettling mood, ethereal but palpable, nonetheless. There were also material indicators that the seminary was floundering: the dwindling recruits, the lack of funds, the malaise among the faculty (but for, of course, *Dr. House's* gusto) . . . All seemed lifeless, an institution once thriving but now bankrupt—fading into a wavering, whimpering collapse. Indeed, the vigour he found in his friend Theodore, in *Walden*, in the spiritual autobiography class, and in Dr. House himself were the sole sparkles on an otherwise dim canvass...

But then Dr. House, too, had now met with tragedy. Eden's disease could prove deadly— *God forbid*! — and it was already vicariously draining Dr. House's vigor, his teaching ability, his life. How Damian yearned to spare him from the pain of losing a loved one. But how? Such matters could only be abandoned to God's will, or at least that thought proved comforting now. . .

Damian stood to test his skates. Theodore pushed him down, pointing at the whiskey bottle leaning against the log.

"Let's see a big swig," he said. Damian nodded, prayed another quick forgiveness, and then opened his coat as cover. He unscrewed the bottle, plugged his nose, and swallowed for three consecutive seconds. The bourbon scorched his throat and burned his belly. He lurched forward and gasped, coughing.

"Dear God!" he said. The booze rushed to his head, leaving him blinking, reeling. Theodore appeared satisfied, however, so Damian, sputtering, recapped the bottle. And now Theodore spun around and charged the pond. He skated confidently, displaying his skill as an experienced hockey player, carving wide circles as he glided with one arm—where his bottle was hidden—

swinging straight at his side, like a pendulum.

Damian likewise tucked his bottle into his sleeve, and, wobbly from the bourbon and the rickety skates, but also suddenly warm and relaxed, he approached the ice. He'd only skated five or six times in his life, (always having to borrow skates from neighbors because the Kurts couldn't afford their own), but today he wanted to do his best for Theodore. To please his friend.

He stumbled as he stepped toward the pond, digging his blades into the pebbly shore to gain stability. He carefully lowered his left foot onto the ice; it cracked—a narrow, surface splinter. He was about to draw back when Theodore burst past him, slashing across the pond, slicing up the ice.

"Look at me, Lord!" Theodore screamed. "You aren't the only one who walks on water!"

"Shut up!" Damian yelled, and then added in a strained whisper: "No scenes, remember?"

But Theodore kept gliding swiftly around the pond, swinging his stiff arm at his side like a speed skater and smiling with rosy cheeks.

Meanwhile, Damian slid his left foot forward, tried to ignore the deep echo of ice splitting beneath him, and pushed off the bank. As he glided away from shore, the sound of wobbling sheet metal shot across the pond. A jagged crease followed the sound, but the cool wind poured over Damian and the sensation of gliding tingled from feet to stomach to fingers.

He tilted back his head. The grey sky was bordered by pine trees. He closed his eyes. He pushed himself along with his right skate, keeping his left toe pointed forward to direct himself. This rhythmic gliding, along with the bourbon in his belly, hypnotized him, it seemed, and his thoughts drifted pleasantly. . . .

He couldn't help marvelling: *he*, it had turned out, was the best Mt. Angelus had to offer. *What does that mean?* He wasn't sure whether to pity the seminary or expand his sense of self-worth. He wondered how could he have known, when he wrote his vocation story half a year ago, that it would become a template to attract men to the seminary? He'd been so desperate to escape from home, that he wrote as striking, as impressive, a story as he could, but who'd have thought he'd advertised himself—his "type"—so well?

And, for that matter, if indeed he was the model seminarian, wasn't he then entitled to a little winter fun on the ice? As for the bourbon, well, he wasn't drunk—and he swore to himself that he wouldn't sip a drop more, no matter what and regarding the gulp he'd already taken, which had been solely for Theodore's sake, well, even the saints had *one* drink once in a while, didn't they?

Damian breathed in deeply the crisp chilly air, and savoured the brisk, bracing tingle in his lungs, fully expanded, as he swelled his chest and then slowly exhaled, feeling steady, calm, content. Indeed, the pine-circled clearing, the pond, the expansive, dome-like winter sky—grey-blue and brushed with strokes of white wispy clouds—this day was available for his enjoyment. The frost was tender, the breeze brisk but not biting, his surroundings were God's gifts, and the bounty of natural beauty complemented the charge given to his ego earlier in the chapel. Today seemed to open itself up to him, to offer the possibility of living with gusto, even saintly passion.

Pleased, he opened his eyes and skated over the grooves carved by Theodore around the pond's edge. Following in these deep tracks stabilized his wobbly skates, his waning ankles, and soon he found himself enjoying the loops around the pond, until . . . until he spotted, just past the shoreline, the exact location in the brush where Father Rector had spied on him months ago.

He stared at the spot, suddenly angry, embarrassed at the horrid memory of his sneaky superior watching him, swimming privately, *naked*. He recollected the Rector's lurking figure in the bushes that morning, a peeping pervert. . . And he wondered if Father Rector ever acted similarly before, spying on other men on the hilltop—at the pond, perhaps, or more likely in the showers, stealing glances in the gym locker room, even peering through dorm windows at night? If so, had he then gone even further . . .?

Damian hesitated, guilty that he was even considering that the Rector might have actually violated vulnerable young men—easy prey, though, given Father Rector's position: parishioners or youthful seminarians, trusting sheep supposedly secure under *his* clerical leadership, submissive to a *rector's* authority.

But these troubling suspicions were likely groundless, of course, and hopefully they would, in time, fade away—as long as nothing suspicious occurred again.

Damian still struggled to accept that this humiliating incident had ever even occurred. It left lingering implications that loomed grim—first, for his long-held conviction that seminaries were safe havens, sanctuaries for fostering sanctity, or at least decency. Worse, though, were those suspicions raised about the Rector's character, his moral core. His possible corruption posed implications that perhaps his was not the only perverse clerical character. Did deception and manipulative abuse infect several, or some, or even *many* ordained ministers? Damian wrestled with such a shocking scenario. *There's no way . . . is there?*

Surely *most* priests lived upright lives but did some use their position as a means to prey on those feeble *and* faith-filled. Damian wasn't sure he wanted to know. As for the Rector himself, was he grotesque, or maybe just gruff, abrupt? And such features as those, attributes of an abrasive disposition, were boons, perhaps, to a leader— and also prone to cause intrusiveness, say, which was what the pond encounter had revealed, nothing more.

Indeed, Damian likely was mistaken, misinterpreting what he perceived—or thought he had. Besides, months had now passed, leaving his memory suspect. Had the Rector *really* been spying on him that day? Or had Father Rector more likely been walking nearby when he heard Damian splashing, and innocently trekked down the slope to the pond to simply see what was happening?

Just then, from where he stood on the slope, Damian saw a young woman mounting the top of the path that climbed all the way from the base of the mountain, snaked through the wooded slopes, and, as it reached mountain peak, led along one side of the pond's shore before finally opening out onto the lawn behind the cathedral.

How pretty, he thought. Her face so beautiful, like art—a sight to behold, to admire. . . *And best ignored,* his conscience told him, and yet the danger of impurity somehow seemed far away. Gazing at this woman, her stride so elegant, presented such a contrast between appreciating her grace with what lude delights the Rector possibly glimpsed from this same spot.

Damian smiled at the woman. She smiled back. He stopped to watch as she began rounding the pond. Her blue eyes peered in radiant azure below her grey fur hat, and her long wool coat split above the hem around her black leather boots.

She held a book bag with *Mount Angelus Abbey Library* written on it. Above these words was the seminary's logo, a stencil of the abbey church perched atop the small mountain, its steeple pointing up. Damian glanced at Theodore, but *he* was absorbed in his antics, slashing about on the opposite side of the shore, prone to miss this charming new arrival circling their formally private pond.

"Hey, asshole!" Theodore screamed to Damian, obviously oblivious that they now had company. "Watch this!"

"Um," Damian groaned, rolling his eyes for the woman to see, trying to convey disapproval of what Theodore had just said, and was probably about to do. Over his shoulder, he gently said, "Maybe just settle down, there. Okay, pal?"

"Damian, you dumb shit, turn around and watch this!"

Cringing, Damian turned to face his friend. He gasped. Theodore had already removed his coat, cassock, and shirt, and had piled them in a heap in the middle of the pond. On the far shore, topless and apparently still unaware of the woman, Theodore was backing up with his bottle peeking out from the crotch of his pants.

"Here . . . we . . . go!" Theodore yelled, slurring badly.

He dug his skates into the pebbly shore, then charged the pond—sending up shaved ice, slices slashed up like waves—and then raced across the ice. He swung his arms viciously as he approached his pile of clothes, squatted about a foot before it, and then sprung his legs straight. Lifting his knees, Theodore appeared to be seated on an invisible dirt bike as he soared—arcing—over his clothing.

Damian held his breath as Theodore descended to the pond. He dropped one leg, his skate pointing to the ice to absorb his descent. That skate touched down, but it got stuck and Theodore pitched forward. Leading with his bare chest, he flew onto the shore, slamming hard, face down. He slid forward; his legs curled up behind him.

"Motherfuger!" Theodore yelled; his voice garbled by pebbles. "My bourbon flattened my balls! Oh, Damian, oh!"

Theodore rolled over and pulled his bottle from his pants. He checked it—miraculously intact—and then he spread out his arms, lying as though crucified.

"This is a disgrace!" the woman said, bellowing across the ice.

Theodore's eyes opened; they appeared strained, suffering, panicked.

"You boys should be ashamed!" Now the woman leaned in, glaring more intensely at Damian. *"And you! You there, Damian!* I have you, your maniac friend's lookout, and your superiors will be getting a nice little letter from me, boy!"

"Ma'am," Damian said, beginning a plea for mercy.

"Don't you dare!" The woman pointed at Damian, filling him with dread and guilt—a terrifying sight and yet, somehow, *familiar*: the shame and sense of sin. He vaguely recognized this scenario: facing a pointing accuser, standing still and guilty, frozen in fear. The woman, pointing at him, draped in her long coat, resembled the spectral figure he'd faced in his nightmare on his first night at Mount Angelus.

Both of them dreadful figures, condemning, frightening.

Yet this woman before him was real. She spun around—her library bag swinging out, fluttering as it sliced the air—and then she stomped up the path and out of sight.

CHAPTER SEVENTEEN
HELPING HAND

Two days later, Damian sat at a table in the crowded, murmuring cafeteria, staring at his dinner, dry chicken and rice, and moving the food silently, mechanically, to his mouth. He frowned, even while he chewed.

He'd sunk into despair since the woman's threat at the pond and now her letter's impending arrival loomed over him like a dangling noose, just overhead, ready at any moment to snare him, suffocating any pleas for mercy, cries of defense. When that letter reached the Rector, Damian's seminary career would surely end, and all priestly—as well as all *saintly*—ambitions would be crushed.

Father Rector would probably react violently to the woman's account of events, namely, that Damian had been standing lookout, as it'd likely seemed to her, overseeing with approval Theodore's charade at the pond. And then there was the *timing*—deeply damning. On the very day he'd been showcased as the model seminarian, he'd dived straight into debauchery, first chance he got.

Now Damian swallowed his last mouthful and rose from the table. Outside blew a cool evening breeze. His gaze followed the ground as he walked, and he didn't look up until he was inside the dorm's foyer. There he turned to the Twenty-Four-Hour Board and gasped: printed in large, bold font, a new announcement was posted on a fluorescent pink sheet: *"Father Rector Requests Every*

Seminarian's Attendance Tonight, at 7:00 p.m., in the Crypt Chapel." He stood gaping, stunned, then spun around and charged upstairs to find Theodore. Three knocks on the door brought a sleepy moan from inside Theodore's room and Damian entered flicking on the lights.

"Assembly tonight," he said, breathing hard. "I-I think, he's . . . he's—he's going to read her letter out loud!"

"Wha—? Why are the . . .?" Theodore said, stammering. He blinked and squinted at the sudden light, grabbing for the sheets to pull over his head and, in this commotion, his swollen black eye and shredded cheek became clearly visible. Damian shuddered.

"Oh, God—gosh!—your face is worse!" Damian said. He raised his open hands—a final plea, desperate—and then slapped his thighs. "We're finished. I'm publicly ousted tonight—just watch. And you, you can't pretend to be sick forever, so everyone's going to see your eye and know it was us. We can't deny anything in that letter. I'll be sent home! *Home!*"

And for the first time since last year, when he'd returned to Grandma Shiller's after running away to Scott's and then encountered his remorseful mother at the front door, Damian sobbed.

"Hold on, hold on," Theodore said, sitting up. Damian slumped into Theodore's chair, put his head in his hands. Theodore squeezed Damian's shoulder. "Look, I found someone who can take care of this—make it right. These things happen."

"These things?"

"Clerical mishaps—and this guy, he sorts 'em out, cleans 'em up. Developed *quite* a reputation when things got dicey for a few priests in a nearby diocese. Even handled some unsavory matters in the monastery, I understand. Pull yourself together, man—I found us a cleanup guy."

Damian kept his face buried as he hunched over. Tears streamed through his fingers. Theodore continued nonetheless, merciful but stern, his gaze steady, eyes alert and focused on Damian.

"Look, her letter's probably already here, right? But Father Rector returns *tonight*—so stop worrying about the assembly! No way he'd bother with the mail the moment he's back. Not before addressing *all* of us. No way!"

"You sure?" Damian looked up.

"Br. Tim said so." Theodore smiled knowingly.

"He's the—*Br. Tim?*"

"Yup. He's our guy. Now listen . . ." Theodore swung his feet over the side of the bed and lowered his voice. "Have you ever seen that monk who looks like Lucifer?"

"The huge guy?"

"Uh-huh."

"Spiky silver hair and pointy goatee?"

"*That* guy."

"He slumps around, like he's injured."

"Yup—and he's nuts, totally crazy. But he's also in charge of delivering the mail."

"Ohhh." Damian's heart slowed, retuning to a normal rate. He now spoke softly. "Can he intercept her letter?"

"Said he'll do it but wants us to come."

"Why?"

"Wants to show us something, some seminary secret. Hidden in those vaults."

"Are you kidding?"

"That's what he said. So just come along, and he'll get you your letter. . ." Theodore paused, raised an eyebrow. "Before he entered the monastery, Brother Tim dated Simone de Beauvoir."

"The writer?"

"Said so. 'I dated Ms. Simone de Beauvoir.' He said so."

"That's weird. Just blurted out her name?"

"He asked what we were reading in Harold's class. I said *The Mandarins* by de Beauvoir. And he just goes and says, 'I dated her.'"

"Probably someone else—namesake."

"Well, he *did* live in France—the guy's done everything! Mailman, detective, computer engineer, reporter, and then he studied cooking in Paris and dated Simone de Beauvoir—that's why he didn't become a monk until he was fifty-five."

"Hmmm." Damian shook his head; he needed to focus on the plan. "Where do we meet him?"

"After assembly tonight," Theodore said. "We'll pretend like we're going for a stroll around the grounds. Once everyone's back in their dorms, we'll walk into the cathedral's foyer—he'll be waiting inside. Mumbled something about 'the vaults.'"

"In the basement?"

"He's down there all the time—says that's where the mail goes until he delivers it the next day."

"Great," Damian said, and then, having now calmed down, his curiosity piqued. "Wonder what's down there."

"Something worth keeping secret."

"Like that letter," Damian said, returning Theodore's sly smile.

The tower bell rang out, a deep, slow *daaawwwwnnnnng* that swelled into the autumn evening and then dissolved into the soft hues of the setting sun, fading as it thus expanded into dusk, into silence. Through this languid atmosphere, Damian and Theodore cut a purposeful hustle—brisk steps that betrayed none of the reluctance Damian felt for where he was headed.

Inside the crypt chapel, Father Rector stood at the podium, scanning the room as it filled. Theodore took a seat in the back row, and Damian joined him, feeling somehow safer because the exit was closest here. Theodore looked like Roy Orbison behind thick, black sunglasses that did little to hide his scratches and bruised eye.

The room erupted in applause as Father Rector raised his hand and cleared his throat.

"No need to clap," he said, pumping his palm to the crowd. "Always this senseless clapping. . . All right, men. Bishop Spur adores my—*our* vocations initiative!"

Applause bombarded the Rector.

"Please, men, please" Father Rector said, frowning. "So tonight, we're gonna kick things off, get this operation underway. Now I'll call out your parish assignments along with the date you'll be speaking. . . Oh. Except Damian, that is. Damian! Damian, where are you?"

Damian trembled. He stood and nodded at the Rector.

"Something's come up," said Father Rector. "See me privately after the assembly."

Damian's knees shook as he sat, numb, and stared straight ahead. One look at Theodore could implicate his friend.

"Theodore!" Father Rector said, holding up a sheet of

paper. "Theodore, here's your assignment."

Handing the sheet to Theodore, the Rector glared at his sunglasses. Damian gulped."And I realize you guys find the chapel lights glary," Father Rector said, "but please don't wear eye protection when inside. . . All right now, Peter M! Peter, here you are. Cameron! Cam—here you go. Peter S. . . ."

After Father Rector finished calling names and distributing assignments, Damian listened to him very carefully, trying to decipher his mood. Father Rector said, "Now, men, I have great hope for this initiative, and that's because I have confidence in all of you. Now I—"

Applause again fluttered up from the chapel seats. Fr. Rector's hand was on his hip, his mouth hung open, gaping, and he shook his head.

"Why?" Fr. Rector asked. "Why are you clapping? It's simply . . . All right, look. Just mark your calendars with the date and location I've given you. Have your story ready by then and arrange for vehicles with my secretary. Our Lady of Priests . . ."

"Pray for us!" the room responded. Someone clapped once, drew the Rector's glare, and then fell silent.

"I'll take a lap around campus," Theodore whispered. "When he's done with you, come up and walk around. I'll look for you."

Damian nodded, then waited as the room emptied. The Rector still stood at the podium, shuffling sheets, his face serious, stolid. Damian's heart pounded; he felt faint. When only he and Fr. Rector remained, he walked to the front of the chapel to face his fate.

"Ah," said the Rector, folding his hands atop the podium. "Take a seat."

He seems serious, Damian thought, *but not mad exactly.* He sat down with a flicker of hope. Fr. Rector sat one row ahead of him, draping his arm over the back of the chair. "Damian, I received some bad news today."

"Y-yes," Damian said, trembling.

"You seem upset. Have you already heard?"

Damian shook his head.

"Okay, well, Eden is very ill and—"

Eden! Not the woman's letter! Damian sighed, and the Rector fell silent before saying, "Now hold on, son. I know you're upset."

"Yes, Father," Damian said, his voice steadying. He considered the sudden turn this conversation had taken— to Eden's illness, not *his* behaviour. No scathing letter. Had the woman even sent it?

"Sorry," he said. "I'm just, um . . . please, go on."

"Well," the Rector said, "this is the worst sort of thing to hear, I know, but I believe you can help."

"Anything."

"Good." Fr. Rector nodded. "I knew you'd be up for it. Well, Professor House has asked for you to visit Eden in the hospital. Now, I'm aware that you freshmen have a very packed schedule, and I don't want to pile on too many extra commitments. So instead of going out to advertise for the seminary, I'm going to let you visit Eden and his dad. In the evenings. Just let me know what day works for them."

"Yes, Father."

"Good." Fr. Rector smiled. "Good man. Ok, dismissed."

Damian sighed and relaxed his shoulders as he climbed the chapel stairs to ground level and then stepped into the fresh evening air. Outside he sighed again, more deeply, and tried to expel the guilty feeling that he somehow benefitted from Eden's plight. The fact was, he was so terrified of the woman's letter and the Rector's wrath, that any other outcome—such as the one he got—was welcome. But now, circumstances settled as they were, *how could he best assist Eden on these upcoming visits?*

For now, though, he just gazed at the stars. Eden would've delighted in their bright sparkle tonight. Damian stopped his leisurely scan of the night sky: he ought to get moving on tonight's mission. He walked slowly, glancing around and still beaming: *he wouldn't be expelled.* The moon was a perfect circle that bathed the seminary grounds in a soft, silver hue—its glow was indeed like the gratitude he felt.

"Hey!" Someone whispered from behind a bush. "Does he know?"

Damian jumped, then laughed as he recognized Theodore's voice. "No, no. Everything's fine. Let's go!"

After passing the Rector on the path, and nodding solemnly, Damian and Theodore approached the cathedral. As they neared the entrance, the cathedral's front door inched open, then a few inches more. . .

"Tim," Theodore whispered. The door swung open, its hinges creaking, and revealed Br. Tim's towering, corpulent silhouette.

"Come," Tim whispered. His belly protruded, filling the doorway, which forced Damian to squeeze by, sucking in his stomach as he passed. Br. Tim smelled sweaty, with a lingering hint of wine in his pointy beard. He shut the door gently, coaxing the hinges to squeak as little as possible. With the moonlight shut out, the three men had to navigate the pitch black. Then Tim's voice from out of the dark—husky and mysterious, "Hold onto my hood."

Damian placed his hand on Br. Tim's broad back and slid it up to the tip of the monk's hood. He then offered his right hand to Theodore, who grabbed it. Thus connected, the three men inched through the foyer and progressed up the body of the church. As they neared the tabernacle lamp, the soft red glow allowed their hands to fall to their sides and they proceeded independently, with Tim still leading the way.

They shuffled into the sacristy, where a streetlamp just outside the window streamed in yellow light. Tim led the boys to a closet along the sacristy's back wall. This was a wide, open closet, full of vestments hanging in a tightly packed row. Tim spread the vestments apart in several places, and Damian leaned in to see. *Searching for what?*

But then, near the centre of the closet, Tim spread the vestments wide enough to reveal a short, narrow door, which suited the entrance of a cottage; made from thin, white planks nailed together vertically, the door rounded into an arc at its top.

Tim twisted the round, white knob and pulled the door open to reveal a staircase that descended into darkness. Stuffing himself through the cramped doorway, Tim descended several steps and then stopped. A bulb brightened above his head and revealed a thin, hanging cord in his hand.

The boys followed Tim down a white-walled stairwell. They reached a shadowy wine cellar, its walls stocked from floor to ceiling with bottles and barrels, before descending a second concrete staircase. These stairs led to the seminary's deepest level, and the air thinned to a musty consistency.

Tim flicked on a light which revealed a large, boxy, high-ceilinged, windowless room encased in concrete. A ledge level with Damian's head wrapped around the room. Upon it were monstrances, a spinning wheel, pointy bishops' hats, brass tabernacles, several ancient gravestones so thick even *he* probably couldn't lift them— *so how'd they get up there?* There was also a thin writing desk that would surely crumple beneath his weight, an antique, wiry wheelchair, and wooden chests shut with thick leather belts. From a railing below this ledge, red and gold vestments hung in clear plastic cases. These vestments seemed like those his mother described from forty years ago, when she attended Latin Mass in her youth.

In the far-right corner was a tall, narrow throne. Lions' heads carved into the front of each armrest growled with mouths wide open. The seat and backrest bulged with maroon velvet cushions. Bronze studs bordered these cushions, making velvet dimples every few inches. Damian had seen such a throne as a boy, during Christmas Mass celebrated by a bishop.

To the left of the throne was a wide iron door built into the wall. Bolts bordered the door, and long lines of bolts crossed at its centre in an imposing "X." Tim stepped up to the door's handle, above which was a dial. He turned the dial left, right, and then left again. A loud click and Br. Tim opened the vault door.

A light automatically brightened inside the safe, and Damian went numb. Encased in a glass cylinder and propped on a little stand was a severed hand in an upright position. The hand appeared to support itself lifelessly, without wires or any visible assistance, and the skin held a ruddy tan complexion, much like Damian's. *But how?* By its posture—with fingers extended in a tight row, pointing straight up—it looked like it was granting a blessing. A jewelled bracelet, wrapped around the wrist, presumably concealed a garish cut.

Damian stood breathless, then retreated several steps to distance himself from the too-lifelike hand. He stepped further and further back, and then suddenly tripped backwards and found himself on his back on the floor and in pain. He slowly sat up. In his tumble he'd bumped into a low cabinet—the only item in this bizarre room that looked modern and wasn't dusty. It clashed terribly with the rest of this tomb-like vault.

He looked over his shoulder to locate Theodore and Tim, who were both obviously entranced by the incorrupt hand. They were so attentive, in fact, that they appeared to be willing the fingers to flinch—or just give a quick tap on the glass cylinder. Torn between the hand and retrieving the letter, he turned to the cabinet, opened its top drawer, and found hanging file-folders. Each file was labelled with a seminarian's name, and Damian quickly found his file and opened it.

There was his vocation story, the original, marked with pen and covered with sticky notes. He read the Rector's remarks, and then flipped the first page to continue. . . By the time he finished reading his altered story, Damian was very anxious to find the woman's letter and then leave this scary place. He returned his file to the cabinet, but then when he turned to ask Br. Tim where the mail was, he found he was alone.

If he yelled, he might be discovered by someone other

than Theodore and Br. Tim, so he silently searched behind some crates and chests, and then approached the vault. It was still open, and the hand appeared as though it might wave. He dropped his eyes in fear as he pushed the heavy door shut. The lock clicked deeply, echoing through this cavernous space.

He turned and moved away from the door, looking for Theodore and Br. Tim . . . but then he stepped on something soft: lying flat on the concrete floor was Br. Tim's black habit, the hood pointed up, the sleeves crossed in a fig-leaf position. An envelope poked out the wrist of each sleeve; Damian gathered them.

One letter was self-addressed by a woman, Elaine Jepson, who shared the seminary's zip code. Thrilled, Damian sighed and relaxed after having been tense these last few days. Truly her written accusation would never reach the Rector, its stated recipient, as Damian tucked it into his pocket.

The other letter was from Uncle Rick! Damian turned toward the stairs and began walking in haste so he could open Rick's letter as soon as possible, but just then knocking came from behind him. He jumped. His neck hair rose. He was about to flee, to escape these horrid caverns, when snickering issued from inside the vault.

"Damian," Theodore said, his voice muffled as he called. "Get us out of here! We can't breathe. And this hand might kill us!"

Damian closed his room door and slid both letters from his sleeve. He sighed deeply, relieved. The moon was so bright, he decided to read Uncle Rick's letter with the lights off. He rolled to the edge of his bed, opened the envelope, and held the papers near his window.

First, there was a newspaper clipping of his father's generic obituary, which Damian purposefully hadn't read since the day it appeared, over four years ago:

February 30, 1994
It is with heavy hearts that we announce the sudden passing of beloved father and husband, George Kurt. Born in New Zealand, George grew up on a farm and then played for the All Blacks before immigrating to Canada. He opened his own plumbing business in Calgary after marrying Cynthia Kurt (nee Reinhold). Together they had four children—Damian, Bernadette, Mary, and James. He will be dearly missed by all his family. A funeral Mass will be celebrated this Tuesday at 11:00 am at Canadian Martyrs Parish.

The obituary captured nothing of who his father really was, did not even hint at his saintliness. *Who'd written it?* Probably his mother. It would not be a useful resource for his assignment.

Now for Rick's letter. It was thankfully typed—Rick's handwriting was illegible—but his uncle's voice came through clearly nonetheless:

Damian:
I hope your year at the seminary is going along fine. I knew a guy from Tennessee, an army doctor who flipped out in Vietnam and entered the seminary, Gus Tisdale—Dr. Gus—we'd call him, and he wrote himself prescriptions for amphetamines to keep himself alert and one morning in the seminary I heard a gun go off and thought the Russians

had invaded. But no—it was old Dr. Gus in his house coat and his rifle. He thought he saw a mouse. Anyway, I think he`s a military chaplain now, or something.

Damian, I tell stories to teach you things, so it bothers me that your mother told you something that isn't true. I overheard her offering a prayer intention at the rosary, thanking God that Fr. Geraldo`s prophecy had come true since you were in the seminary.

There was no prophecy. You ought to know that. Fr. Geraldo said to me if you want to help people be a priest, but if you want to help yourself, then keep to yourself. I tried the seminary out, you know, for a couple years, but realized it wasn`t for me because I wasn`t there to help. I think Fr. Geraldo would be proud I left.

What he told your mom—as she described it to me—was the same thing. That God sent him to her to inspire someone who wants to serve. That doesn`t have to be you or me.

If you don't want to help others, maybe just find something else. That's advice your dad gave me when I was in the seminary. Your dad, in fact, wrote me letters when I was a monk, and I've sent one of them here. I've always kept them private, but I think they would help you now. The rest are hidden in various cracks and crevices in my room. When I find one, I'll mail it to you.

Watch out for the crazies.
Rick

Damian was numb. A letter. From dad. And more to come.

He slowly pulled out another sheet from the envelope Rick had sent, and before he could look, he smelled it: yes, his cologne. He opened the letter as though it were an ancient, sacred scroll and held it to the window. The moonlight gave the words a ghostly feel, as if his dad's spirit were here in the seminary room. The letter was only a paragraph, but the handwriting was unmistakable:

June 15, 1976
Ricky,
Just to let you know I managed to sell your truck, but I still think you should have kept her. I hope those monks are treating you decently. Why you're there beats me. Come on back and meet a nice girl, make some cash, live it up. You're still young.
Love ya, Mate.
George

He stared at the words. He stayed totally still. The voice was *him*. But . . .

Why you're there beats me, his dad had said. Implying he saw Rick's religious life as questionable. Pointless, too, maybe. So then what would he think of Damian's seminary studies, his young life led toward priestly ordination?

Terror and doubt left him unable to even glance back at the words. He'd hide the letter under his mattress so no one else could find and read it, but what would he do when more letters arrived? His faith, not to mention his religious vocation, might not withstand further attacks. His dad's words, remembered as encouraging, now potential devastation.

The moon stayed suspended in the sky for hours, keeping his dad's words alive on the page as they churned in Damian's mind.

CHAPTER EIGHTEEN
ENVOY

Fr. Rector placed his tray across the table from Damian. He seemed to enjoy the chili that the kitchen served on Thursday nights as much as Damian did. He had a big bowl of it, topped with cheese and sour cream, beside two pieces of honey-drizzled corn bread on a small plate.

Fr. Rector opened his napkin, pulled out his chair, sat down, and smiled. "I got your message, Damian. Tonight sounds fine."

"Thanks, Father," Damian said, smiling back. "And I'll need a ride, so..."

"I've arranged for one of the monks to drive you to the hospital. He's meeting us here for dinner. You're going to like this guy. Interesting background."

"Who is he?"

"Brother Tim," Fr. Rector replied. "He used to—oh! Here he is."

Just then Br. Tim lumbered up beside Damian and plunked down his tray. As his barrel-like body sunk down, Damian caught another whiff of wine—altar wine, specifically. He recalled the cellar with barrels and bottles from last night and hoped Br. Tim was sober enough to drive.

"Nice to meet you," Damian said, putting out his hand. "I'm Damian."

"Hello, Damian," Br. Tim replied, his smile sly as they shook hands. "I'm Brother Tim"

"So, Tim," the Rector said, his mouth full; he brought his napkin to his lips and then continued: "Any progress with the phone-a-thon?"

"Well," Br. Tim replied, "we would be ready to begin in a couple months—right after Christmas break—but the donor list keeps shrinking."

"Why?" the Rector asked.

"The list you gave me—some of these people haven't donated for twenty years," Br. Tim said. "When I call their number, they've either moved, entered a nursing home, or died."

"Can't you find younger people—the children of the dead donors?"

"I've been trying," Br. Tim said. "But church attendance is so low, it's tough."

Damian ate silently. He was mentally preparing for his visit to the hospital tonight, and he was still pondering his dad's letter to Uncle Rick. Now a lull fell over the table, so he felt obliged to contribute to the conversation. He turned to Br. Tim and asked, "Are you going to call the donors yourself?"

"No," Br. Tim replied. "We're getting the seminarians to do the work—just like with the vocations' initiative. I'm going to compile a list, write a spiel for you guys to give the donors over the phone, and we'll have a prize for the seminarian who raises the most money."

"Damian can help you write the spiel," Fr. Rector said. "We're using his vocation story as a template for the talks in the parishes—he's a good writer."

"That could work," Br. Tim said, smirking at Damian. "The model seminarian, eh?"

Damian nodded, bashful.

"Whatever the case," Fr. Rector said, already scraping out his bowl with his spoon, "we need more men—look at this dining room. When I was a seminarian, it was packed on chili night!"

Damian turned and beheld the five full tables surrounded by at least twenty empty ones. Had his father been correct to advise Uncle Rick to abandon seminary life? What if his dad had seen Mount Angelus today, with its dwindling numbers and lack of funds? So far, besides Dr. House's class, the primary focus of Damian's life on the hilltop had been the vocations' initiative, which was based on half-truths, and now he was helping Eden and would perhaps assist with the phone-a-thon. The seminary was just trying to survive—fighting extinction, in fact—rather than serving others, as his father had served his family.

Perhaps Damian's desire for holiness, for goodness, would be better satisfied as a family man, as his father had been. But he never seriously considered marriage after suffering Grandma Schiller's stifling home. And yet he wondered, judging from the advice he had given Uncle Rick in that letter, if perhaps his father did not share the stark religious views Damian had inherited from his mother. Possibly, fearing conflict with his mom, his father had never been completely honest about his religious convictions. Except in letters to Uncle Rick . . .

Damian put aside these thoughts. He had enough concerns for tonight, so for now he just enjoyed the autumn dusk outside: the sun was setting on the Okanagan Valley, so orange light shone through the dining room's large windows. Dusk reminded him of death, and he braced himself for tonight's endeavour. He had promised Harold that he would be at the hospital no later than six o'clock.

"Tim, can we go?" Damian said.

"Yeah," Br. Tim said, placing his spoon in his empty bowl. "Let's go."

"Good evening, men," Fr. Rector said as Br. Tim and Damian stood with their trays. "And remember, Damian— you're our envoy tonight. Even just with your presence, give Eden and Harold comfort and strength."

"All right, Father," Damian said. "I'll do my best."

"Did you actually date Simone de Beauvoir?" Damian asked Br. Tim minutes later in the long, blue Buick that the seminary lent out for ministry assignments. He wanted to clear his head of doubts, his father's letter, sickness, death, Eden.

"Yup," Tim said. "Best waitress who ever worked in my restaurant."

"Waitress?"

"What did you think she did?"

"A writer!"

"No, no, no." Tim shook his head. He pulled out of the seminary's parking lot and then descended the hill. "Girl couldn't write her own name. You've got the wrong de Beauvoir."

"You probably should have specified that to Theodore," Damian said, laughing. "He thinks you dated the writer—before Sartre did."

"*That* de Beauvoir. Well, you never know—she got around."

Damian laughed again, glad to have Br. Tim's company. He liked this massive monk and wanted to know him better. He asked, "And why are you leading the phone-a-thon?"

"Business background. Got an MBA from Cornell, and then I worked for IBM in California."

"What have you *not* done?" Damian asked. He was awed by Br. Tim's seemingly immense life experience. He felt happier and gazed at the darkening sky. He needed to stay calm tonight, for Dr. House and Eden, and he was determined to bravely fight off what traumatic memories this visit might trigger.

As they rolled into the valley, the setting sun glowed in cloudless streaks of pink and orange. The fading light seemed to soften the mountain peaks in the distance. Tall pines lined the road that led from the hilltop to the vineyards and farm fields below, and as the car whizzed by, the trees' normal angles and points blended into a greyish green blur. Perhaps death was not as stark as he had always imagined, a plunge into darkness followed by an eternity of either joy or misery. Perhaps death was more mysterious, a bleeding of life's colours into something unknown, barely apprehensible. What had his father believed? If only they had discussed it privately, without his mother's interference, before he had died.

At the intersection at the bottom of the hill, Br. Tim turned left and rolled into town. Damian opened his window and looked back at Mount Angelus. The seminary loomed atop the mountain that towered over the town, casting an alpine ambience on these sidewalks and roads below. He could imagine how the brick structures and robed men who lurked on the peak might strike the townspeople as strange, a constant reminder that temporal existence leads up to eternity.

Or did it?

"Willkommen to St. Hansburg, B.C.," the sign read in Germanic script at the edge of town. Along Main Street, the store fronts were white, with black shutters and carved wood decorations below their slanted roofs, giving them the appearance of cuckoo clocks. Tourists posed and snapped photographs before these Main Street shops—the butcher, German bakery, crepe house, the gift shop—and people back home would think they'd been to the Alps.

St. Hansburg was only ten blocks across, and soon the Buick emerged from town and cruised through the endless vineyards and fields of dried hops. The hops—brown coils of leaves—clung to the long rows of X-shaped frames that supported them. Roadside vendors pilled ruddy apples in slated wood buckets, and past them crops of drooping corn hung ready to harvest. The sun set behind these fields, bathing the countryside in a golden hue. When a pumpkin stand whizzed by, he had glimpsed all the materials needed for an autumn cornucopia. Dusk was like autumn: the slow dying of a day, a year. But it granted abundant beauty.

"So, Harold's son," Br. Tim said. Damian braced himself, waited for him to say more, but then realized Br. Tim wanted *him* to supply the details.

"Leukemia," Damian replied. He wanted to elaborate, how Eden had just started chemotherapy but that his chances of survival were slim, but he could not. Nevertheless, Br. Tim nodded somberly and Damian felt himself getting upset. He changed the subject and asked, "Tim, do you have to crawl through that small closet every time you get the mail?"

"No," Br. Tim replied, seemingly willing to discuss another topic. "There's a staircase that leads to the vaults from outside. It's just that Fr. Rector keeps it locked after 5:00 pm—because he's got the files down there. He thinks nobody knows about the other way."

"How did you find it?"

"Can't sleep," Br. Tim replied. "I wander around the campus at night. A couple years ago I discovered that they never lock the cathedral. I explored down there, and one night I was inspecting the vestments and came across that little door. Found it leads to the mail room where I have to go anyway. Spooky, eh?"

"That incorrupt hand doesn't help."

"That belonged to Saint Alban. He was hung, drawn, and quartered. Before he died, he blessed his executioners. They hung his body in the street, but that hand that blessed them—it stayed fresh."

"Wow." Damian imagined himself faced with such excruciating torture. Would he deny his faith, or accept a grizzly death like Saint Alban? Just then a tall sign with a glowing red H appeared ahead, and his insecurities were wrenched into the present: how was he going to face a dying boy? He suddenly felt like he had been escaping death, trying to vault over it and land in Heaven, his whole life. He had failed to grant his father's dying wish. He had fled Abe. He would probably flee Eden too. His palms moistened.

"Here we go," Br. Tim said as he pulled into the parking lot. "Right on time."

The hospital was small compared to Rocky Peak—about a tenth the size, and had only a ground floor. The small parking lot spread before a drive-through emergency entrance, which also seemed to serve as the non-emergency front doors.

He felt slightly embarrassed that he had not changed out of his cassock before leaving the seminary grounds, but, to cheer himself, he anticipated the nurses' reactions when two robed men—each over six-feet tall and two-hundred and fifty pounds—entered the hospital.

The front doors slid back automatically, releasing the antiseptic smell that seemed universal to hospitals. He breathed rapidly, but prayed to his dad for strength. The hospital's bright white lights reflected off the clean linoleum floors, and the walls were lined with harvest-themed paintings that, judging by the misshapen pumpkins and over-sized corncobs, appeared to have been drawn by elementary students.

As he and Br. Tim approached the front desk, he couldn't help hoping that visiting hours were over, that this visit would be postponed. But the young, round-faced receptionist with blond hair looked up, gave a quick start at the pair of mammoth clerics, and then smiled. Damian said, "Hi. I'm looking for Eden House."

"Are you family?" she asked. "Because visiting hours are over."

Damian sighed in relief, hating himself for doing it, but then Br. Tim spoke up: "We're chaplains."

"Oh. That's fine, then," the receptionist said. She checked her chart and then pointed to a hall with her left hand. "Room 101."

Damian nodded grimly and forced a smile.

"I'll wait in the car," Br. Tim said, and walked away. Now Damian was alone, and the antiseptic smell suddenly seemed stronger. He tried to compose himself as he walked down the hall. Was he actually a chaplain? Maybe he shouldn't even be here. He passed several young nurses, who raised eyebrows, it seemed, at his clerical attire. He found room *101*. He closed his eyes, breathed deeply, and shook his trembling hands: the same preparation, he realized, as before a heavy lift. He knocked on the door.

"Come in," Dr. House said, his voice muffled from within the room. Damian entered. The small room was dark but for a lamp glowing on a table against the far wall. It was from the one from his desk: Damian recognized the lampshade's blue and green glass. That lamp had illuminated his conversations with his professor back on the hilltop, and here it glowed between father and son.

"Hi, Dr. House," Damian whispered. Dr. House nodded and closed his book. "Please. Call me Harold."

Damian nodded.

Eden was sleeping below a silver IV bag of clear liquid. The liquid dripped from the bag into the clear tube that led to Eden's wrist. The chemotherapy pouch gave the feeling of chemical contamination, of acid or poison. He had to remind himself its purpose was to heal.

He stepped closer. Eden was slender and had a mop of his father's sandy blond hair. But patches had already started falling out. His eyelids were veiny, translucent, and his face was as pale as his dad's had been after his heart attack. Damian's eyes welled up. He cleared his throat to stifle a sob.

"Are you the priest?" Eden asked, suddenly awake and eyes wide open. Damian was startled.

"No, no—he's not," Harold said, patting his son's hand. Eden looked at his father with panicked eyes. "It's not time for *that* yet, son. I'll tell you when the priest is coming for *that*. This is my student I told you about."

Eden smiled and struggled to raise himself upright in bed. Harold stood and lifted his son's pillow as Eden bent forward. Settled against the wall, Eden smiled and said, "The Albertan."

"That's me," Damian said, discreetly wiping his eyes.

"So, you're not the priest." Eden sounded desperate for reassurance.

"No," Damian replied. He pulled a chair beside Eden's bed. "I think I'm only four years older than you, actually."

"But you'll be a priest someday?" Eden asked.

"Yeah." Damian nodded. "Someday, I suppose."

"Are you excited?" Eden asked. His voice, although clear, wavered.

"Well, I want to help people." Why did the doubts triggered by his dad's letter have to return now, when he was trying desperately to remain placid, steady, ministerial?

"Can't you help people now?" Eden asked.

"Umm," Damian said. Eden was surprisingly lively for someone so ill, and his question exacerbated the doubts Damian had tried to stifle earlier. Still, he scrambled to formulate an answer: "If I was a priest I could, well, perform the sacraments."

"Like last rites," Eden said, looking at his father.

"And Mass and confession," Damian stammered, trying to avoid the awkward feeling in the room.

"You love going to Mass?" Eden asked, looking back at Damian.

"My family went daily," Damian replied. "Now I go on the hilltop—with the seminarians."

"Do you ever go alone?" Eden asked.

"No," Damian said, smiling awkwardly. He *had* to

change the subject before his private, vocational confusion became apparent. "What do you want to be, you know, when you're older?"

Harold smiled at Eden, whose eyes lit up; this had been the right question to ask.

"I want to be an astronomer," Eden said. "At home I have a telescope and pictures of Galileo and Ptolemy and Einstein and Sagan on my bedroom walls. Above my bed I have a poster of Stephen Hawking. He's my favourite, and he's sick too, you know—just not like me."

"He knows all the constellations," Harold said. He looked out the window, then turned back to his son. "In fact, since you slept so much this afternoon, why don't we take advantage of Damian's strength and spend some time outside?"

"You can wheel my bed?" Eden asked.

"Sure," Damian said. He was happy to have found something other than sickness and his religious vocation to discuss. Calm replaced the anxiety from minutes ago: here was a chance to serve someone by using his talents. Surely his dad, gazing from above, would approve.

Moments later, he was pushing Eden's bed through the hall as Harold wheeled the IV's stand alongside. The hallways were empty, but had anyone seen their threesome—a bedridden, amateur astronomer, a disheveled academic, and a robed weightlifter—Damian was sure the sight would elicit gasps, giggles, even photographs for the local paper. The receptionist at the front desk was on the phone and did not notice them, which was a shame.

They parked Eden's bed in a handicapped parking spot near the hospital's front doors. But the light from the hospital impeded their celestial view, so they pushed Eden's bed to the far edge of the lot. There, the clear autumn sky cooperated—the stars twinkled like diamonds—but Harold had to run inside to get blankets for Eden. When he returned, he had a metal fold-out chair for Damian.

"You two get acquainted," Harold said. "I'm going back in to sleep for a while. When you're done, just come to the room and wake me up. I'll help you wheel him back in."

"Sounds good," Damian said. Harold smiled and turned back to the hospital.

Damian sat in his chair and stared up at the stars. Eden pointed up, and Damian leaned onto the bed so he could follow Eden's finger as he identified stars and constellations. The chemical odor of the chemotherapy oozed through Eden's skin; it smelled of sickness and suffering, and it enveloped them—a smell that one knew only through bitter experience.

The longer they looked, the more stars appeared. The hospital behind them seemed increasingly remote. As Damian stayed at Eden's bedside, the less he noticed the parking lot, the highway traffic, or any of the sounds from the earth's surface. He was travelling through space with his new friend, drawing lines between specks of light and then discovering the characters they made.

"And that's Orion's Belt, of course," Eden said. "He's the first I learned. Just connect the three dots and imagine a strong, courageous man wearing it."

Damian imagined, and he felt himself a better man beside this courageous boy who navigated the stars from his bed.

CHAPTER NINETEEN

MINISTRY OF PRESENCE

Anticipating release, Damian pushed open the refectory door on the last Friday evening in October and looked up at a starless sky. At first, he thought the light pouring through the glass doors behind him was hampering his view, so he stepped forward and climbed several of the stone steps that led up to the cathedral, but the sky was still dull black. The darkness, which hid the clouds that were obviously blocking the stars, disappointed Damian—for Eden's sake—and increased his sense of constraint on the seminary hill.

He had visited Eden again yesterday, and, like their first meeting two weeks ago, they bonded easily and enjoyed their time together. Last night, Harold brought Eden's telescope to his hospital room, and they mapped the sky through the window for hours while Harold slept. Eden was precocious, and their discussions included astronomy and the Okanagan Valley, lost parents and death. Talking with Eden about the pain of losing his father had proven healing for Damian, and now he felt captive on the hill. He missed the intimacy he shared with his young, sick friend.

Damian walked up the remaining stairs to get away from the refectory. Dinner had been brutal: he had sat at an empty table to eat his fish sticks alone and read the novel Harold had assigned—Joyce's *A Portrait of the Artist as a Young Man*. But then Fr. Rector joined him, complimenting the disgusting meal and reminding Damian about tonight's conference. His company was unbearable, so, after eating three of his six sticks, Damian stood, excused himself by saying he needed some fresh air (which he did), dumped his arid food in the trash, and hurried outside.

Now, strolling under the undecorated canopy, he cleaned his teeth with his tongue to get rid of the fishy flavour. Harold had mentioned that the chemotherapy parched Eden's mouth and left a metallic flavour. Eden never mentioned it, so focused was he on showing Damian the constellations of stars, the same stars that were—even on closer examination—totally, cruelly hidden tonight.

"Poor guy," Damian muttered, wondering what Eden would do on a night like this. What *could* he do, constrained to his bed with nothing to see through his telescope and his only company a lonely father? At least he had a father. But for how long would Harold have a son?

Soon Damian found himself at the dormitory door. Through the glass he could see light pouring into the hall from one of the classrooms, and he remembered the day— a month ago now—when Harold had fled the classroom and then, in his office, divulged Eden's condition. Hearing his despair, his worry over losing a loved one, Damian had felt at home on the hilltop for the first time. He had grown accustomed to seminary life since then and—glancing up at the dull, dark sky once more—sighed and opened the door to continue this seemingly endless week.

Inside the dormitory's foyer, a new, pink sheet on the Twenty-Four-Hour Board confirmed Fr. Rector's reminder from minutes ago: "Meeting in Room 101, Friday, 7:00 pm." No end time mentioned. *101* was Eden's room number at the hospital. Damian wanted so badly to visit him again tonight, but how could he? He walked down the empty hall, his shoes clacking echoes on the marble floor. The hallway was dark but for the harsh light coming through the open door of Room 101 ahead. Along the white walls hung class portraits of years past, the 1920s, and he noticed the same style of black dress shoes worn by the men back then.

This sound I'm making, he thought, *has probably been constant for decades—same hard heels, same hard floor, same reluctant pace.* While his first months at Mount Angelus had gone well—he enjoyed his courses, particularly Harold's class, and the hilltop's daily Mass and prayers satisfied his longing for spiritual progress—he wanted more. He wanted to know Eden intimately, to befriend him, to connect with him deeply as he never had with a young man before. He also wanted to work up the courage to read the rest of his father's letters to Uncle Rick during *his* seminary days, and he was convinced that if he could upon their arrival, his biography of his dad would finally be complete. But would it sound saintly?

He squinted as he entered the classroom: long, fluorescent bulbs buzzed so brightly along the ceiling that their glow was reflected in the scuffed, black-and-white checkered floor. The only relief from the glare lay along the rows of old wood tables with thin metal chairs behind them. As he sat down in the back row, he saw that the table's surface, a dull tan, had been scratched by seminarians of generations past: "Vancouver '72," and, barely visible in pin-width cursive, "Brother Lawrence OSB, 1936." The ghosts of Mount Angelus seemed alive tonight.

On the dusty, yellow-smudged blackboard at the front of the classroom, the words "Ministry of Presence" were written in baby-blue chalk. The style of these tall, loopy letters was easily recognizable: it belonged to Br. Robert Hernandez, likely tonight's speaker. The traces of boredom scratched onto the tables' surfaces would receive additions tonight.

Above the blackboard, the clock showed two-minutes to seven and seminarians began arriving, their eyes downcast, their feet slow and heavy; they had already had a long week of studies, and one more commitment—especially on a Friday—seemed excessive. His toes curled when he considered how he, and the others in the room, might otherwise spend this evening: in prayer, spiritual reading, visiting the sick. But seminary initiatives—from this meeting to the vocations' talks to the upcoming phone-a-thon—consumed their time and seemed only to justify Mount Angelus' existence—or to preserve it.

Then Theodore dropped into the chair beside him and whispered into his ear, "Stickers."

Damian leaned back to escape Theodore's fishy breath. For the first time since the accident, Theodore was not wearing sunglasses. His cheek was still scratched, but his eye was hardly swollen and only faintly bruised. But what was he talking about?

"Stickers?" Damian asked.

"Oktoberfest's tonight," Theodore said. "Beer tent opens at seven, but they'll still let people in until ten."

"No," Damian whispered. "No more drinking. Look what happened last time."

"This is different. There're girls there. And they hand you stickers at the beer tent's entrance. Then, when you're inside and everyone's drunk, girls stick them on us and we stick them on girls, *anywhere.*"

"No way!" Damian whispered fiercely. Theodore shocked him. Was he even trying to be holy?

"Suit yourself," Theodore said, shrugging. Damian turned away and crossed his arms, trying to show his disapproval. But then a memory of Veronica, soft in his hands, upset his sense of moral superiority, and he shook his head in frustration. Who was he to judge?

"When is this over?" Theodore asked.

"Who knows?" Damian replied.

"Well," Theodore said. "Old Downtown Bob has to get back to Kelowna, so he can't keep us *too* late."

Several weeks ago, Theodore had learned that Br. Robert did not reside at the seminary, but rather lived alone in an apartment in downtown Kelowna. His order, once beggars, paid for his residence. Since then, he had referred to Br. Robert as "Downtown Bob." Damian couldn't help chuckling at the name, and just then the room hushed as Br. Robert himself—his long Spanish curls flowing—entered and walked to the lectern, where he removed some sheets from a manila envelope. Then he clasped his hands behind his back and extended his beach-ball belly toward his audience. The friar smiled contently as his eyes seemed to settle above the seminarians' heads.

"Boys," Br. Robert lisped. The white lights above him illuminated his waves of brown hair like a halo. He wore a white shirt with ruffled bib and a tight purple cardigan with brown buttons that appeared ready to explode off the material. The lines of his pressed green slacks led down to shiny, black leather loafers.

"Boys," he said again, dropping his eyes to flip through

his sheets once more. Theodore mumbled "Downtown Bob," and Damian smiled, though he tried not to.

"Boys," Br. Robert said a third time. He seemed to have found his place on his page. "You can't give what you haven't got. At times during your ministry this year, you may feel like you have nothing to give— no advice, no comfort, no encouraging words. But you always have yourselves to offer, the gift of your presence. And that's what I want to discuss tonight, boys—how, for two hours every Thursday, you will offer yourselves to prisoners, addicts, students, patients, or retirees, and you will do so *willingly.*"

"Here we go," Damian muttered; Br. Robert seemed to notice, but continued speaking:

"That's why I, Downtown Bob..." Br. Robert said. He paused as Theodore's eyes widened and nervous laughter escaped several seminarians. A knowing smile on his face, the friar arched his brow at Theodore and then finished his sentence: "...want to speak to you about the ministry of presence."

Theodore turned to Damian and whispered, "He knows."

Damian bit his lip and shrugged, but then—because he did not want to lean in toward Theodore's smelly mouth—he whispered loudly: "The Feathered Friar. That's his new name."

"Mr. Kurt," Br. Robert said, staring at Damian now, "why don't you help us since you seem talkative tonight."

"All right," Damian said, frustrated at Theodore for always getting him into trouble.

"If you find yourself in a ministry situation where you don't know how to help, what should you do?" Br. Robert asked.

"Stay," Damian said, but suddenly he was bothered by the memory of sitting at his father's bedside, stuck in his chair because of his mother's command.

"Why?"

"Because I have to," he replied.

"No," Br. Robert said. "You stay because you choose to. Now, boys, imagine you are preparing for a journey..."

Br. Robert began guiding his audience on an imaginary trip, where the *journey* was a metaphor for the seminarians' weekly excursions to their pastoral ministry placements, and the *preparations* he described were meetings like this one. But Damian was distracted by the parallel sense of constraint he suffered tonight, told by the seminary he had to stay here on the hilltop, and the helplessness he had felt while watching his father die, parched.

What could he do? He couldn't just get up and leave. And besides, he had no way to get to Eden. Frustrated, he lifted the side of his cassock and pulled out Joyce's novel. He opened the book on his lap, where it was available for him to read but visible to no other eyes and found the pen he had used to mark his page.

Br. Robert swirled his arms so that his cardigan stretched even tighter around his belly. Then he spun around to write on the chalkboard and compiled a loopy list of possible ministry placements: "Hospital, Addiction Centre, Retirement Community." Damian took the opportunity to quickly scratch something onto the table: *"St. Eden of Mt. Angelus, 1985—"*

He stared at what he had written. How did he know when Eden had been born? He must have figured the year subconsciously since talking to Harold. But why had he written *"St."*?

He reeled in his chair. The room seemed to tilt as his pulse raced. If he scratched out the words now, he would surely get caught. No one would know it was his doing if he just left it, but the whole message disturbed him: did he want Eden to die? Of course not. Was he preparing himself? Perhaps. But why did he care so much?

As Br. Robert continued speaking, Damian shook his head, leaned back slightly in his chair, and read his novel. The message on the table—and his present mental state—was overwhelming, so he latched his attention onto young Daedalus. He felt better as he followed the narrative; a young man struggling to become an artist and form his aesthetic worldview. After several chapters he looked up at the clock: 9:00 p.m. Br. Robert was still going strong, so he rubbed his eyes with his fingers, letting his book shut in his lap around the empty pen.

Then Fr. Rector arrived at the door.

"Excuse me, Brother Robert," Fr. Rector said, and Damian's pulse quickened. He realized how tense he still was, how he needed to relax. Around the room, heads rose and eyes opened as Fr. Rector walked to the front of the classroom. Br. Robert—silenced—stepped away from the lectern as Fr. Rector took it.

"I'm sorry to interrupt, gentlemen," Fr. Rector announced. "As you may have heard, doctors stepped up Eden's chemotherapy this morning. Dr. House just called me to say they are doing well, but that Eden is quite nauseous. Please keep the House family in your prayers, and I'll update you with any news."

Damian clenched his fists. He had to see Eden tonight!

He would make a deal with Theodore: a visit to the beer tent in exchange for a ride to the hospital. Now Fr. Rector frowned and looked at his watch. He turned to Br. Robert and said, "Should be wrapping up here."

"Yes, Father—just have to distribute the assignments," Br. Robert replied. Fr. Rector nodded and stomped—his shoes clacking as everyone's did—out of the classroom. Br. Robert returned to the lectern and flipped to another sheet.

"All right, boys," he said. "Oscar and Chase, Saint Margaret's Parish for religious education at 7:00 p.m. Brian and Sam, Sun Valley Treatment Center at 1:00 p.m. Damian and Theodore, Mount Angel Towers at 3:00 p.m. Reynaldo and..."

Theodore turned to Damian and smiled: "Mount Angel Towers is a retirement home. It'll be a sweet—"

"I'll go to the beer tent," Damian blurted. "But then I need a ride to the hospital."

Theodore eyed him closely, obviously confused by this sudden change. Then he looked at the clock and said, "We have ten minutes. If we run, we might make it."

"Let's go," Damian replied. He and Theodore ran out of the room and raced down the hall, passing the glass door of Harold's dark office. Outside the clouds had cleared, and an orange harvest moon hung low. The van rattled as they sped down the hill. In town, they drove down First Street, but the crowds of people milling about slowed their progress. Damian saw a parking spot and said, "There! Just pull in and we'll run the rest of the way."

Theodore screeched to a halt and jerked the wheel, nearly hitting the cars before and behind them as he parked. When Damian opened his door, he heard polka music coming from no farther than a block away. He and Theodore ran toward the music and soon saw the tent. Erected in an empty lot, the beer tent was a portable structure, but it had a flat, Bavarian façade that gave it the illusion of permanence.

Girls patched with stickers were walking out of the tent. Damian silently prayed that he could escape these temptations. The girls, obviously drunk, giggled and staggered into each other as they passed, and he got a close look at the stickers, which were of cornucopias full of vegetables. Theodore ran faster, and Damian followed. They charged up to the ticket booth, where a pimple-faced employee shook his head and said, "Sorry. We stopped letting people in about a minute ago."

Damian sighed in relief: his soul was safe tonight. His prayer had worked! But Theodore appeared distraught.

"Please," Theodore said, pleading with the man in the booth. "Just the two of us."

"Nothing I can do, pal," the young attendant said and slid shut the opening through which he passed people their tickets.

"I can't believe this," Theodore said, shaking his head and turning to Damian. "Downtown Bob screwed us!"

"Well," Damian replied, trying to hide his gratitude for having avoided the beer tent.

"Come on," Theodore said. "Let's just go back."

Theodore turned to walk back to the van, his shoulders slouched, his head hung forward. Damian felt sorry for him, but he needed to press on and get to Eden.

"Just one more stop," Damian said, his voice friendly but firm.

"The hospital?" Theodore said, turning around.

"Still?"

"That was our deal." And then Damian caught another glimpse of the low, flat-faced harvest moon. He tilted his head back: sure enough, the stars were twinkling. "Come on. This'll cheer you up. I promise."

"There," Damian said ten minutes later as Orion's Belt came into focus. "You try."

Theodore positioned himself behind the telescope, which was pointed at Eden's hospital window, as Damian sat on his young friend's bed. He now found the chemotherapy smell comforting because it meant he was with Eden—the two cocooned in each other's company; still, though, he shuddered to think that the silvery bag had not stopped dripping into Eden's body for weeks now. The moonlight traveled through the glass window and illuminated the suspended chemical pouch, making it glow in the dark room.

"I see three stars in a row," Theodore said, his left eye squinting. "But no belt."

"Use your imagination," Eden said. "And connect the dots."

"What should I imagine below the belt?" Theodore asked.

"Theodore," Damian warned.

"Sorry," Theodore said. "I guess my mind's still set on stickers in the beer tent."

Eden, curious, tilted his head at Damian, who said, "He's kidding. We saw the Oktoberfest tent on the way here."

"Gave us the idea to stop and perform some *hands-on* ministry," Theodore remarked as he swivelled the telescope and surveyed the night sky.

"Theodore!" Damian warned again.

"What's this group called?" Theodore asked. "It's like a slanted cube with one bright star poking out the bottom."

"Let me see," Eden said. Theodore moved the telescope toward the bed as Damian stood, grasped Eden under his arms, and lifted him to the eye piece.

"You're not too nauseous?" Damian asked. Eden shook his head. His ribs felt like they might snap in his hands, so he relaxed his grip as Eden closed his right eye and peered into space.

Almost immediately Eden said, "Cassiopeia. I thought that's what you saw. She's a princess with her skirts up over her head."

Damian, anticipating a crass remark, shook his head at Theodore, who kept silent.

"I told you he's smart," Damian said. But he worried: holding Eden's emaciated body was effortless.

"Do you think we could see the beer tent if we pointed that thing toward town?" Theodore asked.

Damian shook his head again, but Eden—his eye stuck to the telescope—replied, "Probably. Let's try."

Damian gently swung Eden into the middle of the room, his thin body horizontal; careful not to let Eden tug on his IV tubes, Damian watched him lower the telescope, so it was parallel to the ground and pointed back at town.

"I can't see past the houses," Eden reported.

"Thank God," Damian said. He arched his brows playfully at Theodore, who finally smiled.

CHAPTER TWENTY
BECKONED FROM ABOVE

On the second Thursday in December, Damian sat before an elderly couple in their suite in Mount Angelus Towers. The furniture in the living room was pink, as was the thick plush carpet. Framed paintings of Rocky Mountain landscapes graced most walls, and above the fireplace hung portraits of the couple's children, grandchildren, and great grandchildren. The apartment smelled of antiseptic and body odor, which was better than the halls' stench of urine and gravy.

"Another cup of tea?" Grace asked Damian for the second time in five minutes. She'd been a nurse for thirty years, back when they wore crisp white uniforms and were supervised by nuns. Damian enjoyed speaking with her about Eden's condition—something he was regularly apprised of by his almost daily visits to the hospital. These visits were unknown to Fr. Rector, who thought Damian only saw Eden on Thursday nights, after his ministry at Mt. Angelus Towers. But Damian knew Eden needed him, as *he* certainly needed Eden, and since he always got his schoolwork done throughout the week and faithfully ministered to the seniors, as he was doing today, he felt little guilt for his actions.

When he arrived every Thursday, Grace would ask about Eden and they would discuss it while Theodore and Frank—Grace's husband—would talk about cars and engine repair. Frank was a retired mechanic, but he constantly begged Theodore to look under the hood of his van. He was senile and would forget he had asked before. Or he was just determined to come out of retirement, and Theodore's van was one of the few opportunities he had to do so: the residents at Mount Angelus did not typically have vehicles. But today Theodore had agreed—his van's fan belt was squealing—and Theodore and Frank were braving the snowy parking lot, leaving Damian and Grace to chat.

"No thanks," Damian replied. "But it's just so awful to see him skin and bones."

"I know dear," Grace replied. "But with a young man in chemotherapy, it's what you'd expect."

"He's sleeping all the time. But when I come—"

"Well," Grace said, "then I bet he just perks right up. It must be so nice for him to have you by his side when he needs to be so brave."

Damian nodded, smiled, and blushed. He knew Grace was right. And so how could he deny Eden, who was suffering so badly, a daily bedside comfort? It would be wrong and he would regret it, just as he regretted failing to fetch his father that last cup of water.

Grace tilted her head as she sipped her tea and smiled at Damian. Her eyes disappeared in wrinkles. She was short, plump, and had a pinched face. She wore a pink nightgown beneath a cream cardigan. She didn't smoke, but she still reminded Damian of Grandma Schiller, whom he would see in less than a week for Christmas holidays.

Just then Theodore burst into the room, panting.

"We gotta go!" Theodore said.

"Now?" Damian asked, worried that Eden's condition had worsened and Harold had notified the nursing home.

"Now," Theodore said. "Downtown Bo—Brother Robert called us for an urgent meeting on the hilltop. Everyone's quitting ministry early today, or at least that's what he told the nurse at reception."

"Ok," Damian said, relieved that the emergency didn't seem to relate to the House family. He turned to Grace, "Sorry. Better go."

"You go," Grace said. She was calm, her years of nursing having left her accustomed to emergencies, Damian guessed.

Frank was just closing Theodore's hood when they reached the van.

"Should be all good to go," Frank said.

"Thanks," Theodore replied. "What do I owe you?"

"My hands," Frank said, showing his palms to Theodore, "are covered in oil. I say we're square."

Theodore raced through town, his van no longer squealing, and then navigated up the icy hill. He parked in one of the few stalls remaining in the seminary's crowded lot. Damian saw crowds walking into Anselm Hall and followed them. Inside, seminarians, priests, and professors were congregating in Br. Robert's usual classroom.

Damian and Theodore sat apart, lucky to find chairs in the crowded classroom. Br. Robert, pressed and polished, stood at the lectern with Fr. Rector behind him. Damian quickly surveyed the room; everyone seemed nervous.

"Boys," Br. Robert said. "Thank you for coming on such short notice. Thank you for leaving your ministry placements early, and I want you to know I will make calls to apologize for your absences.

"If you've been watching the news lately, you've seen

the scandals involving clergymen. Well, now the news is close to home. Three religious brothers in our diocese, at De Sales High School, have been charged with sexual abuse. The accusers are their students, and they've filed suit against the diocese."

Gasps and whispers traveled around the room. Appearing frustrated, Fr. Rector shoved Br. Robert out of the way as he took the lectern and said, "If successful, these suits will bankrupt this diocese. According to Bishop Spur, the accusers may want millions each and we can't afford that. But I want you all to know that we will fight this!

"Also, Bishop Spur has asked that no priests or seminarians minister to minors for the foreseeable future. Those of you at schools or anywhere with access to youth will be reassigned. We will approach this obstacle with confidence," Fr. Rector said loudly, his knuckles bulged as his large hands gripped the lectern. "Our Lady of Priests..."

"Pray for us," the room responded. Seminarians shook their heads and got up to leave. Others stayed to chat, murmuring excitedly. But Damian stood and approached the Rector.

"Father Rector," he said. "Is Doctor House with Eden?"

"Oh, Damian," the Rector said. "I heard from Harold this morning—very bad news."

"What?"

"Eden took a turn for the worst."

"*What?*"

"He fell into a coma early this morning. I was going to announce it at evening prayer, but then..." The Rector waved his hand at the still-crowded classroom.

"I'm going," Damian said, more to himself than to his

superior. He had already turned away when the Rector spoke sternly:

"Not happening, Mr. Kurt—Eden's underage."

"You can't be serious," Damian said, spinning around to face the Rector.

"You're not going," the Rector said. He glared down from the lectern with an arched eyebrow, and then collected his papers and walked away. Damian walked back to Theodore, who was sitting by a window.

"I'm going to see Eden," Damian announced. "Give me the keys to the van."

"But you can't drive," Theodore replied. "And if anyone finds out . . ."

"I'll talk to you later," Damian said fiercely. Theodore handed him the keys, and Damian left the room. Looking up and down the hall, he did not see Fr. Rector, so he casually jogged to the seminary's front doors and then burst outside.

The cool December air refreshed him as he raced across the parking lot. He unlocked the van and jumped inside. He turned the keys in the ignition, as he had seen Theodore do, but it groaned loudly as he engaged the starter motor too long. He jumped at the jarring sound, let go of the keys, but then, thankfully, the engine ran normally. He pulled the gear to reverse and the van shot back, so he stomped on the brake and screeched to a halt. Easing off the brake, he continued backing up gently, and then crossed himself before shifting into drive.

As the van rolled out of the parking lot, he looked up momentarily at a small group standing on the sidewalk: Fr. Rector stared into him as he drove past. Damian snapped his gaze back to the road, but he could still feel his superior's glare even as he descended the hill, turned onto the highway, and increased his speed along the country roads that led to Eden.

The hospital lot was nearly empty, so Damian pulled into a parking stall near the entrance. His front tires hit the concrete block, so he backed up and saw that he was in a handicapped spot. Unwilling to waste another moment, he pulled forward, shoved the gearstick into park, and jumped out of the van. He had the presence of mind to pull off his cassock and leave it on the driver's seat.

He ran past the receptionist, who called something he didn't hear. He saw Room 101, twisted the door handle, and entered without knocking. The room was dark but for the lamp glowing on the table against the far wall. Harold sat in a straight-backed wooden chair, but he slumped forward with his elbows on his knees and his hair hung in his face. He looked up, nodded at Damian, and then dropped his gaze back to the floor and closed his eyes.

Eden lay motionless. Damian had to step forward, letting the door close behind him, in order to detect Eden's breathing.

Convinced that his young friend was alive, a strange calm came over him. Through the shadows he saw a chair against the left-side wall. He walked to it, picked it up, and placed it beside Harold. Without speaking, he squeezed Harold's shoulder and then sat down to wait.

He kept vigil with his friend in despair. As darkness passed and dawn arose, Eden's condition was stable, Damian's presence constant. He realized that this might be the end. And if it was, if this was when his young friend would be sucked away into his diseased body, Damian would be right here to watch the flame of a young life withdraw, disappear, and then be thrown back up into the starry night sky.

CHAPTER TWENTY-ONE
WORKS WITHOUT FAITH

"Father Rector is displeased," Br. Robert said. He had rolled his desk chair to the centre of his office, and now he sat with his legs crossed, bobbing one black leather loafer inches from Damian's knee. Br. Robert tilted his head and the sunlight shining through the windows illuminated his Spanish curls.

"I had no choice," said Damian, shifting in the metal fold-out chair Br. Robert had had waiting for him. "Harold's my friend. So is Eden."

"But he's underage," said Br. Robert. The friar frowned and then rested his note pad on his lap. Sighing, he crossed his arms and began chewing on the end of his shiny black fountain pen. He stared at the red carpet, apparently gathering his thoughts before continuing.

Damian had never confided in anyone but Harold and his mother, and he wasn't about to help Downtown Bob now. Last Wednesday, when he had returned from his all-night vigil at the hospital, he had found an envelope beneath his door. At first, he had wondered if it was from Uncle Rick.

But when he read his name on the front, one look at the tall, loopy letters had identified who had left it. In his letter, Br. Robert had ordered Damian—by the Rector's authority—to meet for spiritual direction every Monday at 1:00 p.m. for the rest of the year. Now he sat in the friar's hilltop office, inhaling musk cologne and trying not to look at the miniature statue of David on the desk.

"Why are you here?" Br. Robert finally asked, raising his eyes from the carpet.

"Your letter said the Rector demanded I be he—"

"No, no, no," Br. Robert said, shaking his head. He sighed again and removed his pen from his mouth. "Why are you in the seminary—why are you studying for the priesthood?"

Now Damian sighed. This question had plagued him after Uncle Rick's letters had arrived, but lately the busyness of seminary life had kept his doubts at bay. He did not want to appear uncertain, however, so he mumbled, "I feel called."

"You'll have to do better than that, Damian." Br. Robert sat upright, grasped his notepad, and lowered pen tip to page. "Father Rector claims you have a great vocation story—an ideal background, and that's why the seminary's basically advertising with it. But then you shocked us by blatantly disobeying an order from the bishop so you could visit your friend."

"Who's dying."

"What part of obedience do you not understand? It's a promise you'll make at ordination, along with simplicity of life and chastity." Br. Robert rolled the "s" in chastity, and the thick gold rope around his wrist bounced against the page as he wrote. Br. Robert annoyed him, and he couldn't help comparing the fancy friar to his plain, hardworking father. "Do you pray, Damian?"

"You see me at morning and evening prayer," Damian replied. Br. Robert slapped his pen against the page.

"You know very well that I do not," Br. Robert said, his brown eyes glaring. "My life in pastoral ministries requires that I live in the city and commute to my office here when I am needed. What prayer commitments you keep, Mr. Kurt, are—as you know—unknown to me."

"I pray the liturgy of the hours with the community," Damian said. "It's the prayer required of Catholic clergy."

"See, this is the defiant attitude that concerns the Rector." Br. Robert picked up his pen again and wrote furiously. Damian grew frightened. "I want you to keep a journal of spiritual progress with a list of prayer commitments. You'll write what prayers you do—on your own, not just communally. Believe me, I've lived as a religious for twenty years now, and you need to develop a *personal* prayer life. Second, I want you to journal about your vocational discernment—what you're feeling and why you believe God is calling you. Be sincere, Damian, and then hand your reflections in to me."

"Why?"

"So, Mr. Kurt, I can provide Father Rector with a favourable report regarding your being here at all. Believe me, with the scandals plaguing the church right now, there will be zero tolerance." (Br. Robert's "c" in "tolerance" reminded Damian of skating on the pond.)

"Zero tolerance for what?" Damian asked.

"Boys who shouldn't be here," Br. Robert replied, drawing out the first word.

"I'll have something for you next week," Damian said. He got up to leave.

"Same time, same place," Br. Robert hissed. Damian nodded, but he wondered: while writing this newly assigned journal entry, would he mention his father's letter to Uncle Rick? Would he describe the doubts burgeoning within him? He certainly couldn't reveal his daily visits to Eden. His seminary life, it seemed, was increasingly buried in secrecy. And he knew what his father would have thought of that.

Beeps instead of bells woke Damian for the first time in four months. He waved his hand around his alarm clock—which sounded louder than he remembered—and finally hit the button to silence the grating beeps. He forced his eyes open, and glowing red digits showed 4:15 a.m. The December morning was black as night. He sat up, blinking and rubbing his eyes. As he stood the bed springs squeaked, and he nearly expected to hear James mumble in his sleep. But when he flicked on his light, he saw his empty cot and clean, orderly seminary cell.

He blinked back fatigue as he pulled on his trousers, slipped into his still-laced shoes, and threw his cassock over his head. He was walking down the hall when he remembered his rosary, breviary, and journal and turned back to get them.

Outside showed a starry sky and the fresh winter air blew through his cassock. His nipples hardened and he shivered, realizing he had forgotten his undershirt on his chair upstairs. He would have run back, but Eucharistic adoration—organized by the monks in the crypt chapel an hour before Morning Prayer—was about to begin.

As he hurried to the crypt, a low hum grew into recognizable Latin words being chanted by two male voices in perfect unison: ... *uni trinoque domino sit sempiterna gloria, qui vitam sine termino nobis donet in patria...*

He descended the stairs and plunged into the thick aroma of incense. He opened the chapel door as the two monks kneeling on either side of the altar chanted the final word slowly: *Ah—men*. The first syllable rose from their mouths, before the second began with a hum and then descended to earth.

A censer hung from a chain that hooked to the top of a thin brass stand. The stand stood beside the altar, which was enveloped in the ribbons of silver smoke that billowed from the cone-shaped vessel. He stepped past rows of empty chairs and sat to the left of the centre aisle. Behind the pair of monks, he was alone in the chapel. He deposited his journal, breviary, and beads on the chair beside him and knelt. He closed his eyes to pray and immediately began falling asleep. He looked up: both monks were kneeling with their chins on their chests, so the points of their black hoods stuck straight up. On the altar, a gold monstrance glowed in the candlelight. In the centre of the monstrance was a small round window with a white host behind it. Emanating from around the host were wavy gold rays that reminded him of the sun that would not rise for another hour.

His knees ached, just as they had when his family prayed the rosary on their grandmother's living room floor, so he sat and opened his journal on his lap. He grabbed the pen he kept hooked over the front cover, and when he clicked it, one of the monks snorted and raised his head momentarily. He knew he could not keep awake either, not unless he stimulated his mind by working on Br. Robert's journal assignment. Inhaling deeply, he shuddered back sleep, opened his eyes wide, and wrote:

December 2, 1999
Brother Robert:
This is my first journal entry for you. I got up early this morning for some personal prayer and now I am sitting in the crypt chapel, reflecting.

Being up this early reminds me of all the mornings my mom used to wake us kids up to go to Mass. I used to dread the Canadian winters, but before we left for church each morning, she would sit us down on the living room sofa and read the life of that day's saint. I loved those stories and thought about them all day after hearing her read them.

My mom never knew, but I had my own copy of Butler's Lives downstairs, under my bed. It was the older version—I had found it in my grandmother's basement— and I would read the stories in stiff, antiquated language at night on my own. The older version was better, it had more gruesome details, martyrs eaten by lions, heads chopped off, and crazy miracles with corpses talking and stuff.

I miss those stories because now, well, I only feel that kind of passion and joy when I'm with Eden, or when I read the books for Harold's class.

I came to the seminary to live passionately, but

He stopped. The censer's spicy smoke had drifted back to where he sat. He blinked, and when he shut his eyes, he kept them closed. His thoughts drifted to the story of a robed bishop whose name he could not recall. The bishop's robes billowed in warm puffs of wind that carried the smell of a foreign spice. The bishop may have been on a boat, gently rocking in the sea. . .

He woke to the sound of his fellow seminarians intoning the opening hymn upstairs. Somehow, he had slept even through the bells. Smoke lingered in the grey chapel. The candles were out but sunlight came through the glass door at the back. The two monks were gone, as was the monstrance. His journal was open on his lap; his pen lightly cradled in his right hand.

He ran up the crypt's stairs and burst into the cathedral just as the hymn ended. His shoes tapped against the marble floor and echoed through the massive cathedral. He hurried his step, but before he could shuffle into the pew behind Br. Tim, the Rector turned back at the noise. Their eyes locked, just as they had the moment before Damian rolled the van out of the parking lot to visit Eden.

He dropped into a genuflection to break their gaze and try to redeem himself, but when he arose the Rector was still staring. He stepped into the pew and found himself behind Br. Tim's wall of a back. He opened his breviary, found the right passage, and joined his side of the church in praying aloud:

It is better to take refuge in the Lord than to trust in men: it is better to take refuge in the Lord than to trust in princes.

He prayed for deliverance from Fr. Rector's wrath, but at the moment he was grateful for the refuge found behind his corpulent friend.

The next day he woke to the bells, with the fifth and final toll swelling through the dawn before silence settled again on the hilltop. When he sat up, making his bed creak, his alarm clock showed 5:01 a.m. in red digits that appeared gentler in the grey morning light. He dressed and gathered his breviary, journal, and rosary. Outside he saw the beginning of a cloudless day, and he felt the advantage of his undershirt against the brisk air.

The cathedral's white walls were bright from the sunlight shining through the high rows of windows. He felt refreshed in the cathedral's clean air, and the crisp clacking of his shoes against the marble floor reinforced his sense of being awake and alert.

He saw the Rector in the front row and wished he would turn around to see his punctual arrival. He did not, so he genuflected and then sat beside Br. Tim. He kept his back straight against the hard pew and looked ahead as the final few seminarians straggled in. Then the Rector stood and intoned the opening hymn. Damian sang lustily and prayed loudly throughout the morning office.

When the final hymn ended, he pulled his rosary from his pocket and dropped to his knees. The Rector would soon turn to exit the church, and he would see him in silent prayer.

"Damian," Tim whispered, standing at his side.

"Sorry," Damian whispered back. He stood and stepped into the aisle to let Br. Tim pass. Br. Tim bent his knees in a short genuflection—preventing a rumble through the cathedral by touching his knee to the floor—and Damian tried to squeeze past him to resume his pious posture in the pew. But Tim whispered:

"Phone-a-thon meeting today. Crypt Chapel. Four o'clock. Rector will be there, so…"

"Got it," Damian replied. He knelt and perched his beaded hands atop the pew in front of him. He squinted with his right eye, hoping to catch an approving glance from Fr. Rector, but the priest was nowhere to be seen. He glanced back and saw the Rector chatting with Tim in the cathedral's foyer. He must have walked past just as he had been talking to Tim.

Sighing, he closed his eyes again, crossed himself with the rosary beads, and began praying the Joyful Mysteries. He pictured Mary kneeling alone in a room at the temple, praying to do God's will. Her face was white and beautiful, and her eyes were closed so she did not see the small light hovering in a corner of her room. The light grew into an angel, floating with thick-feathered wings and outstretched arms. Mary opened her eyes and gasped—

"Damian." Br. Tim pounded his finger into Damian's shoulder. "Rector wants you."

Damian opened his eyes and gasped. He stood and spoke before he even knew what he was doing: "All right."

He followed Tim back to the foyer, feeling his friend's heavy steps through the marble floor. He stared at Tim's blue socks in black sandals until the foyer door opened. Fr. Rector's face was steady and serious.

"Damian, I need you to write a spiel for Tim," the Rector said. "Something generic for the phone-a-thon—he'll give you the details."

"Yes, Father," he said. He nodded at the priest and then nodded at Tim.

"Your morning's free, what with Harold away," the Rector continued. "I want you to have it written by noon."

"Sure," Damian said, but his heart sunk at the mention of Harold's name.

"And Damian," Fr. Rector said, arching his eyebrows.

"Yes, Father?"

"Don't chat in the church. Ask the person to come back to the foyer—like I just had Tim ask you."

"Yes, Father," Damian said. He returned his gaze to the floor and sighed when the priest walked away.

Having endured what Brother Chef called "seafood salad," Damian left the cafeteria with the fishy flavour of lunch lingering in his mouth. He blew into his hand to determine if he needed to brush his teeth and was surprised to *see* his breath (which needed freshening). Even with his undershirt, the wind whipped through his cassock and he reminded himself to pull his coat out of his closet when he got upstairs. Shivering, he folded his arms around his chest and ran into Aquinas Hall.

The air was warm inside, and he quickly closed the door behind him. He was happy to see that nobody was around. He had purposefully eaten quickly and then hastily returned to the dorm building so he could run upstairs and finish praying his rosary without distraction. Other seminarians seemed to still be eating their miserable lunches, so he turned to quickly scan the Twenty-Four-Hour Board.

And his heart sank: a posting from Harold with today's date. A quick read, however, informed him that Eden was stable, but that the second last essay for Spiritual Autobiography was due tomorrow! Having spent the entire morning writing the phone-a-thon spiel with Tim, he had hoped for a quiet, prayerful afternoon.

He shook his head as he walked up the stairs, already piecing together his favourite passages from Thoreau and Saint Augustine and extracting some unifying theme that Harold had asked for on the posting.

He was warm by the time he got to his room, and the sudden shift in temperature—along with the heavy lunch—made him feel sluggish. He locked his door, went to his sink, splashed cold water on his face, and looked at himself in the mirror: *one more essay, one more week before Christmas holidays. Lord help me...*

He channelled his frustration into his writing, and two and a half hours went by fairly quickly. He wrote about qualities shared by Augustine and Thoreau, one a Father of the Church, the other a secular saint. Damian argued that both men, however, lived with unyielding passion that ultimately led to joy. He titled his essay "One Goal, Two Answers," and, after rereading his work, decided his long-hand copy was legible and did not need to be typed.

He reached into his drawer and found a single paperclip, which he took as a sign of having properly completed his semester's work. His pages stacked and clipped on the center of his desk, he stood, pushed in his chair, pulled his beads from his pocket, and knelt. He closed his eyes, inhaled through his nose and— with his exhalation—expelled academic assignments and seminary initiatives from his mind.

But then he recalled his father's letters tucked into his journal, and the daring plan for his final essay came to mind. Compared to the essay he'd just written, which was adequate for the class, his last work could instead describe his father's life—an un-canonized saint, a man perhaps doubtful of religious life, but one who served his family and exemplified goodness.

This revised biography of his father, this spiritual autobiography of the man he admired most, would be updated and improved by the letters to Uncle Rick. He just needed to hope they would arrive soon and be of an entirely different tone. This plan was risky, required faith, but the rewards it promised were worth it: he would pray that it worked, and knelt on the floor of his cell with his rosary clenched tight in his hand.

The Second Joyful Mystery was a favourite of his because it involved a sign, and one more forceful than finding a final paperclip at the semester's end: he imagined Mary, pregnant, riding a donkey to her cousin's home. When she arrived and Saint Joseph helped her dismount, Elizabeth approached and John the Baptist leapt in her womb.

"Damian!" Theodore yelled and knocked loudly, making Damian start and stumble.

He called, "Yeah?"

"We're late!" Theodore replied through the door.

"For what?"

"Ministry! Come on! Why is your door locked?"

He tried to stand but stepped on his cassock and tripped. His left butt cheek slammed against the floor, and his hip snapped. The sound was loud—a clean, sharp break. He was shocked. He held his breath.

"What's going on in there?" Theodore yelled.

"Help!" Damian yelled back. Theodore rattled the doorknob. Damian writhed in pain. Lying on the floor, he shifted his weight away from the break and felt the bone sag, then the prickly end of his femur shot pain into his torso, which laid him flat on his back. He screamed, "Go get help!"

"I'll get a key!" Theodore said. And Damian could hear him run off down the hall. He continued to lay in agony, unable to get up. While he waited, through his tears and the stabbing pain, he thought: *Why am I being punished like this? All I was trying to do was pray in the seminary. A sin, it seems.*

Damian, suffering on the floor, waited for what felt

like an eternity for Theodore to return with a key.

That night, Theodore pushed Damian in a wheelchair down the main floor of Aquinas Hall. Hours earlier, Theodore and Br. Tim had finally arrived upstairs with a spare key. After unlocking the door, they helped Damian up, got him down the stairs and into the van, and then driven him to the emergency room. There X-rays had shown that Damian had suffered a fracture in his hip—likely related to stress he'd placed on it from weightlifting. Luckily, because of where the fracture had occurred, he would not need surgery. Just rest. The doctor gave him painkillers and a wheelchair and released him. But he would not be going home for Christmas. The injury made travel too difficult.

Now, rolling down the smooth, linoleum floor, Damian felt no pain, and in fact felt pleasantly dozy from the medication. He asked Theodore to stop in front of Harold's office, where he slid a note under the door. In it, he described his plans for writing about his father as the topic for his final assignment. He felt confident that Harold would agree to this idea.

"Okay," Damian said to Theodore, "now to the Bishop's Suite!"

"Sounds good," Theodore replied, and pushed him off down the hall. After Damian had returned from the hospital in a wheelchair earlier today, the Rector granted him permission to temporarily stay in the main-floor suite normally reserved for visiting bishops—so that Damian could avoid the stairs during his convalescence.

And now Theodore pushed Damian into that room,

which overlooked the Okanagan Valley.

"Thanks," Damian said. "I'll see ya tomorrow."

"For the Phone-a –Thon" Theodore replied.

"Right."

But Damian didn't want to think about the Phone-a-Thon now that he was through with this horrible day. Theodore left, and Damian wheeled over to the bed, struggled from his wheelchair, and collapsed onto the mattress. The springs squeaked, and his rosary beads fell from his pocket.

He knew that if he waited too long, he would just fall asleep, so he decided to finish his rosary now. He had, earlier in the day, already managed to get to the Third Joyful Mystery, The Nativity. As he prayed the words of the Hail Mary, he imagined Mary and Joseph kneeling beside the manger. Baby Jesus was asleep, and after their exhausting search for a place in Bethlehem, the family was happy in their stable.

Happy in their stable, he repeated silently, and he prayed that some messenger would come give him a mission as the angel had to Mary in the temple. Her mission, a noble, saintly journey that had led to the stable in Bethlehem, was announced by a star. After Damian finished his rosary, he crossed himself with the beads, climbed on his bed, and gazed out at the stars.

"Eden," he whispered, and he prayed that his mission, whatever it was, would take him back to Eden.

CHAPTER TWENTY-TWO
BROTHERS BEGGAR

The next day, Damian pulled up his wheelchair to the wide oak desk in the Bishop's Suite. The desk faced the window and overlooked the rolling farm fields below. The Rector, in an unusually generous allowance, had granted him permission to make his calls for the Phone-a-Thon from his new, plush room.

And now, as Damian gazed out the window, he confirmed what he guessed yesterday when the Rector told him what direction this room faced: he could see, far off in the distance, the small, country hospital where Eden lay. The sight brought Eden's suffering to mind. Damian reached into his pocket and grab another painkiller—to dull the mental pain.

While he waited for the medication to take effect, to blur his consciousness pleasantly as it had for the past twelve hours, he stared at the small building in the distance that imprisoned Eden, and he wondered: from his bed, did Eden gaze longingly at the window in his room, wishing he was strong enough to peer through his telescope and pan the stars?

Already his mind became dozy. Could Eden turn toward his window and see the hilltop seminary? Could he see this window, and Damian's sad face, gazing down from it? But this was silly because there was no way Eden could know which window—which room—was his. Did Eden even know why Damian couldn't be with him? Maybe

Harold had explained that clergymen had been abusing boys Eden's age, and that now the ministry those corrupt priests should have been doing was off limits to Damian.

The December wind began to whip snowflakes down past the window and off, over the pine-crowded slopes of Mt. Angelus that led to the farm fields below. Damian moved the black, long-coiled, dial telephone to the centre of the desk. Maybe he could race through ten or fifteen donors, rattle off the script he and Br. Tim had composed, and then, every hour or so, call the hospital to check in on Eden—be his guardian angel, his patron saint contacting him from above. His voice would follow the fast-moving flakes as they raced down the hill toward the hospital. Harold wouldn't mind. Fr. Rector would never know. Likely no one was about to knock on his door, except maybe Br. Tim, and he would be happy to find Damian putting the Phone-a-Thon to actual ministerial use.

The bell tolled. 9:00 a.m. The solemn tolls seemed to roll off more briskly in the white light that poured through the window, and Damian felt the urge to stand and begin his usual morning routine: prayer, Mass, class with Harold. All that was temporarily gone.

So, sighing, he resigned himself to making calls for the day, to casting out his net for the seminary's finances and reeling in a much-needed money haul.

Who was first on his list of names? Mrs. Stella Fishbean. A friendly name. He lifted the script to review it once for practice, but why? He had written it, hadn't he? He dialed Mrs. Fishbean.

"Hello," a feeble female voice said. Had he woken her, or was she just old? He realized the early hour would have him speaking to retirees.

"Hello, am I speaking to Mrs. Fishbean?"

"Yes."

"Mrs. Fishbean, can you imagine a world without priests?"

"Without what?"

"Without priests." (The wind howled past the window, so he spoke louder.) "A world without any priests to say Mass, hear confessions, visit the sick, and"— (here he tried to personalize his plea)— "comfort the elderly."

"Without priests?"

"That's right, Mrs. Fishbean—not one left."

"Are they persecuted?"

"Worse, ma'am. They're frustrated young men in law offices, classrooms, zoos, and what have you, all because seminaries had to close from lack of funds."

"Zoos?"

"What I'm saying is that without donations from good people like you, Mrs. Fishbean, young men like me will no longer be able to follow God's call."

"You're a seminarian?"

"Yes, ma'am—first year at Mount Angelus Seminary."

"Mount Angelus!" Stella said, as though recognizing the name. "Do you know Theodore?"

Theodore? What was this? "Yes, Mrs. Fishbean— Theodore's a close friend."

"He's such a holy young man—from a big Catholic family and wanted to be a *saint* all his life!"

"Yes, ma'am," Damian said, proud to hear his vocation story's effect, proud too—in a way—to hear *his* qualities praised by another name. But *Theodore's?* "Excellent young man. Now, can you imagine if Mt. Angelus closed because it couldn't afford to form men like Theodore?"

"No."

"Neither can I. I can—"

"Theodore prays for hours, on his *knees*."

"Right," he replied, and could not help smiling because Stella was inventing now: Damian had not put that in his vocation story. "I can take your credit card number or a cheque, Mrs. Fishbean. If you donate one hundred dollars or more, your name goes on our list and seminarians—*like Theodore*—pray for you at our daily Mass."

"Two hundred. Cheque."

"Thank you, Mrs. Fishbean. I'm writing down your pledge and we'll send a card reminding you of our prayers." Damian checked her name and wrote two hundred dollars with an exclamation mark beside it.

"Thank you, Theodore."

"Damian."

"What?"

"You're welcome, ma'am." He hung up the phone. *Two-hundred dollars!* And *she* had thanked *him. At this rate, I'm going to—whoa!* He jumped at the wind howling outside. He needed to continue, maybe he could hear himself praised under the guise of even more names. He would list them beside the tally of his earnings. The image of all those dollar amounts written down, the sound of all those names that actually described *him,* was exciting.

Who was next on his donor list? Stanley King. He dialed the number. Someone picked up, but Damian—hearing the wind wail again—spoke first: "Mr. King?"

"Yes?" (Another old voice.)

"Can you imagine a world without Eden?"

"What?"

"A world without *end.*"

"Who *is* this?"

"A world without—" Damian said, desperate to correct himself, but he could not continue.

"Is this a joke?" Stanley sounded cross. Damian hung up, numb. Outside, the wind wailed: it sounded like a voice saying, *choose!* What had he just said on the phone? *World without Eden, world without end?* Why had he said that? His pulse raced—a splashing sound in his ears. He took another painkiller, and he suddenly reminded himself of Fr. Dennis back in Calgary—inebriated in the morning. Was this kind of indulgent lifestyle what he was actually promoting by soliciting donations for the seminary?

He closed his eyes and imagined the world under a deep, white blanket of snow. Silent. Still. Cold. And when it melted, so did every priest's collar, every vestment, breviary, cape, and cassock. All the portraits that hung around him in this room—portraits of visiting bishops who had stayed here, who seemed to collectively glare down at him, commanding him to perpetuate an institution of deception and control—all these portraits on the walls would melt into puddles that would wash away the smell of incense so that the seminaries, turned into a museum, would just smell old, never sacred. All that would remain would be the stories of valiant priests, corrupt priests, saints, sinners—stories worth remembering, like *his*.

The wind wailed, but he forced himself to focus, to not look back at the window: *If parishioners still attended priest-less churches, as mom certainly would, and still recited prayers to themselves at home, like Grandma Kurt, then they could preach to each other, to themselves, and the Church's stories would live after the clergy had melted. It's easy to imagine. Too easy.* Shame stopped these thoughts. Had he lost his faith? Suddenly he felt like he was falling. He scrambled mentally for purchase—something to rest upon, something permanent, eternal—something he could not imagine the world without. *Eden,* he thought, *it's you I can't imagine losing.* Without thinking about what he was doing, he dialed the hospital's front desk.

"Hello?" he said just as someone lifted the phone at the other end.

"Hello," the nurse who worked reception—he recognized her voice now—said. "Is this an emergency?"

"No, no. This, this—" he said, not wanting to reveal himself, to show how desperate he was. He dispelled the fantasy ice age, the anti-clerical thaw: his feet—in his mind—touched earth. But what to say? He could think of nothing, so he opened his mouth and, again without thinking, said, "Can *you* imagine a world without priests?"

"Oh—is this Mount Angelus?" "Yes," Damian said, hearing the relief in her voice and feeling relieved himself: the seminary's finances and the clergy's future were not, he realized, pressing dilemmas to him, but calming distractions from death, cancer, Eden, his father, his dwindling faith: reality. "And seminarians like me are, um—"

"Asking for money."

"Yeah," he said, breathing in relief again. He was now very high from the pills. "And, and, what would the world be like without priests? With young men like me frustrated and out of place—trying to find satisfaction?"

"Awful," she said.

"Yeah," Damian said. "It's awful. And what if these young—"

"It's O.K., it's O.K."

"It is?"

"Yeah. I'll donate."

"Oh," Damian said, almost disappointed. "How much?"

He recorded her information, realizing that now she would recognize his voice as belonging to the money-begging seminarian. He could not comfortably ask about Eden. He was stuck here serving Mother Church and *Her* temporal needs, worried that he secretly wished those needs would go unmet. But he didn't want that. He had rejoiced at the money Stella had given. But that was pride, not his sense of service.

He *was* stuck at this desk, serving the Church with his talents, feeling like the confused young men he asked his potential donors to imagine: he could imagine them well, since he felt lost and yet trapped—how he was supposed to feel outside the seminary—as he served the Church from within, protected and imprisoned on this sacred hill.

The End of Part Two

PART THREE

CHAPTER TWENTY-THREE
DESCENT

Damian was dreaming about the seminary's tower-top bell, how Fr. Rector had ordered it rung to celebrate Damian's winning the Phone-a-Thon (which he actually had, the day before), when a deep, solemn toll, swinging sadly, strangely, in the pitch darkness, woke him. The sound, unique to bells rung from towers, faded spatially like the volume diminished as the tone travelled out and away, wherever it's location the volume preserved. A signal to eternity.

That first toll faded, and he momentarily wondered if he had, in fact, dreamt it, when a second filled the air with vibrating alarm. His skin prickled, and he opened his eyes to the black night as the bell's hum swelled in his ears and then receded, leaving him with a sense of urgency and a strange suspicion that he was about to experience something he would never forget.

His clock read 3:17 a.m. He flipped back the wool blanket that was his Phone-a-Thon prize and wondered: *has Eden died?* No. Harold would have contacted him directly, somehow, with *that* news.

Wouldn't he?

Damian struggled to sit up on the edge of the bed. His hip didn't hurt badly, but it was stiff and sore because the Bishop's Suite was surprisingly cold. His bare feet touched the thin rug, and he shivered without his blanket, rubbing his arms, assuring himself: *surely Harold would've sent me another note, called Father Rector so he could tell me privately.*

The bell rang out a third time, its grim tone raising the goose bumps on Damian's arms, and he curled his already-numb toes. *The bell's not for Eden,* he thought, and he wanted to say it aloud—to hear some comforting words and assure himself that all was well. *It's for something else. Something.* But what? The bell never rang before six o'clock in the morning, when the moon had already descended but dawn was still hours away. Unless some rare, public tragedy had occurred, and then the bell was rung to alert the hilltop community—like a flag at half-mast. What was happening now was very rare.

He struggled into his wheelchair and wheeled himself to the door. The bell rang again, relentless, as he entered the dark hallway, where the air was thin, dry, and even colder than in the Bishop's Suite. Oddly, given the early hour, dim white light shone through the glass door at the end of the hall. Was the moon's glow that strong?

His wheels rolled smoothly on the marble floor, squeaking quietly in the silence. The bell rang again. He opened the glass door and immediately snow hit his face: all he could see ahead of him were flakes streaming out of the darkness.

The bell rang, humming deeply, louder now that he was outside, and he pushed himself toward the deep sound. The snow blinded him. He struggled onward, and his wheels crunched through the fresh fall. In this blizzard, he could not distinguish the green squares from the black on his blanket—it simply looked dark and dusted with snow.

The bell—again it sounded— told neither the time nor

gathered seminarians for prayer. These clangs broke out sharply through the dark, sharp and sounding mercilessly until . . . they were adding up at this black hour to a number he dreaded but somehow knew was coming, a number that had now come and gone, a number of years that had ended tonight.

Sweat poured into his eyes as he progressed; tears—the snow could not hold them back—streamed down his face. He turned his head to wipe them, and through the blur he saw seminarians in black cassocks streaming by, making their way to the cathedral, toward the bell tower. Another toll. Thirteen.

When the fourteenth—and final—deep sound of the bell sounded directly above him, someone strong grabbed the back of his wheelchair and quickly pushed him up to the cathedral doors. It was Br. Tim, who now reached around the wheelchair, opened the cathedral door, and pushed Damian into the warm foyer, where seminarians were stamping their shoes and breathing on their fingers. Incense mingled with damp robes: the aroma of the clergymen who filled the cathedral's pews. They were burning white candles, wearing black cassocks and habits. They were praying with breviaries, reading from ancient Bibles.

The seminarians milling around began joining a long line that stretched from the foyer to the front of the church, though what was up there Damian couldn't see. And now the line of seminarians seemed to be slowly moving forward, single file, up the centre aisle. What were they doing?

Br. Tim pushed him forward so that he joined the long line, and Damian leaned side to side but still couldn't see what lay ahead. But there were no more tolls. He willed another to sound so that the number didn't match Eden's age, but his wish met with silence. And so he knew. Eden. He was dead.

But Damian couldn't ponder the loss of his friend because the line was moving quickly. The cathedral was dark, shadowy: only the lights above the altar and along the sides were on. Directly ahead of him was a tall, thin seminarian, the snow already melting on his back, disappearing into the cassock's black material; he had a rocking gait. And there, sitting in a pew to the right, was Br. Robert, his arms hanging over the pew ahead of him. He was shaking his head, crying.

Br. Robert's presence angered Damian: did *he* even know Eden? His tears were likely fake, like everything about him. Suddenly Damian wanted to flee.

But Br. Tim's strong arms kept pushing him forward, as though he was locked in a cart on a roller coaster—indeed, his stomach rose in his throat—and now he was almost at the front of the church. Seminarians ahead of him seemed to pause before the altar and then peel off the line, looking sad as they returned to their pews.

The thin seminarian ahead of him was now at the front of the line. Damian rocked left and right as he approached the steps just before the altar, and now he glimpsed what was up there: a blown-up photograph of Eden in a frame on a wooden stand

The seminarian before him stopped, stooped, and kissed it. Damian's toes curled, and at that moment he realized he'd forgotten to wear shoes. He twisted back in his wheelchair to protest.

"Stop! Turn around!" he said to Br. Tim, but Br. Tim

ignored him and just kept pushing, straight and steady. The thin seminarian walked off to the right, and Damian found himself facing the portrait; he stuck his feet out in frustration as Br. Tim pushed him towards it.

Here was Eden's face. The portrait stood on the step before the altar. It was surrounded by flowers. The photograph appeared to be from about a year ago—from before they'd met. Eden looked healthy, heavier, more robust, his face bright and round. Seeing him like this, at a time when he'd been a stranger, and knowing that he was now gone forever, seemed to erase their entire relationship, as did the presence of all these other people in the cathedral. Damian had to escape. He pushed back with his feet on the marble floor, and he clawed and slapped at Br. Tim's thick arms. Then he grasped the still-cold rims and pushed himself off to the side, finally free of Br. Tim. He rolled off as fast as he could.

The church's side aisle was bright. His mind felt light, crackling, *blank* as he rolled quickly past the pews. He reached the foyer, kicked open the door with his right foot—it hurt, but he was so frustrated and desperate he liked the pain—and wheeled himself through the now-empty space.

He kicked open the second door, harder than before, and the wind caught it and slammed it against the side of the church. The bang echoed behind him. *I don't care,* he thought. *All of them—they never even knew him.* And they'd kept Eden's death from him, so that he was the last to know.

Outside snow was pouring down in heavy sheets, the flakes thick and wet. He pushed himself forward, not back to the Bishop's Suite but straight ahead, wondering,

Where's Harold? Why didn't he call me?

"Fuck him!" he screamed, not sure if he meant Harold or Fr. Rector, who had obviously kept Eden's death a secret so Damian wouldn't dash off to be with him and get himself kicked out of the seminary. Damian had likely been collecting donations when Eden had died, helping the institution that had kept him from his dying friend. The thought made him grind his teeth.

He rolled down the main road. The snow—though thicker—was so wet it immediately melted on the road's surface. Moving through the frigid air chilled his bare toes. He wrenched down on the wheelchair's rims, faster and faster.

He crested the top of the hill. The tall pine trees along the sides of the road were barely visible through the thick flakes, but they still seemed imposing on either side of him.

He was really flying down the hill now, the wind whistling in his ears. His wheels squealed, the chair shook. He squeezed the wheelchair's armrests to steady himself— the wheels were moving far too fast to try to stop them. His head was soaked, his cassock frozen to his heaving chest as the wind beat against it. He sobbed.

The long, tall, black bars of the iron gate stretched across the road at the bottom of the hill. At this hour they were still closed and locked, and they resembled prison bars against the falling snow: Damian was speeding towards them, about to crash.

He dug his right foot into the road. The old pavement was jagged and sharp, and it grated his foot raw. The pain rose to his shin bone, but he didn't slow down.

He flew towards the gate, cringing as he prepared to

hit it, and then he saw a man in a coat trying to open it from the opposite side.

"Hurry!" Damian screamed.

"Damian?" Harold screamed back; his voice muffled by the wind but immediately recognizable.

"Harold! Help!" Damian said, and then he dug his heel even harder into the pavement, but the chair spun to the right. His foot caught under the front right wheel and the chair flipped over, pitching him out of it about four feet from the fence. He flew through the wet snow, through the whistling wind. Then he smashed into the gate and dropped onto the pavement. Reaching through the bars, Harold caught his head and protected it from the road.

"Ouff!" Damian said, the wind knocked out of him. His spine felt snapped. He lay prostrate, the snow falling into his eyes. Harold's hand was shaking under his head. Harold was breathing hard, too, crying as well. Damian was still angry, and said, "Why didn't you call?"

"Damian."

"*Why?*"

Harold gazed down, fatherly, forgiving, concerned. He said, "You can't run from the truth!"

"That Eden's dead?"

"Yes . . ." Harold said, pausing, "but also the truth about your life—why you're here."

And looking up at Harold, with the iron bars between them, Damian knew he was right. He could avoid the truth no longer. There was no running away.

CHAPTER TWENTY-FOUR
ALL TOO HUMAN

Damian's spine hadn't snapped, but it felt like it had.

After he'd slammed against the iron gate last night, Harold ran up the hill to fetch Br. Tim, who came to Damian's rescue. He and Harold helped Damian back into his wheelchair, pushed him up to the Bishop's Suite, and deposited him in his bed, where he lay, having rested, sleepless, for a few hours.

A package swished under the door. A parcel. Bright brown and clear tape with a rectangular bulge in the centre. He knew: the rest of his dad's letters from Uncle Rick. Now. Of course, it had to arrive right now.

And yet in a way it was perfect timing. With Eden's death and Harold's advice to face the truth, Damian was finally, though still reluctantly, resolved to accept the past and record it as it really was.

An old oak cane leaned against the wall. An aid to an awfully tall bishop long passed away. The cane reached the package on the floor, though dragging it towards himself bunched his back in biting lumps.

In the package was a note from Uncle Rick:

Here's the rest of them, bud.

A few were slid between my sheets, so I had to hang them up to dry for a few days. May now be a touch crisp.

Found a few other items in the process. My, they don't print them au natural anymore. Good times.

Uncle Rick.

Even from hundreds of miles away, Uncle Rick's room and habits lifted Damian's gut into his mouth. Disgusting. If he left the seminary, would he become like Uncle Rick? He had to take the chance, to face the truth regardless of where it took him.

He opened the first letter:

August 20, 1976
How are ya, Ricky?
Or should I call ya Friar Rick?

I've been thinking about where you are now, and I have to say I think it's a queer state of affairs. A real man has a woman and works the land, owns a business. I remember back when I was a boy in New Zealand. We were raised to be real men back there, plowing mother earth, using our hands.

The missus dragged me to the pew last weekend, and those priests wear the queerest robes—and I do mean queer! I hope they don't have you in one of those velveteen getups.

To be frank, your sister's driving me nuts with her devotions, her kind of faith. A little of all that's fine, but church every day? Too much. Once a week is even more than I like.

Love ya bud, and hope to see ya back soon!
George

Damian closed his eyes and considered. On one hand, his father hadn't said anything awful, but clearly piety wasn't his life's purpose. His criticism of priestly vestments particularly hurt, as Damian recalled the pride he'd felt that morning he first donned his cassock. His father's criticism of his mother pained Damian also, although maybe his dad had a point.

He read all of his father's letters. The theme was the same: persuading Rick to leave the seminary because the clerical life was not the life of a real man.

And now he turned to his father's story in his journal. Harold's class required a composition of a life of someone he admired, and Damian decided, in light of the letters, to leave his father's story just as it was—how he'd managed to write it so far, but to now abandon the desire to add fantastic, saintly elements. In fact, he would even add to his father's story the few forgivable faults revealed in the letters. Like finding his wife too religious. Like criticizing clerical vestments. These peccadilloes humanized his father rather than canonized him.

And as Damian set out a fresh page from his journal on which to write his new version of his dad's life, the version he'd submit to Harold, he tried to get comfortable with a new idea he realized he now had to accept: that he could no longer imagine his father was a saint, and that, therefore, he himself did not need to keep trying to be one.

CHAPTER TWENTY-FIVE
REVELATIONS

Three days later, after Damian had composed his father's realistic biography and sent it to Harold through the seminary mail, he received a response—a packet from Harold, including a letter-sized envelope and another, larger envelope holding what felt like a hardcover book.

He opened the smaller envelope first and found a letter.

Damian,

Tolle Lege!

Thank you for your assignment. You have now completed Spiritual Autobiography, as I knew you would. I am so impressed with your account of your fine father's life. What a talented storywriter you are! Your grade is your usual "A." Well done.

In fact, so fine was your tale of this admirable life lived well, that I have another project for you to take on, one you may find manageable during your convalescence. The editors at the Kelowna Sun have heard about Eden's sickness and death and they want to profile his young life, as an extended obituary of sorts. I am too distraught to take on this task right now, or to leave the house, for that matter, but then I thought of you. Would you, please, compose his tale for the newspaper?

And then, just as I'd thought of you for this project, God's providence struck! While cleaning under dear Eden's bed in his now-empty room, I found what appears to be his journal. I simply cannot read it. I'm in no state to do so. Hearing his voice through the words would surely break my heart entirely.

But maybe you can give it a look and see what might apply to your account of his short time on this earth. And I believe you should have no qualms over invading his privacy: you should know that after one of your last visits, Eden told me he trusted you more than anyone else he knew. As do I.

Now, take and write, dear Damian!

Love and inspiration,

Harold

Damian was moved: to be charged with the task of recording dear Eden's life! What an honor. He felt solemn before such a noble responsibility.

However, he was ambivalent about reading Eden's journal. On one hand it did seem like a violation of privacy. But, at the same time, Eden's keen mind and precocious wisdom was worth recording and spreading. Surely some of his insight would be captured in the pages of his journal, and Damian could prudently preserve what treasures he found and then communicate them in the extended obituary he'd now write. If, while working with Eden's private reflections, Damian came upon embarrassing private revelations, he would quickly skip them, out of respect for his lost friend, and certainly keep such information to himself. After all, Harold had mentioned in his letter that Eden trusted him deeply. Such trust needed to be honored, to be respected and valued.

Having thus considered the endeavour and grown

comfortable with it, Damian opened the second envelope and found a hardcover journal bound in red canvas. The spine was creased, the pages wrinkled and worn, and a blue ribbon marked a spot near the volume's end. Before opening it, he pictured Eden's face and recalled his voice; then he began reading.

The entries began about four years ago, when Mrs. House had left Harold and Eden when Eden was eleven years old. In tight, neat, blue cursive, which stretched in straight, narrow lines across the pages, Eden recounted his grief over his mother's leaving. He described how he both loved and missed her, yet resented how she had abandoned their family. He also wrote at length about his father's grief, how a part of Harold had seemed to die with his wife's departure.

But then Eden's thoughts seemed to change focus. As the months passed, his grief lifted and he became increasingly concerned with astronomy and his homeschooling. And the entries were less frequent—once every two weeks rather than the near-daily entries that opened the journal.

Then, several months after his mother had left, Eden made an entry describing a strange visit to his home by Fr. Rector. Damian's attention piqued at this, as he found it very odd the Rector had never mentioned that he had been on personal terms with Eden in the past, prior to his falling ill. Damian read the entry closely:

September 22, 1995

Today marked three months since mom left us, and Father Rector made a visit to our home. I assumed he came to assist, to minister to the grieving in our time of need. Our period of pain.

But today was a day I want to forget forever. Father Rector arrived when my dad was at work and I was home alone, sick with the flue. I thought it was strange that he arrived when he did because I thought he'd only visit to see dad, and that he'd surely know when dad would be teaching.

He knocked gently on my door, which startled me because I hadn't heard him enter the house. But then he gently opened the door and with a voice so soft it was almost a whisper, asked how I was managing, if I needed anything. He said he'd come to keep me company because dad had told him I was laid up in bed at home alone.

He sat on the bedside, blessed my sweaty forehead, and then coaxed me to unbutton my shirt so he could bless me with holy oils. As he rubbed the oils on me, he lamented my being sick and comforted me about mom's leaving. He claimed priests could make a decent substitute for a missing parent. He kept rubbing the holy oils all over my front, and moved lower, to my stomach, then my waist. I must have shown my discomfort with this because he began assuring me I'd get better soon if he blessed my whole sick self.

But then, as he told me a story about being sick when he was a boy and how a priest had anointed him just this way and he'd recovered in a day, he moved his hand into my pants and rubbed me down there, differently, grasping, pulling.

He touched me like this for a few moments, then he heard my dad come in the front door and quickly said we didn't want to worry him with holy oils lest he think my *sickness required the last rights. He pulled his hand away, buttoned up my shirt, and covered me with my blanket.*

My dad came in and the Rector was again feeling my brow, acting like any normal person concerned with someone sick in bed. He blessed my brow one last time and said God would come now and cure me for sure. Nothing to fear. And that we should keep this visit quiet. "Eden," he said to my dad as he winked at me, "is certainly a special little guy." He consoled us again over mom, then left.

Damian couldn't lift his eyes from the page. He gasped, loudly, and could not regain his breath. Several minutes passed before he could move on to the following entries. In them, Eden recounted a half dozen similar visits by the Rector, similar sexual abuse, along with Eden's confusion and guilt. He claimed he kept silent because his father was already so burdened with sorrow. Harold's only remaining joys in life were his son and his work at the seminary, and Eden to tell him what the Rector was doing, both those joys would be damaged—complicated at the very least.

Damian wept hard as he finished reading the journal. He closed it and held it in his hands, caressed it, in fact, pressing it to his heart and kissing the cover to express his sympathy for Eden. He yearned to comfort him after such cruel abuse, such violation by the Rector's horrible hands.

Rage and revenge. Remorse and regret. These emotions churned within him, leaving him frozen, stuck. Paralysed with negativity.

What could, what *should* he do with this terrible, new-found knowledge?

Three days later, having reread Eden's journal

countless times and pondered nothing but the Rector's abuse of his dear young friend, Damian now stood on crutches in the cold, wide hallway outside the Bishop's Suite. The smooth, black and white checkered linoleum beneath his feet felt hard and smooth—strangely so, in fact—after two weeks in a wheelchair.

He stepped forward with his right foot and quickly put weight on it. Then he swung his crutches forward and gingerly lifted his left foot. He had not used his left leg in two weeks, and to lift it he had to lurch to the right, tilting his body and gripping the handles on the crutches tightly before hauling up his atrophied leg, which felt like it would pop from its socket. He eyed the floor before replacing his left foot onto it, avoiding a particularly deep crater in the linoleum, and then stepped down. His left leg felt like it would crumple beneath him. But would it?

What a struggle to walk! But then what an infinitely more terrible struggle Eden had faced while alive, such a terrible secret to keep—and during a horrible illness!

Then, behind him, the door at the end of the hall opened and brisk steps approached from behind.

"Damian," the Rector said before he came into view. "Up on your feet finally, I see. Good, good."

Then the Rector stepped in front of Damian, blocking his way. He crossed his arms, frowned.

"Heard about Eden, I suppose. Terrible, terrible."

Damian just glared at him. The Rector glared back, then tilted his head, as though curious as to why Damian wasn't responding.

"But don't you worry about Harold, son. Time will pass. He'll heal. These things—" the Rector twirled his finger, "these things, they happen. Nothing you can do."

There's something I can do, Damian thought, grinding his teeth. And while he couldn't push the Rector out of his way right now, although he would have liked to had he been stronger, more mobile, he knew how to bring him down. He would write Eden's story and give it to the police, along with Eden's journal, and then send the story to the Bishop, the local newspapers, and, finally, to Harold. To thus ruin the Rector, bring him to justice. And hopefully get him locked up, too.

Yes, he thought. *I'll write the story right away.*

But, for now, he said, "Yes, Father. Nothing you can do."

At this the Rector nodded, and then walked away. Damian stood still on his crutches, but he was now certain of his next move.

CHAPTER TWENTY-SIX
WHAT WAS HIDDEN SHALL COME TO LIGHT

The next day, Damian held the story he'd written about Eden. It had taken him all of yesterday afternoon and the better part of last night, but now he was proud of his work and carefully read it over at his desk in the Bishop's Suite.

Eden's Star

What does a saint's life look like?

The answer to that question is: it depends. Some saints attain heavenly status by what they achieve: miraculous feats like levitation and the stigmata. Or grand ventures like founding a religious order or leading a crusade.

But other saints live humbler lives, quiet, in the shadows. Eden House was one such as these. He was born in 1985 in Kelowna BC to Harold and Matilda House. He was an only child, the apple of his father's eye.

Eden was primarily raised by his father, Professor Harold House of Mount Angelus Seminary. Eden was gifted, and his father homeschooled him. As a young boy, Eden developed a love for reading and cultivated a particular interest in astronomy. He became so focused on the stars that he neglected his other studies. This imbalance actually worked to his benefit, since astronomy kept him occupied during the disease that ended his life. He set his sights on the stars, unsatisfied with dwelling on earth—which was good because he didn't stay here long. In the tradition of the ancient astronomers who had no universities or observatories to belong to, he taught himself to navigate the stars from his bedroom in the Okanagan Valley—spending hours alone with his telescope.

Eden endured three great sufferings in his short life. The first was the loss of his mother, Matilda. She abandoned Eden and his father when Eden was eleven.

But much worse was the second suffering he endured. In his vulnerable state after his mother had left, Father Bernard Bunyan, Rector of Mount Angelus Seminary, preyed upon Eden and sexually assaulted him in his own home. Eden recorded these ruthless attacks in his journal, and by this the abuse was discovered—for Eden never mentioned it to anyone.

Thirdly, Eden endured—and was finally over-powered by—the scourge of leukemia. This disease consumed him, killed him, and the writer of this obituary believes that given the treatment of Eden at Father Bunyan's hands, Eden's early demise was, in a way, a mercy.

Some are saints by what they achieve, others by what they endure.

Eden once claimed that he had discovered an unnamed star while gazing through his telescope in the hospital. He named the star Celestaurus, but now, as his friends and loved ones below look up and remember him, we think of it as Eden's Star.

Damian realized, as he read over his work, that the lives of the saints were about the only thing left in Catholicism that he still admired and valued. The past year's events, from hitting his head at the gym to leaving home to live with Scott, from applying to the diocese and writing his vocation story to entering Mt. Angelus: this path he'd taken had wrested him of the religious beliefs his mother had instilled in him. While he'd met Harold and Eden and grown personally over the last twelve months, he'd lost his faith. The year after he'd pledged to become a saint.

A week ago, he thought the primary cause of his lost faith was what he'd found in his dad's letters—his having had to abandon the saintly story of his father and his own ambitions of becoming a saint. But now, holding this story in his hands trembling with sadness and rage, he knew his exit—mentally, spiritually, and soon physically—from the Catholic Church was made certain by his discovery of the Rector's abusing Eden.

At least this story will find redemption for Eden, he thought. *As for me, I can walk again now, clumsily, and so I need to venture out into the world and stumble forth as best I can in this life—leave thoughts of heaven behind.*

And he knew he would do just that. For now, he started addressing envelopes, five in all: to the local police, to Bishop Spur, to the Kelowna Sun, and to Harold. The agony and anger it would cause Harold might only be mitigated, he thought, by knowing that making Eden's pain public could bring justice and spare other victims.

He worked with resolve; with new-found certainty. And, for the first time in a long while, with some hope for the future.

CHAPTER TWENTY-SEVEN

OVERHEARING HIMSELF PREACH

Three months later, Damian sat beside his mother in the front pew at Canadian Martyrs Parish. He'd returned to Calgary from Harold's house—where he lived now, working as an obituary writer—when Grandma Schiller had fallen ill with pneumonia. He'd arrived last week, and she was currently in the hospital.

After Damian mailed his story about Eden to the police, to Bishop Spur, and to several newspapers, he went to Harold's house and delivered the story in person. Harold cried upon reading it, and then he and Damian sat down to talk. Damian explained that he obviously could no longer live at Mt. Angelus, and that he did not want to continue in the seminary regardless of the Rector's past actions. Harold immediately offered his home to Damian, and Damian moved in that night—in a spare bedroom across the hall from Eden's old room with the telescope.

And there, during the first week at Harold's place, while Damian was adjusting to his lovely, peaceful new home, his story began to take effect. The police, to whom Damian had sent the story and Eden's journal as evidence, arrested the Rector at the seminary. And though he was granted bail, by the time he got out he was informed by Bishop Spur that he was no longer Rector of Mt. Angelus, would be placed on probation at a local retreat centre until an investigation could be done. Also, the Kelowna Sun published Damian's story and an article of their own about the Rector. This prompted several ex-seminarians to contact the paper and claim that they too had been victims of his abuse.

Now the Rector was awaiting trial, as the charges against him mounted. But Damian's story had another effect, too: that of spreading his reputation as a powerful writer. When an opening to be an obituary writer for The Kelowna Sun appeared in the classifieds, about a month after moving into Harold's, Damian applied and immediately got the job. He was happy in his new life, writing to Uncle Rick regularly and receiving visits from Theodore and Br. Tim.

Now, sitting in the same old pew in his childhood parish, Damian felt strange: a new, independent person, but back where he no longer belonged, and again under his mother's control.

Today was Easter Sunday and the church was decorated with white altar cloths and purple tulips and radiant sunflowers. The people around him stood up and the organ began to play *Come Holy Ghost*. Damian stood and turned. Father Dennis processed up the centre aisle with a young man Damian didn't recognize. The young man wore an alb and held some pages. Damian guessed he was a new seminarian, freshly accepted and soon on his way to the seminary.

Fr. Dennis began Mass. He looked healthy, well—no sign of his drinking was apparent in his appearance. He proclaimed the Gospel, and then introduced the young man, who, it turned out, would be the guest homilist.

"I'd like to invite Peter," Fr. Dennis said, "our diocese's newest seminarian, to come up and share his vocation story on this, the feast of our Lord's resurrection."

Immediately Damian wondered if he was about to hear a personalized version of his own vocation story. Was it still in circulation? Being used as the model template?

Peter nervously took to the pulpit and shuffled his papers. He began by describing his home and family life—but not in a way that matched Damian's tale. Damian relaxed. He didn't want to be reminded of the words he had crafted to make himself sound like the ideal priestly candidate.

But then Peter bellowed out some very familiar lines, yelled them at the congregation:

"I will commit myself to seminary formation, continuing the pious lessons I learned in my family's home."

This *was* Damian's story—the diocese was obviously still using it. Probably the seminary, too. He was sitting here with the other parishioners, overhearing himself preach.

Peter continued: "And I will pray and study until I am confident in my abilities to save souls for Christ."

That's not me, Damian said to himself, suddenly calm, recognizing the sentence but also seeing the divide between himself sitting in the pew today, experienced, almost independent, more sure of himself, and the scared teenager in the basement of his grandmother's home last year, writing these bold words to bolster his own wavering courage. He knew the next line would pledge allegiance to the bishop, to the Church. On cue, Peter, a thin, pale boy of eighteen or nineteen, said with feeling,

"And I pledge my loyalty to Bishop Spur and the Church's hierarchy."

That's not me, Damian repeated, realizing that his

choice to visit Eden on his deathbed over Bishop Spur's mandate for seminarians to stay away from youth had severed the pledge he had made in his vocation story. But he had never really known what that pledge entailed when he made it, as Peter likely did not know now. Damian pledged fidelity a year ago because he wanted the Church's protection. Now he wanted to protect himself from the facade he had seen put up around the seminary's reputation, a combination of vestments, lies, and ceremony to preserve the corruption within. He had rid himself of his fear, his inferiority, and his trembling submission to authority. These words he had written, that he rejected now, were promises to allow no such healing to occur.

But then why was he here, in the pew, and not with Harold? Why had he succumbed to his mother's pressure again? He cared for Grandma Schiller, but he felt under the power of his mother's thumb again. He glanced over at her, saw her grinning proudly, and began planning his escape.

Peter was closing his homily, unless he had added an ending that was different from the one Damian had written. He said: "And I will do my best to give good example to other young men, so they follow in my footsteps, toward Christ's altar."

Nope, Damian thought as he heard the same line that had concluded his vocation story when he had written it last year. *Nothing original here,* he thought. And then, considering the meaning of that final sentence, he thought, *But that's definitely not me,* and almost had to hold himself back from going up to Peter now and warning him not to pursue the priesthood. But Peter would have to discover his life's path on his own. He, appearing proud with himself, walked back from the pulpit and sat beside Fr. Dennis, who also appeared satisfied with the words that had just been preached.

Let them have my story, Damian thought, *but my future starts today.*

Mass continued, Fr. Dennis seemingly healthy and well, but who knew the truth? After the consecration Mrs. Kurt stood to join the other Eucharistic ministers around the altar, and then she came down and stood with the chalice beside Fr. Dennis who nodded at Damian. He was in the front pew, after all, and should be first to receive. Now was his moment—the chance for a physical expression of a choice he had already made and would now stick to. He stood, fit his crutches under his arms, but then put them down again, leaving them lying on the front pew. He needed no support. Not for this. Let people call it a miracle.

He walked out of the pew, looked at his mother and nodded at her. Then he nodded at Fr. Dennis, whose smile waned. He glanced at Peter, and then walked away from the front row where his family had sat so many times. Damian passed the full pews, from which parishioners, most of whom he recognized, gawked at him. He passed the vases of fake flowers, realizing that without his crutches walking was easier. And, finally, he passed the baptismal font at the back of the church, longing to leave this building and exchange it for his future, which enticed and slightly scared him at once.

As he reached the doors at the back of the church, he considered turning around for one last look at his past. But why? He would never forget it. He opened the church doors, the sun blinding him. And when he stepped outside, the world shone so brightly he could not quite see what was before him.

ACKNOWLEDGEMENTS

Thanks, Eugene, for your guidance at the start of this project. Thanks also to Roy Hoffman, K. L. Cook, John Pipkin, Kirby Gann, and Phil Deaver for mentoring me during my drafts of this novel. Thanks, Robin, for editing. Finally, thanks, Kyle and Nick and Cammie, for cleaning up and publishing this novel.

ABOUT ATMOSPHERE PRESS

Atmosphere Press is an independent, full-service publisher for excellent books in all genres and for all audiences. Learn more about what we do at atmospherepress.com.

We encourage you to check out some of Atmosphere's latest releases, which are available at Amazon.com and via order from your local bookstore:

The Farthing Quest, a novel by Casey Bruce

The Black-Marketer's Daughter, a novel by Suman Mallick

This Side of Babylon, a novel by James Stoia

Within the Gray, a novel by Jenna Ashlyn

Where No Man Pursueth, a novel by Micheal E. Jimerson

Here's Waldo, a novel by Nick Olson

Tales of Little Egypt, a historical novel by James Gilbert

For a Better Life, a novel by Julia Reid Galosy

The Hidden Life, a novel by Robert Castle

Big Beasts, a novel by Patrick Scott

Alvarado, a novel by John W. Horton III

Nothing to Get Nostalgic About, a novel by Eddie Brophy

Home is Not This Body, a novel by Karahn Washington

Whose Mary Kate, a novel by Jane Leclere Doyle

Stuck and Drunk in Shadyside, a novel by M. Byerly

These Things Happen, a novel by Chris Caldwell

ABOUT THE AUTHOR

Aaron Francis Roe teaches English and Communications at Bow Valley College. He lives with his family in Calgary, Alberta. *Saints and Martyrs* is his first novel.

CPSIA information can be obtained
at www.ICGtesting.com
Printed in the USA
BVHW072027200121
598108BV00001B/3